By Xenia Melzer

A Dom and His Writer
Love Wins (Dreamspinner Anthology)

Published by Dreamspinner Press
www.dreamspinnerpress.com

A DOM AND HIS WRITER

XENIA MELZER

Published by

DREAMSPINNER PRESS

5032 Capital Circle SW, Suite 2, PMB# 279, Tallahassee, FL 32305-7886 USA
www.dreamspinnerpress.com

A Dom and His Writer
© 2017 Xenia Melzer.

Cover Art
© 2017 Aaron Anderson.
aaronbydesign55@gmail.com
Cover content is for illustrative purposes only and any person depicted on the cover is a model.

ISBN: 978-1-63533-826-3
Digital ISBN: 978-1-63533-827-0
Library of Congress Control Number: 2017910300
Published October 2017
v. 1.0

Printed in the United States of America
(∞)
This paper meets the requirements of
ANSI/NISO Z39.48-1992 (Permanence of Paper).

For Michael. Thank you for the constant inspiration.

Acknowledgments

I WANT to thank my readers, who make it possible for me to write.

I also want to thank Simon from Dead Soft for giving my book a home in Germany.

And, as always, I have to thank the best editors in the world (I'm laying it on thick because I need to stay on their good side): Anne Regan for her patience and vast knowledge. Kelly for her sharp eye and the ability to smooth out my grammar blunders. Liv for cheering me on and finding the small mistakes that can have a big impact. And Anastasia for her deep knowledge of everything legal and real estate. If there are any mistakes in this book, I'm the one to blame.

CHAPTER 1

"To FIVE wonderful years with the best sub ever!" Richard Miller raised his glass, filled with a truly excellent Merlot. He was in an exceptionally good mood, and it showed in the way he beamed at his sub and lover of five years. Dean smiled right back. He, too, was in the mood to celebrate, although his enthusiasm was a bit hampered by the sting in the sensitive flesh of his ass and the occasional shudder that ran through him whenever the plug buried inside his hole hit his prostate.

Richard grinned knowingly. "Feeling troubled, boy?"

Dean knew better than to make a face or complain. He lowered his gaze to the crisp white tablecloth in front of him and spoke as softly as possible. "Yes, Master. I can feel your hand on my flesh every time I move."

Richard patted Dean's hand. "As it should be. You are mine, boy, and don't you ever forget that."

Dean loved the possessive tone. It turned him on even more than the memory of the spanking he had received before they came to Mamma's, their favorite Italian restaurant. Of course, it hadn't been just the spanking, although Richard was a genius at pushing Dean until he thought he couldn't take it anymore. It was also the fact that he hadn't been allowed to come, not even when Richard had teased him with the brand-new plug now resting between his asscheeks, or while Dean had given Richard a blow job. The leather cock ring Richard had put on him as a finishing touch prevented him from coming while keeping him painfully aroused—which was exactly what Richard wanted. Dean shuddered and then moaned softly when the movement caused the plug to nudge his prostate in a most delicious manner.

"It seems I have a very horny boy on my hands tonight." Richard's tone suggested he wasn't troubled by that.

Dean dared to look his Dom right in the face. "It's your fault, Master. You make me ache and need so much, I can hardly stand it."

Richard reached over the table to caress Dean's cheek. There was a hint of steel in his voice. "Are you complaining, boy?"

Dean shook his head vehemently. "No, Master! I would never do that! I know you always give me what I need. I trust you."

"That's my sweet boy. I have your best interest at heart, never doubt that. And tonight is special, because it's our anniversary. I want to push you farther than I have in a long time." An evil grin appeared on Richard's lips. "I'd advise you to enjoy your food. You're going to need the sustenance."

Again Dean felt his entire body tremble, but he cut off his moan quickly when the server came with their appetizers. Mamma's was a very small restaurant with only ten tables, hidden on a side street close to their own apartment on the Upper Eastside. The place was owned by an Italian woman everybody just called Mamma.

In Dean's opinion, she was the best cook in all the world. Since neither he nor Richard were gifted in the kitchen, they often came here to eat or had Mamma deliver meals to their place. Dean looked down on the bruschetta the server had placed before him. The enticing scent of fresh, very ripe tomatoes mixed with garlic, basil, a hint of marjoram, and a superb olive oil on top of a roasted, homemade slice of bruschetta bread made his stomach growl. He didn't reach for his cutlery, though. He waited for his Dom to give him permission to eat. While Dean inhaled the wonderful aroma and listened to the clinking of Richard's knife and fork, he wondered if this was part of his torture today—not being allowed to enjoy the food. He quickly regretted this treacherous thought when Richard offered him a piece of his own bruschetta with his fingers. Dean opened his mouth and closed his eyes to concentrate fully on the explosion of tastes on his tongue. There were the tomatoes, the garlic, the bread, and, underneath it all, the salty temptation of Richard's fingers. Dean whirled his tongue around them, sucking lightly, which drew a moan from his master. "Dean. Boy. So good."

Dean licked his lips, slowly, carefully, knowing what that did to his master. Richard was a very visual man, after all.

"Naughty boy. I should have spanked you harder."

The words made Dean ache in all the right places. Another bite of the bruschetta was offered to him, and they both reveled in the sensuality of their game. After the bread, the server served them a plate of antipasti: grilled peppers, zucchini, eggplant, and mushrooms in a dressing of the same heavenly olive oil and scented balsamic vinegar.

When he got a plate with spaghetti and seafood next, Dean knew Richard had ordered this feast especially for him. All his favorites in one evening. Between bites he looked at his handsome master, whose ebony skin glistened in the light of the solitary candle on their table. Dean was no longer surprised that he felt a little flutter in his stomach every time he looked at Richard, even though it was their fifth year together. Something about the man kept him hooked, and it wasn't just the Dom/sub dynamic of their relationship. Richard appealed to him on levels far deeper than that. Dean smiled at his wonderful man.

"Thank you, Master. This is delicious."

Richard grinned, full of male pride. "I'm so glad you approve. Only the best for my boy. I need you happy and relaxed for the things I have planned."

Suddenly Dean couldn't wait for dessert to come. Tiramisu with fresh strawberries, another favorite of his. Richard fed him the sweet temptation in small bites, and Dean practically tongue-fucked the spoon. Every time he swallowed, he felt the plug move in his ass, sending his already prickling nerves into sensual overdrive. The combination of the sweet tiramisu, the full flavor of the strawberries, and the constant tingling in his backside would have made him come right there in the restaurant, if not for the cock ring.

Richard sensed his distress, which sent him into full Dom mode. Dean could tell by the way his master held himself, how he flexed his impressive chest muscles and biceps under the expensive, dark red silk shirt he wore. Dean felt his entire body heating up while his mind settled firmly in his sub headspace. This was no longer an anniversary celebrated by two equally successful men who happened to like their sex with a little spice. It was now Richard's show, the scene he had come up with for both their pleasure. And Dean would submit, like he always did, because deep down, he knew this was how his life was supposed to be. He lowered his head, since eye contact was no longer allowed, waiting for his Dom to give him directions.

CHAPTER 2

RICHARD MADE a deep, rumbling noise in his chest when he saw Dean lower his gaze. His boy was in the scene now, showing his consent to whatever Richard might come up with, which was quite a lot for tonight. His cock, which had been hard the entire evening, felt like a baseball bat in his slacks. Seeing Dean submit to him so readily always did that to him. Richard stood, and his boy followed suit with graceful movements. They left the restaurant, knowing tonight's meal would be added to their tab just as always. When they reached the car, a customized BMW Z8 in a beautiful dark blue, Richard made sure to squeeze Dean's ass and to push the base of the plug with his thumb, drawing a firm circle on it. Dean yelped in surprise, his body jerking forward before settling back into the touch. Richard was pleased.

"Good boy. You make me ache so good."

Dean whimpered, while his body glowed from the praise. Richard held the car door open for his boy, who gingerly sat down on the black leather seat. "Do you feel it?"

Richard knew it was cruel, but he couldn't help himself. Torturing Dean, be it with tools or words, was the one thing in the world he would never tire of.

And his boy knew. The slender limbs trembled for him, the answer spoken oh so softly. "Yes, Master."

"Then brace yourself. You'll feel it even more once we get to the club."

Richard went around the car, sat down in the driver's seat, and started the motor. While he tried to find a gap between the other cars, he gave his instructions. "Open your trousers and let your cock out."

Dean complied immediately, his cock springing free. Richard threw a glance at the fully aroused, heavy prick. The tip was glistening with precum, the balls were obscenely full, and the veins on the shaft stood out in stark relief. It was a sight of pure beauty.

"Pump yourself twice, then swipe up the precum."

Moaning, Dean did as instructed, his body jerking in anticipation of something he wouldn't get tonight.

"Give me your fingers."

A desperate whimper was the answer to that order. Dean knew what was coming, and he dreaded it. Richard chuckled, then used his sternest Dom voice on his boy. "Remember, no coming without my permission."

"Yes, Master."

The words were more like a whine than coherent speech, a sure sign that Dean was already far gone. Perfect. Richard saw Dean's fingers, glistening with moisture, hovering in front of his mouth, and suddenly he felt the urge to be really cruel. "I'm going to suck your fingers now, boy. Caress them with my tongue, taste your delicious juice. And every time I pull, you will clench your tight little ass around the plug, make it move inside you. Can you do that, boy?"

Dean blanched but nodded. When Richard raised one of his brows, Dean hastened to answer. "Yes, Master. I can do that."

"Good boy."

Just like that, Richard took Dean's index and middle fingers in his mouth, swiping his tongue around them, savoring the unique, salty taste of his boy. He played with the digits as if they were his boy's cock, alternating deep sucking motions with quick swirls and gentle bites. Dean made the most adorable whimpering noises in the back of his throat. When he had to stop at a red light, Richard glanced at his boy to check if he was being obedient. He sucked hard and at the same time, Dean clenched his ass muscles, squirming because the motion made the cloth of his slacks scrape over the sensitive skin on his backside. It was so hot, Richard almost came in his pants. Luckily for him the light turned green, and he had to concentrate on traffic again.

They were not far from Whisper, the high-class BDSM club located in downtown Miami he owned together with his partner, Martin Carmichael. They had started out as fellow Doms on the scene. Martin owned a large security firm together with his twin sister, Olivia. One night, Richard and Martin had gotten drunk and both expressed their displeasure about the lack of sophisticated BDSM clubs that could meet their admittedly high standards. There were a handful of decent ones in the States, but not one that had their absolute approval. They stopped their drinking and started planning, writing down what they wanted and needed from a club and how they would run the place. A year later they opened Whisper, and the club had been an immediate hit. It was now going into its fifth year, with counterparts in New York, London, and Paris. At the moment they were discussing opening one in Berlin as well. Just like all of Richard's other business ventures, Whisper was a huge success that lined him up with even more money than he already had.

Richard steered the car into the fenced parking lot in front of his club. A bouncer checked his car plate and ID before letting him through the gate. Since the club was so exclusive, they had a lot of very rich, highly reclusive members who valued their privacy above all. The bouncer at the gate was the first of a number of security obstacles anybody who wanted to get into Whisper had to overcome.

The next of these obstacles was the iron entrance door, where two bouncers checked the IDs and the membership cards of those who wanted in. Once inside, a long corridor with a dark red carpet and beautiful BDSM photographs on the walls led to a counter where up to four subs took all electronic devices, keys, and jackets from the visitors. Then a bouncer checked the membership cards once more and took a picture of everybody before opening the grand wooden door with the iron fittings that led into the actual club area. Even though there were days when the Doms, eager to play with their boys, loathed all the procedures it took to enter the club, they were a necessary evil, and the members payed hefty six-figure fees per year because of the legendary security at his place. For Richard, this was no problem. As the owner, he could just walk into the club without bothering with the pesky security.

It was a Saturday night, and the club was packed. On the stage in the main area, a *shibari* demonstration had just begun, and normally Richard would have been very interested to watch it, for he loved tying his boy up, but not today. Today he had something more important to do. He led Dean to the back of the club, where the private rooms were. For tonight he had booked his favorite suite. He opened the heavy wooden door with the key integrated in his membership card and stepped aside to let Dean enter.

"Strip, boy, and then assume your position on the mat. I'll be right there."

Dean strode over to the small wardrobe in the far corner of the room. When he started to undress, Richard closed the door and went to his office. It was located at the end of the floor with the suites, behind a small, unobtrusive door that led into another hall where his and Martin's offices were, as well as a conference room and a small coffee kitchen. In the office he changed into his leather pants and a harness that highlighted his heavily muscled chest. He wanted to look good for his boy.

"Somebody's eager."

Richard turned to see Martin leaning on the doorframe, a saucy smile on his lips.

"Hello, Martin. Nice to see you too. You know it's our anniversary today. And even if it weren't, my boy deserves eager anytime."

Martin sauntered into the room, and they hugged briefly. "Of course he does. He's one of the most intriguing subs I've ever met."

Richard growled low in his chest. "He's mine!"

Martin laughed. "Just yanking your chain, bud. You know my tastes run differently."

Richard snorted. Martin preferred his subs to be airheaded twinks, unable to function without a strong hand guiding them through their lives and, preferably, also financially dependent on him. Not that he ever took advantage of them; Martin was the very picture of an honorable Dom, but he needed the added dependence. Unfortunately for him there weren't that many subs out there who would accept his need to provide for them completely, except for the gold diggers, and those Martin didn't touch. He had been burned once, and Martin never repeated a mistake.

Richard smiled. Dean was a handsome man with his shoulder-length blond hair, the long, slender muscles that pegged him as a runner, and grace that came from years of practicing yoga, but a twink he was not. At almost six foot, he was a little too tall for Martin's tastes but perfect for Richard, who loved the way Dean fit against his own six foot five. Dean was also anything but financially dependent. He was an insanely successful writer who made millions with his books. He didn't earn as much money as Richard, who played in the billionaire league; still, by any reasonable standard, Dean was independent. He just had no interest in money or business at all. Only his writing mattered to him, which was why Richard took care of all the tedious things that came with making a lot of money, like taxes, investments, and long-lost friends and relatives who wanted in on the wealth. It was a different type of sub dependency, one Martin would probably never understand. Richard only wished his friend would find that special someone he craved so badly, and soon.

Martin patted him on the shoulder. "You look good, man. Go show your boy who's boss."

Richard rolled his shoulders and flexed his biceps. "That I will do."

CHAPTER 3

IN THE playroom, Dean knelt on the mat, his knees spread wide, his ass resting on his heels, his hands folded behind his head to showcase his muscles. He was still rock-hard from the drive there, and the anticipation of what was to come made him wince. Richard knew him better than anybody else in the world. He could play Dean's body like an instrument, make him sing.

The door opened, and Dean's entire focus went straight to the man who entered. Richard was one fine-looking man with his dark skin against which the silver D-ring of his leather harness shone like a beacon, the hard muscles that gleamed in the light, the sensuous lips that could kiss so well, and the large hazel eyes that seemed to look right through him and shone with love every time their gazes met. Dean knew he was one lucky bastard.

"Nice positon, boy. You did well."

Dean kept his gaze trained to the floor but felt a flash of pride surge through him. His master was pleased! Richard approached him slowly, letting his eyes take in every inch of Dean's pale skin.

It was an intimate caress that made Dean tremble with need. Richard finally stopped in front of him, his voice deep and demanding. "As I said, I have great plans for you today, boy. But you made me so hot on our way here, I need your mouth first."

Richard opened his pants to let his impressive cock free. Dean was not a small man himself, but Richard was huge, and sometimes Dean wondered how he managed to take the man in so easily. It was, most probably, because they were made for each other.

He opened his mouth to lick at the first beads of precum on the thick, dark head. His master's taste was intoxicating, and Dean started his ministrations in earnest. He swirled his tongue around the head just like his master had done with Dean's fingers in the car. Then he started to suck and swallow, trying to take in as much of the thick meat as he could.

Dean had never managed to deep throat Richard. His gag reflex was too strong for that. He made up for it by creating as much suction as possible and by using his highly flexible tongue to bring his master the ultimate pleasure. Dean loved sucking his Dom; it gave him a chance to reciprocate the wonderful things Richard did to him.

Richard's hands were buried in Dean's hair, fisting the strands as he pistoned into Dean's mouth, his movements already rapid, warning of his oncoming orgasm. Then he suddenly stilled, his dick pulsed inside Dean's mouth, and hot cum shot down his throat. Dean tried his best to swallow it all, gulping down his master's seed greedily. He kept on sucking, trying to milk the last drop from Richard, before he slipped his cock out from Dean's eager lips.

"You really are a needy slut, boy. But don't worry, I'll take care of you."

Dean licked his lips but couldn't answer. The act of sucking his master had made his own cock even harder, and the need to find release was riding him hard. He had to fight to keep himself from coming right then. Richard touched his shoulder lightly, both to reassure him that he was doing well and to get his attention.

"Rise, boy. Go over to the cross."

Gracefully, Dean walked to the huge St. Andrew's cross situated in the far left corner of the room, opposite the four-poster bed. It was a massive thing of beauty, the oak wood polished to a sheen, the surface as smooth as the finest silk. The cuffs dangling from the cross were made of soft, padded leather and already set to Dean's height, another small service the club offered to make its customers happy. The measurements of all subs were in a database so a Dom didn't have to waste precious time adjusting the equipment.

Richard was right behind Dean, his hot breath like a breeze on Dean's cheek. "Lift your arms."

Dean obeyed immediately, letting out a needy whimper when the cuffs closed around his wrists. Richard bent down to secure his ankles as well. His big hands glided over Dean's skin in a reassuring manner, setting his nerve endings on fire. When he reached Dean's ass, Richard pinched the two globes hard. Dean let out a pained cry, his cock jerking, begging for release. Richard reached around him to grab the throbbing shaft with his right hand, and started pumping lazily.

"We haven't even started and you're already at your limit? Don't make this too easy, boy. I want to challenge you tonight. I want to push you way past your limits. Hold it in. Do it for me."

"For you, Master. For you. Yes."

"For me. Only for me. I'll use the flogger on you, boy. I'm going to mark this beautiful back with stripes, show everybody to whom you belong. Do you want that, boy?"

"Yes, Master. Please, do it. Mark me."

Richard placed a kiss on Dean's nape. Then he stepped back to retrieve the flogger he had selected from one of the cabinets on the wall. Slowly he let the leather strips glide over Dean's skin, causing him to wince.

Then he raised his arm and swung the flogger for the first time. Dean let out a grunt when the first blows hit him, the sting something he always had to get used to in the beginning. Soon he started leaning into each strike, welcoming the pain. He sank deeper into his headspace and forgot about everything except the pain and heat radiating through his body and the presence of his master, who made him fly.

When the familiar tingling in his lower back alerted him to his oncoming orgasm, Dean managed to pry himself from his trancelike state enough to beg for mercy. "Master! I'm close. Please!"

Dean didn't know if he was begging to come or asking Richard to help him control his need. It didn't matter. Whatever his Dom decided would be the right thing. The flogging stopped. Richard's hands ghosted over Dean's burning back before he started licking and biting the welts. The new sensation was enough to distract Dean from his need to come. When he was sure he was in control again, he turned his head as far as his bindings would allow. "Thank you, Master."

Richard took Dean's chin in his hands and kissed him deeply before releasing him again. "You're welcome, boy. Even though I do wish to push you, I don't want it to end yet."

His hands reached for Dean's ass and squeezed, causing the plug to hit Dean's gland. "I still haven't abused your ass yet. We will try the riding crop today. See if you can take eight blows."

Dean moaned. The crop was one of his favorite toys. Richard mentioning it alone made Dean's cock jerk and precum flow from his slit.

"You're going to beg me for each blow. And after you receive it, you will count and thank me for giving to you what you need. Do you understand, boy?"

The visuals Richard invoked with his deep voice were intoxicating. Dean couldn't find the strength to speak. He nodded, hoping his master would be satisfied with that. For once, Richard let this nonverbal response slide. Dean could feel his Dom shifting behind him as he replaced the flogger with the crop. It wasn't a long one, merely a foot, but the core, probably birchwood, was wrapped in leather. Dean knew it would hurt just right.

Richard caressed his asscheeks with the flexible length, which made Dean squirm in his restraints. "Please, Master. I'm begging you! Let me feel it!"

Richard brought the crop down hard on Dean's backside. Dean just had time to register the whooshing sound in the air before a trail of fire appeared across his right cheek. He screamed at the intense pain but didn't forget his master's instructions. "One. Thank you, Master. Please, let me feel it again."

The crop flew once more, bringing tears to Dean's eyes. "Two. Thank you, Master. Please, again."

Dean managed to get through the third and fourth before he started to cry. The tears streamed down his cheeks, his breathing became labored, his body so alive with different sensations he thought he would pass out any moment.

Richard paused. "Are you all right, boy?"

Dean sucked in air. He was tempted to call "manga chick," his safeword equivalent to "yellow," but decided not to do it. After all, this night was about pushing himself, and the short interruption had been enough for him to gather his strength again. "I'm fine, Master. Please, don't stop. Make me feel it."

Richard pressed a kiss on Dean's sweat-covered temple before he brought the crop down again. "Five. Thank you, Master. Please, again."

The sixth blow had Dean arching his back in pain. The seventh made stars explode in front of his eyes before his vision darkened momentarily. The eighth blow left him sobbing, unable to form a coherent word. His cock was straining, glistening with even more precum and an angry red, the veins looking like they would burst any moment.

Richard set the crop aside and ran his hands soothingly over Dean's arms and ribs, making soft sounds in the back of his throat. "Shh. You did so well, boy. I'm so proud. Such a good, strong boy. You are my pride, my sweet one."

Between his sobs, Dean felt a smile crease his lips. Richard only reverted to sweet talk when he was extremely pleased. His master's obviously splendid mood helped Dean to regain his composure. "Thank you, Master. This was good."

"I'm going to make it even better." Richard's hands were once again on Dean's cock, stroking and pumping, teasing him. "I'm going to remove the plug now and fuck you good and hard. I'm going to work your prostate until you can only think of coming, but you are not allowed, do you hear me? You have to keep it in. Otherwise I'll punish you for the entire week."

"Yes, Master."

Richard grabbed the base of the plug and twisted it around a few times, making sure it hit Dean's gland and made his hips jerk, before he pulled it out. Then he poured a generous amount of lube on his own cock, aligned the head with Dean's twitching hole, and plunged right in.

Dean threw his head back, screaming like he had under the crop. Nothing felt as good as his master's thick cock buried deep inside him. Nothing came close to the feel of Richard's big hands spanning his hips, digging his nails into the sensitive flesh of his groin while he started a relentless rhythm. Since they were both primed, there was no need to go slow. The pounding grew in intensity, and when Richard changed the angle of his thrusts, Dean knew he would lose this challenge. He cried out, warning his master again that he could no longer hold back. Only this time Richard didn't stop. Instead he grabbed Dean's hips even harder and added a vicious twist to his thrusts.

"Come on, boy. Give me a reason to punish you for the rest of the week. I'm going to put a cock cage on you, the heavy one with the fat plug for your asshole. I won't allow you to come even once until next Saturday, but I'm going to fuck you every chance I get. Your hole will be filled the entire time, either by me or the plug. And every evening you will lie down and spread yourself for me, beg me to whip your hole before I sink my big, fat cock into you."

Dean groaned. The words alone made him dizzy. The tingling in his back was getting more intense. He made one last effort to control his orgasm, but Richard chose that moment to thrust in deep and hit his gland full-on.

Dean was lost. He arched his back as his cock started to pulse, and the cum shot out of him in a thick stream. It seemed as if his balls wouldn't stop, and he didn't even register when Richard unsnapped the cock ring so that his spunk could flow freely.

Through it all, Richard held him tight, finding his own release deep inside Dean's body, his semen filling Dean up. After they were both spent, they remained in their position, Richard buried deep inside Dean, his strong arms encircling his sub like a delicious cage made of flesh.

Once their panting eased, Richard slid from Dean and started undoing the cuffs. He then carried him to the bed, snatched two bottles of water, wrapped Dean in a soft blanket, and cuddled him close. They remained silent for some time, basking in the afterglow of the truly wonderful scene they had just shared.

"You were really good today, boy. I'm very pleased."

Dean snuggled closer to Richard's chest, a lazy smile on his lips. "You're twisted. I disobeyed you. I came. Yet you say you're pleased."

There was a teasing note to Dean's voice. It was clear how well he understood Richard's intentions.

"I asked you to give me a reason to punish you for the rest of the week and you did. What is there not to be pleased about?"

Dean stretched his legs. "Nothing, I guess. My brain's not working properly at the moment. All fuzzy."

"Then sleep, my precious. You've earned it."

The soft kiss to his head was the last thing Dean was aware of for quite some time before Richard carried him to the car to drive home.

CHAPTER 4

THE NEXT morning, Richard woke to the enticing scent of freshly brewed coffee. Sunlight filtered through the drawn curtains, promising yet another nice, sunny day. Richard had set the alarm clock deliberately late, not at the usual seven o'clock. After such an intense scene, he and Dean both needed time to recover.

Richard sat up in bed, glancing at Dean, who was kneeling next to the bed, his gaze cast down, his posture perfect. Next to him was the tray with two cups of coffee and their breakfast. Even though neither of them was any good in the kitchen, they still knew how to push the button on a coffeemaker, and yogurt and cereal were impossible to muck up. Add a little fruit prepared by the housekeeper and left in the fridge, and breakfast was actually enjoyable. Of course, the presence of his lover, naked and totally submissive, was an added bonus. Richard reached down to pat Dean's head in recognition of his services.

"Thank you, boy. That looks delicious. Now hand me the tray and then come in here. I want you to join me today."

Dean did as instructed without questioning his master's orders. They had been together long enough for him to trust Richard completely in everything. Richard pulled Dean close, kissed him deeply, and then put one of the bowls in his hands. "Eat. Yesterday was strenuous."

Dean blushed just the tiniest bit, which was beyond adorable. Richard couldn't resist putting another quick kiss on the man's nose before he started eating himself. "As for your punishment, I will give you the cock cage after we shower. You know why I'm punishing you, boy?"

Dean swallowed the mouthful he had just taken. "Yes, Master. I came without permission."

"You did. We can't have that. You need to learn more self-restraint."

"Yes."

"Now, I've been thinking about taking a trip to Vegas next week. We haven't been there for quite some time, and I'm itching for some fun."

Dean took a sip of his coffee as if to hide his reaction. Richard knew it wasn't that he didn't like Vegas; he just couldn't see the fun in gambling. While he didn't complain, he never lingered in the vast halls with their blinking slot machines, and Richard suspected watching him play poker all night bored Dean out of his mind.

Richard tugged him closer. "I'm going to book you a day at the spa. What do you think?"

Dean put the coffee aside, a satisfied smile on his lips. "You know you had me at the word spa, don't you?"

"Of course I do. It's your kryptonite. Massages and treatments. I don't get it, but whatever makes my boy happy."

"A trip to a spa always makes me happy. Thank you."

"I haven't booked it yet."

"But you will as soon as we're out of bed. I know you, Master. You're a go-getter."

Richard chuckled, pleased by their easy bantering. "That I am. How's your book coming along?"

A shadow crossed Dean's features, and Richard knew something was wrong. He had suspected as much for the last three days but hadn't pressed the matter. Now he wondered if he should have said something sooner. "What's the problem, Dean?"

It couldn't be writer's block. Dean didn't even know how to spell that. He was like a well, constantly coming up with new ideas. If anything, the day had not enough hours for him to follow through with every inspiration he got. Dean looked uncomfortable enough for Richard to start worrying. "Dean?"

"It's the cover for my next thriller. I told them what I wanted, in great detail, but they just went and did something else, and I don't like it. When I told them so, they said something about marketing and the right target group, and then I just kind of faded out of the conversation."

"Dean. You should know better."

"I'm sorry. I didn't mean to keep it from you. I just didn't want to ruin our anniversary."

"Which is noble and also unnecessary. You bring your worries to me, just like you trust me to make the right decisions for both of us. Now get me my phone."

And that was the trouble with Dean. Nothing besides his writing could hold his interest for any amount of time. If he was unhappy with the cover, he would say so once, and if things didn't change, he would simply give up. It still upset him greatly; he just couldn't muster the energy to argue with whoever was in charge.

At the beginning of their relationship, Richard had tried to get Dean a competent agent to take care of things like covers and manuscript changes, but after half a year of fruitless interviews, he had given up. There was nobody out there fit to take care of his boy's needs, so Richard had taken that task on himself.

He was rich and influential enough to be recognized in the literary world without being an actual part of it, and he never wasted time. Saved on his phone were the numbers of all the big bosses, so when there was a problem, he went straight to the top. Just like now. After only two rings, his call was picked up.

"Mr. Miller. It's so nice to hear from you."

"Nice talking to you as well, Sebastian. I'm having a minor problem, and I know you're the man to fix it."

"Of course, Mr. Miller." The man on the other side of the line sounded apprehensive. Richard made no courtesy calls, and when he said he had a problem, that meant everybody else had a problem as well.

Richard had taught Sebastian quickly that it was best to go along with whatever the scary boyfriend of his publishing house's most successful writer wanted. Since Richard always got his way in the end, there was no point in delaying the inevitable.

"Dean just told me about the cover. He's not happy with it, and he told you so. Now can you explain to me why his wishes were completely ignored?"

There was a heavy silence on the other end while Sebastian seemed to mull over his answer. "The marketing team suggested a different approach for this title, since it's not within the series but a rather dark spin-off. They think it would be better to market it differently."

"And Dean's suggestions were not appropriate?"

Richard could almost see Sebastian wince. "They were. Just not what the marketing team had in mind."

"So you're telling me, because some guys at PR think they need to prove a point, my boyfriend had to put up with something that really makes him unhappy?"

Richard knew just the way he'd pronounced the word "boyfriend" was enough to inform Sebastian how serious this was. He wisely remained silent while Richard went on. "Dean's last book garnered you a net win in the seven digits, all with a cover he had personally selected. What makes you think this time will be any different?"

"Nothing, Mr. Miller. I will see to it that Dean gets the cover he wants. Can I do anything else for you?" Sebastian clearly knew when he had lost.

"No, thank you. That was all. Have a nice day, Sebastian."

Richard disconnected the call. "Now, that wasn't so difficult." When his gaze fell on Dean, he raised a brow. "You're flushed."

Dean panted. "Can't help it. I love it when you go all dominant and unrelenting. I'm so horny right now, my hole is itching to feel you."

Richard could feel his inner predator waking. "Let's take care of that. Get the lube and prepare yourself."

A malicious grin appeared on Dean's face. "Already done."

Richard laughed and pulled Dean into his arms. "I love the way your mind works. Let's take the edge off."

RICHARD DIDN'T waste time with preparations. They were both horny and, since Dean was already lubed, good to go. Richard grabbed Dean's hips and maneuvered him onto his lap and waiting cock. His voice sounded a bit breathless from excitement. "You're so beautiful, boy. So fucking beautiful."

Dean held still for a few heartbeats, enjoying the feel of Richard's length stretching him in the most delicious manner, before he started moving his hips. He loved and needed the kinky sex they usually shared, but once in a while, he opted for the vanilla version.

Simple, straight sex without any toys or games, just the two of them. No designated roles, no dynamics determining their actions. Only Richard Miller and Dean Connelly, two men who loved and complemented each other in ways neither of them had ever thought possible.

After their exhausting games of the previous night, they didn't last long. They climaxed together, sealing the orgasm with a deep, passionate kiss.

Richard retreated slowly from Dean's body but didn't let go of him. "Let's have a shower. Then we can talk punishment."

Dean slung his arms around his Dom's neck and let Richard carry him into the bathroom.

AFTER A prolonged shower with lots of groping and lathering each other, they returned to the bedroom, ready to follow up on the punishment Richard had promised. The moment Dean went down on his knees, the phone started ringing.

Dean groaned. He clearly recognized Richard's business ringtone, the one that always took Richard away from him.

Richard sighed but accepted the call. When somebody was suicidal enough to call him on a Sunday morning, it had to be urgent—and if it wasn't, the person in question had made their last call to Richard. "What?"

There was no reason to be overly courteous. He hated to be interrupted when dealing with his boy, especially when it was an occasion as delicious as this one. The person on the other end of the line paused, no doubt intimidated by his gruff tone. When she finally spoke, her tone sounded hesitant.

"This is Amber Smith speaking, Mr. Miller. I'm really sorry about phoning you on a Sunday, but it's urgent."

"Get on with it." Richard wasn't in the mood to waste time with pleasantries. Amber was his lawyer in New York, who handled all the businesses he had there. Her call meant he'd probably have to fly over, and soon, which sent his mood plummeting.

"The manager of your Diamond Spa has been arrested for fraud and identity theft. I've managed to keep it from the press, but the situation is not under control. It would be best if you came."

"What?" Richard couldn't believe it. "Wasn't it your office that did all the background checks on the employees? Didn't you assure me they were all clean as a whistle? What the hell is wrong with you?"

"As I said, I'm really sorry, Mr. Miller. Apparently Mr. DeLuca has been leading a double life for so long, he knew how to slip under our radar."

Richard was pacing the bedroom, barely able to rein his anger in. "If he's that good, how did he get caught? No, don't bother answering me. I'll be in New York in"—he checked his watch—"about six hours. By then, I expect you to have all the facts for me, as well as something we can tell the press."

"Yes, Mr. Miller. Shall I start looking for a replacement?"

That question forced a snort from Richard. "Don't bother. *Your* replacement is going to do that. Tell your bosses it was no pleasure doing business with them. I would also advise you to try to clean this mess up as best as you can, or I might feel inclined to sue you over your incompetence. I'll call you once I'm in New York."

With that he disconnected the call. He knew he was being harsh, but being lenient had never made a successful business. At least being lenient with lawyers. Those leeches charged horrendous sums just for being available to him, and they topped those sums when they actually had to do something other than see to papers being properly signed. For the fortune he spent on them, Richard expected flawless performance.

Messing up a new project was something he was capable of himself. That's why he had the lawyers, to prevent scenarios where he lost money because of wrong choices. He most certainly did not pay them for losing money in his stead. And a scandal like this could lose him a fortune if not handled carefully. He had to call Martin to redo all the backup checks for employees at the Diamond Spa.

"You're leaving?" Dean didn't sound happy.

He never was when Richard had to go on business trips. In the beginning of their relationship, that had been a major problem. Before they met, Dean had lived for his writing and didn't care for the outside world. Once they had become permanent, he started to grow restless whenever Richard wasn't there.

Dean needed structure and stability in his life to function properly. Richard provided both, although it was harder to do when he wasn't there. For a moment he contemplated taking Dean along to New York. After their intense scene last night, everything inside him screamed to stay close to his boy. Unfortunately things would get ugly at the spa. Having Dean there was not a good idea. Which meant he had to come up with a strict routine for the next two or three days.

Richard closed his eyes and breathed in deeply a couple of times to get back into the right headspace before he addressed his boy.

"Present, boy."

Dean's eyes widened. As Richard hoped, the commanding tone didn't fail to jostle him out of his pouting. He hastened to do as he was told, a happy smile tugging at his lips.

"I have to fly to New York, boy. I will try to be back in two, three days, tops, but me not being here does not mean you won't be punished. You will wear the cock cage all the time except when you're in the shower. Since I can't fuck you myself, you will wear the vibrating plug, the one I can control over my cell."

Dean made a whimpering sound. His cock was standing proudly in front of him.

Richard grinned evilly. "You'll have trouble fitting into the cage, aroused as you are. You better start thinking about cold showers and roadkill."

"Please, Master! Just once more before you go?" Dean sounded like a puppy, and Richard loved it.

"I don't know, boy. If I let you come once more, then the punishment has to be increased. Are you willing to accept whatever I deem appropriate?"

Richard could see Dean's mind working. He wouldn't have been surprised if steam had come out of his boy's ears. Dean needed to come, desperately, but he also knew how ingenious Richard could be when it came to punishment. It was a risk he never took lightly. This time his need got the better of him.

"I accept, Master."

"Then get over to the bed. On your back."

While Dean hastily scrambled onto the bed, Richard had to suppress a snicker. His boy wouldn't like what was coming.

As soon as Dean got into position, Richard grabbed the lube, squirted a generous amount on Dean's right palm, and stepped back. "Master? I don't understand."

"You said you needed to come. Go ahead. Give me a show, and don't forget to lube your hole as well. I have a vibrator waiting to go there."

Understanding dawned on Dean, but he did not complain. Only a slight frown betrayed his disappointment.

Since Richard had taken the fun out of this particular orgasm, Dean got over with it quickly. He stroked himself with his right hand while his left fingered his hole, slicking it with lube. It didn't take him long to shoot, and Richard could tell that his boy wasn't truly satisfied.

Well, tough luck. He would be in a week, when Richard would allow him his next orgasm. He went into the bathroom, wet a cloth, and cleaned his boy quickly before he put the cock cage on. Once the device was in place, Richard slapped Dean's thigh playfully.

"On all fours, boy. Show me your hole."

Again, Dean complied without protest, the very picture of an obedient sub. Except Richard could tell by the tense line of Dean's shoulder muscles how upset his boy was.

Pushing his sub was a Dom's job, one Richard took very seriously.

"Well lubed, boy. I think I'll fill you with my seed once more before I go."

Richard poured some slick on his own rock-hard cock before he slid easily into Dean's tight hole. His boy's body welcomed him as it always did, although there was a strain to his moans. Being fucked with a cock cage on was not a pleasurable experience.

Richard felt lenient enough to make it quick. He thrust into Dean with an unrelenting rhythm, trying to hit his prostate in the process. When his boy squirmed and whimpered beneath him, Richard allowed his own orgasm to build. He pumped his semen into the tight channel and then retreated quickly.

"Don't lose a drop, boy. I'm going to trap my spunk inside you."

"Yesss, Master." Richard knew Dean loved it when he did that. It reassured him of his master's love and care.

Richard retrieved the fat, vibrating butt plug he intended to use on his boy from the cabinet. After lubing it up, he inserted it carefully, sliding the thick rubber shaft in and out of Dean's twitching hole before pushing it in all the way. He twisted it a few times, until Dean's desperate moans told him it was nudging his gland. Satisfied with his work, Richard grabbed his phone to test the plug. When he hit the button on the app, the plug started to vibrate, causing Dean's hips to thrust helplessly.

"This is going to be fun. I'm sure you're going to enjoy this, boy."

Dean looked at him dazed. "Whatever you wish, Master."

"My good boy. I love you."

"I love you too, Master."

Richard kissed Dean once more before he got dressed. He took out the bag he had always sitting packed in his wardrobe for emergencies like this, told Dean he would give him instructions on his cell, and went to put the fire out in New York.

Chapter 5

RICHARD HAD been gone for two days.

Dean hated every second of it. He never did well without his master, but this time it was particularly bad. Even though Richard had come up with some truly interesting ideas to keep Dean occupied and took the time to text him new instructions every three hours, Dean felt restless.

It wasn't the cock cage, although that definitely added to his stress. It was a feeling of dread he just couldn't shake. Knowing he was being silly didn't make it any better.

He had spent the better part of four hours going over the edits for his latest novel when the phone rang. Nightwish's "Sleeping Sun" told him it was Richard. Dean fumbled for the phone with trembling fingers, eager to hear his master's voice. "Yes?"

"Good afternoon to you too, boy. Did you have a good day?" Richard's voice sounded as deep and affectionate as always. Nevertheless, Dean could hear the strain in it. Things were obviously not going well over in New York.

"Now that you're calling, my day has turned wonderful, Master."

Rumbling laughter came through the connection. "Flattery won't get you out of the cage, boy."

"I know. So please tell me you're coming home. Please." Dean knew he sounded desperate, but he couldn't shake the feeling of dread.

"I know this is hard for you. I ask you to be strong for one more night. I'll be back tomorrow evening."

"Really? Thank God."

"Dean! What is it? The last time you were so out of it when I left was after we first met. Is something wrong?"

Richard's tone was rife with concern. Dean hated himself for adding to his Dom's burden, but he had learned a long time ago to trust Richard with everything. Telling the man his concerns and worries, letting him deal with them, was part of their relationship. And as much as Dean loathed himself for being so weak sometimes, he was still glad to have somebody to carry him.

"It's nothing concrete, Master. I just feel antsy, unable to concentrate. It's as if I'm waiting for something to happen. I'm restless."

There was a moment's silence on the other end, Richard, no doubt, contemplating Dean's problem and thinking about a solution. When he spoke, his voice had that confident Dom ring to it that always managed to calm Dean down.

"Thank you for telling me, boy. That was very good of you. Now here is what you'll do. I want you to write a story for me, one about a Dom and his sub. Make it kinky. If it pleases you, add a paranormal angle. It's three o'clock now. You keep writing till six. Then you order dinner from Mamma's and, boy, I expect you to eat, do you understand? After dinner, you go into the shower. You're allowed to take the cock cage off and the plug out to clean yourself. When you're done, you put both back on and go to bed naked. Starting at eight, I'm going to torture you with the vibrator. Do you hear me?"

"Yes, Master." Dean sighed with relief. Just like that, with a few well-placed commands, his Dom had given him structure, a safety line he could use to get through the rest of the day. "Thank you, Master. I can't wait for tomorrow to come."

"You're welcome, boy. And not only tomorrow will come."

It was a rather cheesy innuendo, but it made Dean laugh. "I love you, Master."

"I love you, boy. Now get with the program."

DEAN WAS busy writing the story Richard had required from him when his phone rang. His first impulse was to ignore it and keep the story flowing, but the unknown caller didn't seem inclined to give up. The call went to voicemail three times and started ringing again shortly after. Dean finally gave in. "Connelly."

"Mr. Connelly? Elisa Connor from Connor and Partners speaking. Do you have a moment?"

Dean already regretted having taken the call. The woman sounded formal; her tone of voice suggested she was a lawyer, and Dean already knew that nothing good ever came out of him talking to them.

"I'm quite busy at the moment. If it's not too urgent, we can make an appointment sometime later this week." Or never. That would be fine with him as well.

"Unfortunately, it *is* urgent. Very urgent. And nothing I wish to discuss over the phone. If you could give me just an hour of your time…."

The woman was good, he had to give her that. Her voice had just enough drama in it to make him wonder. But he hadn't been with Richard

Miller, entrepreneur par excellence, for five years and not learned a thing or two.

"Can you call me back in ten minutes? I need to check my schedule and arrange some things."

"Of course, Mr. Connelly. I'll call you back."

With that, Elisa Connor disconnected, sending Dean into action. First, he tried to call Richard and went straight to voicemail. Then he typed Connor and Partners into his laptop. When the site of a law firm in Miami popped up, he knew there was trouble.

From the looks of it, it was a big firm, and from the lack of information given, one that dealt with rich clients only. They did have a list of their lawyers, though, and Elisa Connor's name popped up.

Dean stared blankly at the screen for a few heartbeats; then he pulled out his phone once more. Since Richard wasn't available, he had to go for the second-best choice.

"Carmichael."

"Master Martin. It's Dean."

"I guessed as much from the caller ID, boy. What's the matter? You sound stressed."

"A woman named Elisa Connor has called me. She says she has urgent business to discuss. My master is still in New York, and I don't know what to do."

Dean could hear the panic in his own voice and tried to take deep, calming breaths. Martin's voice over the phone helped him with that. He sounded reassuring, strong. Just what Dean needed.

"It's fine, boy. You did the right thing. I assume this Elisa woman is a lawyer?"

"Yes. I looked her up on the web. There is a law firm called Connor and Partners in Miami… I just don't know what she might want from me."

"Can you stall her till tomorrow?"

"She said it was urgent. I don't know if she's just a good actor, but I believed her. Plus, I think she's already in the area. She was talking while in the car."

Martin stayed silent for a moment. "We have several options here, Dean. You can just tell her to come back tomorrow, when Richard is back. That's probably the wisest thing to do. What makes me a little nervous, though, is that she has your cell number. Ask her how she got it, because by any rights, she shouldn't have it. Unless you were careless with it?"

"Never!" Dean did nothing to keep the hurt out of his tone.

His cell number was indeed a well-kept secret. After a crazy fan had hacked his previous phone and left disturbing pictures and messages on it,

Richard had seen to it that it couldn't happen again. His new number was known to only a few people, and he never used it to make random calls. Come to think of it, the fact that there had been no caller ID should have stopped him from taking the call. Dean groaned. When would he ever learn?

"It's too late for that, boy."

Master Martin appeared to have read his thoughts, but that was a Dom for you. "Now we have to deal with the potential fallout. When she calls you back, ask where she got that number. If she has no satisfying explanation, tell her to fuck the hell off. If she has one, tell her you are inconvenienced today and make an appointment for tomorrow, when Richard is back. Can you do that?"

"Yes, Sir. I can do that." When he had strict orders to follow, Dean could do anything.

"Good boy. If there's anything else, call me back immediately. I can't leave here right away, but when you need me, let me know it."

"Yes, Sir. Thank you."

Martin disconnected the call and only seconds later, the phone rang again. Dean took a deep breath and answered.

"Connelly."

"Mr. Connelly. Elisa Connor, again. Have you checked your schedule?"

"I have. But before we talk about that, I have a question. How did you get this number?"

There was a long pause during which Elisa Connor obviously tried to phrase her answer. When she finally spoke again, her words knocked Dean right on his ass.

"Your sister, Tricia Connelly, gave it to me."

CHAPTER 6

"SHE ALSO gave me your address. Can I come over? I'm in the area and could be there in about fifteen minutes. Mr. Connelly?"

Dean managed to focus enough to answer Elisa. "Yes. Yes, you can come over."

He didn't register when Elisa ended the call or how the cell slipped from his lifeless fingers. Something was awfully wrong, he just knew it.

Two years ago, his beloved big sister had moved to Germany. The international law firm she worked for had opened a new headquarters in Munich, and she was in charge. The hours were beyond crazy. In many respects, Tricia was like Richard, always giving everything.

So all Dean had heard from his sister in the last two years were a few letters, sometimes with pictures. The last one had been four months ago, when she told him she would come back to the States soon. Since then, nothing. And now a lawyer contacted him, claiming she had gotten his number from Tricia? That was bad. Really bad.

Dean rose unsteadily to his feet. The butt plug nudged against his gland, but right now he found it irritating, not comforting. Knowing it would earn him an unpleasant punishment, but unable to care at the moment, he went to the bathroom to get it out. Since he was at it, he also unfastened the cock cage.

Memories of him and Tricia flooded his mind, all the more vivid because he didn't know what was going on.

Dean had only been seventeen when his parents found out he was gay. Christopher and Faith Connelly both came from old, conservative money and had raised their two children accordingly. There was not a lot of love lost between them. Not that his parents were particularly caring toward each other either. All that counted was how others, especially their peers, perceived them. It was important to drive the right cars, to make the right investments, go to the right country club, study at the right university.

Both Dean and Tricia had learned early in their lives to never mess with their parents' expectations. Tricia, who was five years older than Dean, had taught him all the necessary tricks to keep his mother from breathing down his neck.

When he realized he was gay, Dean had turned to Tricia, because she was the only person in the world he trusted.

She hadn't let him down. She had supported him, helped him to keep it a secret from their parents. It was Dean's bad luck that one of his father's business partners had decided to hit on him. When Dean turned him down, the man accused him of having made the first move. Dean had been too shocked by the accusation, as well as his father's vile reaction, to say anything in his defense.

Christopher Connelly had thrown him out that same day, telling him to never show his face again. Even though their relationship had been strained at the best of times, it still hurt to see the disgust and hatred in his father's eyes.

Again, Tricia had saved him. She let him crash at her student apartment until he found his own place. With a part-time job as a waiter and the extra cash Tricia sent his way every month, he finished high school and started studying at a small university.

It was then that he wrote his first thriller. Much to his surprise, the book was picked up by NestEgg Publishing and became an instant bestseller. Something about the main character, a female called Laura Ashbourne, seemed to enthrall readers. Apart from the satisfaction, it also brought him financial independence.

Dean tried to pay his sister back, but Tricia refused him outright. Instead, she demanded a hand-signed copy of each new book he wrote.

At twenty-five he'd met Richard, who swept him off his feet and introduced him to the world of BDSM. From that day on, Dean's life had been bliss.

A bliss that lawyer woman was going to destroy, he just knew it.

As if on cue, the landline rang. It was the guard at the lobby, asking if he was expecting a Ms. Elisa Connor. Dean confirmed her story and went to the door to open it for her once she reached the top level where he and Richard lived.

Elisa Connor was a tall woman in her forties, if Dean had to guess her age. She wore her hair in a tight bun. The black-rimmed glasses, her tailored jacket, and the matching pencil skirt with sensible shoes made her look like an expensively dressed version of his elementary school teacher.

Elisa held out her hand in that slightly condescending manner all lawyers showed when dealing with nonlawyers. Dean had always wondered if they had to participate in special courses just to get the intimidating part right.

"Mr. Connelly, I presume?"

"Yes, that would be me. Please, come in."

Dean let go of her hand and stepped aside so she could pass. While he closed the door, he could see how Elisa took in the apartment.

It was huge. The entire upper floor was theirs. Since Richard loved open spaces and full natural light, the entrance hall merged with the living area. An expensive leather couch in the shape of a crescent moon, custom-made, of course, faced a window that gave a spectacular view of the city and opened out to a veranda with a pizza oven and a set of lounges. The floor was Brazilian walnut, the walls painted in an eggshell shade. They didn't have many trinkets around, both of them preferring clean surroundings. They did have paintings and photographs, though, and not of the cheap kind.

To Dean, this was all normal. He had grown up rich, made a fair amount of money with his books, and being with Richard was just a constant stream of all the privileges money could buy. It wasn't something he still noticed. Only when he saw the reaction of strangers to his home—which, admittedly, hardly ever happened because they rarely allowed others in their sanctuary—did he realize how insanely wealthy his boyfriend was.

He had to give it to Elisa, though; she snapped out of her trance quickly. Coming from such a big firm, she was probably used to the blatant display of wealth.

"You have a very lovely home, Mr. Connelly."

Dean had to suppress a chuckle. What a poor shot at being polite. "Thank you so much. The credit for that goes to our interior designer. He's a genius. Now, would you care to tell me what this is all about? Why has my sister given you this address? Which, by the way, should remain confidential."

Elisa Connor looked genuinely sad for a moment, and the feeling of dread knotted Dean's stomach once again. "Of course it will. As well as your cell number. This information was given to me under confidentiality, so you can rest assured."

She took a deep breath. "Can we sit down? This is not easy for me."

Dean indicated the leather couch with his chin. Once they both had settled, Elisa started talking again, as if afraid to be silent for too long.

"I met Tricia when she did an internship at Connor and Partners. She was such a gifted lawyer. Before she went to Germany, she came to me to settle her affairs in case anything should happen to her. That's when I got this number and address."

Elisa paused once more. The wet sheen in her eyes told Dean before she opened her mouth what had happened. "I'm so sorry, Mr. Connelly. Tricia died in a car accident two days ago. Since she didn't want you to be contacted by strangers in case anything happened to her, she listed me as her emergency contact. That's why I'm here today."

Dean just sat there and stared. There was an off feeling in his body, a tingling he couldn't place. As if his insides were about to constrict, to squeeze until there was nothing left inside him.

He could see Elisa's mouth moving, but no sound filtered through. The world had stopped and there was nothing that would make it spin again.

Tricia was dead.

His beloved, laughing, caring, beautiful, brilliant sister was no more.

His only family was gone.

Dean wondered if the feeling of emptiness was normal, or if it was because his heart had stopped. He ached, he needed Richard, but he was alone.

"Mr. Connelly?" Elisa's sharp tone managed to pierce through the haze surrounding him. "I'm very sorry about your loss. Unfortunately, there is more. I don't know if you're aware, but your sister has a three-month old daughter. Her name is Emily. The pregnancy was complicated, and Tricia didn't want you to worry, so she didn't tell you about it. She said she wanted to surprise you when she returned home. Since there is no father registered for Emily, she is now orphaned."

Dean gulped back his tears. There were just too many things crashing over his head all at once, so he clung to the things that came to his mind.

"What does that mean? What will happen to her?"

"In her will, Tricia named you guardian for Emily. She didn't want her parents to take the child. The will is very specific. You are also the sole heir to Tricia's fortune. Emily has a trust in her name that you will control as well.

"Tricia meant to tell you all these things when she came back. I know this must all be very confusing, and I'm sorry I couldn't break this to you in a gentler manner. Emily will arrive in the States in three hours. A woman from the Florida Department of Children and Families Child Welfare Program will take care of her until you have made up your mind and the formalities are cleared. Do you have any questions? Or do you need time to yourself?"

CHAPTER 7

DEAN BLINKED, desperately trying to get a handle on the situation. He had never felt so cornered and helpless before. "Actually, both. This is a lot to process. Tricia never mentioned anything about being pregnant. Emily is already three months old, you say?"

Elisa nodded.

"Then why didn't she tell me?"

"She said she felt it was important to see you personally for this. When she had Emily, she was so full of joy. As I said, there were complications during her pregnancy. It took a toll on her, not just physically. She was always so strong, so used to being in control. And then her body betrayed her, so to speak. It was hard."

"You two were close." It was a statement, not a question.

Elisa eyed Dean warily. "I know, it's not very professional, but we already knew each other and, well, I always admired her. She made it easy for me to like her."

"That was my sister." Dean fought back the tears that threatened to overwhelm him. "What happens to Emily should I not take her?"

Elisa's expression turned serious. "Then the state will take matters in hand. I don't wish to pressure you and neither did Tricia. She never expected for things to turn out like this. None of us did. First, the Child Welfare Program will get in touch with your parents to see if they would be willing to take Emily in. And, yes, that will happen despite what Tricia has stated in her will. If your parents refuse to take the baby, then she will go to foster care. A blond-haired, blue-eyed, white baby girl won't take long to place. There's a long list of couples waiting to adopt a child. She will be well cared for, that I can promise. What I can't promise is that you will be allowed to have contact with her. If her new parents don't want it, which is a high possibility, then they can cut contact."

Dean mulled those words over. He didn't like them. Didn't like the idea of his little niece being with strangers, or, even worse, his parents. Growing up with their lies and hatred and arrogance.

Tricia had always been on his side. When he had told her about his book, she had been nothing but supportive, never once indicating she thought it was a ridiculous idea at best. Emily was now all he had left of his big sister. All the family that remained.

There was no way he could not take her in. She was his.

The thought of what Richard would say about all this hit him like a bucket of ice water, but not even the displeasure of his Dom and lover could change Dean's decision. They would work things out. Richard would understand. He always did. Dean could do this.

"I want her. I don't know anything about babies, but I guess there's books I can read?"

Relief washed over Elisa's features. She managed a shaky smile. "There are not just books. The Child Welfare Program can provide you with the contacts of nurses and capable nannies to help you in the beginning. Remember, when people have their first child, they are usually completely clueless."

"So how does this work?"

"I'm going to inform the authorities that you are willing to take Emily in. There is some paperwork to go through, but that shouldn't take too long. We can schedule your first meeting with Emily for the day after tomorrow. I have to warn you, though. They probably won't let her stay with you immediately. Somebody from the office is going to check your home, to determine if it's okay for a child to live here, and maybe they'll insist on you taking a baby-care course before they leave Emily to your care. If things go smoothly, she can move in with you in a week or two."

That didn't sound so bad. Dean rose from the couch. "Thank you. And now, I need time to myself."

Elisa rose as well. The sad expression was back on her face. She was about to turn to the door when she suddenly stopped. "Do you want to see her picture?"

Dean froze. His heart hammered against his chest as if he'd run ten miles. "You have a picture?"

"It's not a very good one, but the authorities in Germany, who put her on the plane, sent me one. They've been very considerate."

Elisa unlocked her cell, tapped at the screen a few times, and then held it toward Dean.

The picture didn't show much—a little blurry and clearly taken in some sort of waiting room—yet it had his full attention. Emily was sleeping. She was dressed in a cute pink ensemble with a matching cap. Her tiny little fingers held a stuffed animal Dean identified as a mammoth.

His niece was beautiful and perfect, and his heart melted.

"Thank you." He hesitated a moment. He had just remembered something else. "Will Tricia be on the plane as well?"

Elisa shook her head. "Her body is still in the morgue. Once they give clearance, she will be cremated and the ashes will be sent to you. She had no specific wishes what you should do with them. She just wanted you to have them."

Dean already knew there was no way he could spread his sister's ashes anywhere. He wanted her close so she could see her little girl growing up. Elisa shot him one last sympathetic glance before she left. Dean closed the door, sank to the floor, and stared into nothing for a while.

Then he started to cry.

CHAPTER 8

RICHARD TOOK a deep cleansing breath when he entered the lobby of the apartment building. The three days in New York had been hell. He had worked nonstop to minimize the damage that good-for-nothing manager had caused. Things were still not smooth sailing, but it was nothing the assistant to the manager couldn't deal with on her own. If she kept doing a good job, Richard would offer her the position permanently.

He greeted the receptionist and headed for the elevator, swiping his phone on the way. He stared at the vibrator app, not sure if he should activate it. He hadn't heard back from Dean since the day before, when he had missed a call. Richard had been in a meeting then, and when he tried to call Dean back, it had gone straight to voicemail. Since there had been no further calls from Dean, and he also hadn't responded to Richard's texts, Richard assumed Dean had gotten lost in his writing, which happened on a regular basis. In fact, he was glad, because when Dean was in a writing trance, he didn't care about Richard's absence so much. Truth be told, he probably forgot Richard even existed. Only the story mattered then. But now Richard was back home, and it was time for Dean to snap out of work. The vibrator app was the perfect way to announce his return.

At the moment, it would alert his boy to his arrival. If Dean had any sense, he would be welcoming Richard on his knees, in a perfect display position. Richard felt his own cock harden just thinking about his boy. He opened the door to their apartment.

There was no Dean.

An eerie silence hung in the air, one that put Richard on high alert. Something was wrong. This was not the content atmosphere generated by Dean working. Dropping his suitcase, he marched into the wide living area.

"Dean? Boy! Where are you?"

Richard felt panic tighten his chest. Dean not being where he was supposed to be was bad. It meant something had happened. He quickly searched the other rooms in the apartment before he came back to the living room.

Just when Richard was ready to call the police, he saw movement on the veranda. He rushed outside, where he found Dean curled up in one of the lounges, a blanket wrapped around his body despite the warmth of the Floridian evening.

"Dean! My God, what's happened? Are you all right?"

Any idea about a scene vanished from Richard's mind. His boy was in no shape to do anything, that much was obvious.

Dean slowly lifted his head. Dark circles under his eyes dominated his pale face, his hair hung ragged, his eyes were bloodshot. He had a death grip on his cell phone, and the way he looked at Richard made him shiver.

"She's dead. Tricia. She's dead."

There was so much pain in those words, so much hurt and loss. Richard felt it as well. He had always liked Tricia, not only because she was Dean's sister, but also because she was a fascinating person, almost as dominant as himself.

Dean and Tricia had also been exceptionally close, something that had fueled Richard's jealousy more than once at the beginning of their relationship. He could only imagine how the news must devastate Dean.

"What happened?" Richard sat down next to Dean and pulled him close, knowing how much better his boy did when he had this kind of bodily reassurance.

"Yesterday a lawyer called me. She said she had my number from Tricia and insisted on a meeting. She came by and told me. It was a car accident. She… oh my God, Richard, she's gone!"

Dean started sobbing. Given how raw his voice sounded, he hadn't been doing much else during the night. Richard held him close, making soothing sounds at the back of his throat, trying to pour his strength and comfort into his lover. After an eternity the sobbing finally eased. Dean snuggled even closer to Richard, inhaling his scent.

"There's more."

Richard caressed Dean's head. There was always more. "What is it, boy? Tell me, so I can handle it for you."

The words didn't fail to put Dean more at ease. "Tricia has a daughter. A three-month-old. She's called Emily." Dean hesitated a moment. "Tricia appointed me as Emily's guardian in her will."

Richard tensed. This was indeed more. More than he thought he could handle. Guardian for a baby? He had never thought about having children; they were something that happened to other people, people willing to give their lives up for those tiny harbingers of chaos and destruction.

He and Dean had a perfect life, with fulfilling, time-consuming jobs and an even more fulfilling lifestyle, kinky hot sex included. They most definitely had no room for a child. They didn't *know* anything about children. And weren't you supposed to take care of a kitten first?

His thoughts jumbled, something Richard wasn't used to. He was always in control. Always. It was part of who he was. Nothing could surprise him. And Dean needed him. Relied on him. Freaking out was not an option.

"Do you want to see her?" Dean held up his cell tentatively, as if he wasn't sure how Richard would react. Richard managed a nod. He was still thunderstruck.

Dean fumbled with his phone and then shoved it under Richard's nose. There was a blurry picture of something very pink against the background of a boring gray waiting room.

"Umm, nice?" Richard didn't know what Dean expected of him. He didn't even know what he expected of himself, and that made him cranky. Dean's obvious fascination with the little pink bundle made it worse.

"Isn't she beautiful? Elisa, the lawyer, said she'll come by with her tomorrow. I just wish Tricia would be the one introducing her to me. Well, at least I'll get to see my niece for the first time."

Richard hated to break Dean from his bittersweet place. "I'm not sure that's a good idea, boy. We obviously can't keep her, so why don't you spare yourself the added pain?"

The moment he ended the sentence, Richard knew he'd made a mistake. Dean grew stiff in his arms before he slipped from Richard's grasp.

"What do you mean, we can't keep her? She's my niece. She's all that's left of Tricia, and my sister trusted me with her care. How can you even suggest sending her away?"

Dean was getting agitated. He could rarely muster the energy to work himself so up, but when he did, it meant Richard stood no chance.

Dean could be surprisingly stubborn when he wanted to. Now was not the time to upset his boy even more. Now was the time to make a tactical retreat and offer Dean the support he needed. They could talk about it once they both had time to clear their thoughts. Richard was convinced it wouldn't take Dean long to realize how impossible it was for them to take care of a baby. Once the harsh reality hit him, he would see reason. With all their money, they could buy Emily the future she deserved without getting too involved.

"I'm sorry, Dean. I didn't mean to be—thoughtless. But you're very upset at the moment. I'm afraid seeing that baby is going to make it worse."

Dean's features softened a bit. He leaned back into Richard's touch, clearly needing the reassurance. "Her name is Emily, not 'that baby.' And, yes, you're right. I'm deeply shaken. Losing Tricia was never an option in my head. Aside from you, she was the only constant in my life, my pillar of support. I feel like half my life has turned to ashes, leaving only emptiness. I've lost my ground, and I need you more than ever."

"Don't worry, Dean. I have you. Always. I promise. Now how about we go and take a nice hot bath together? I can try to relax you a bit, and then we can order your favorite from Mamma's. Allow me to take care of you."

As predicted by Richard, Dean melted upon hearing those words, spoken in his best Dom tone. "Thank you, Master."

RICHARD LED Dean to their spacious bathroom with the walk-in shower and the gigantic tub that doubled as a Jacuzzi. He sat Dean down on the toilet seat before he started to run hot water in the tub.

After a short hesitation, he selected a lavender bathing oil he had brought home from a visit to France. While he poured a generous amount into the whirling water, he contemplated commenting on the cock cage and vibrator lying abandoned on the floor, but decided against it. He wasn't even sure if he would punish Dean for taking them out without permission. In light of what had happened, their little game seemed almost shallow.

"I'm sorry I took it off."

Dean had followed his gaze and drawn the right conclusion. Richard turned to his boy, his lover of five years, and brushed his lips in a chaste kiss. "Don't worry, boy. You had good reason. I would never punish you for that."

As if Richard's words had taken a great portion of tension out of his body, Dean sagged. Richard pulled him close. "You have to get undressed, my love."

Dean followed the instruction with tired, jerky movements that told Richard louder than words how exhausted his boy was.

When Dean was naked, Richard guided him to the tub. He slid out of his own clothes, stepped in first, and helped Dean. They sat down, Dean cradled against Richard's broad chest. As the heat of the water started to seep into them, Richard could feel Dean relaxing more and more. His head lolled to the side, his breathing deepened, and then he was fast asleep.

Only when the water started turning cold did Richard reluctantly wake his sleeping boy. Dean desperately needed the rest. What he didn't need, though, was getting sick.

Richard toweled him dry as quickly as possible before he tucked him under the covers of their king-size bed. Dean never fully woke from his exhausted slumber.

When Richard slid in next to him, he cuddled close, made a content little noise in the back of his throat, and started softly snoring again. It took a little longer for Richard to find the same peace.

Too much had happened in the last few hours for him to just let go.

CHAPTER 9

THE NEXT morning, Richard woke to the intoxicating smell of fresh coffee. Dean was kneeling next to the bed, the tray with both their breakfast on the nightstand. He looked better, refreshed. There were still lines around his eyes that spoke of the emotional pain he was suffering, but his complexion had changed from ghastly back to a healthier coloring.

"Good morning, boy. Thank you for breakfast."

"Good morning to you too, Master. You're welcome."

Richard reached for his cup to take that first life-giving sip that woke him all the way up. After he had savored the strong flavor for a few moments, he put his own cup away, took Dean's, and held it to his boy's lips. Dean made an appreciative noise as he gulped. Good boy that he was, Richard knew he hadn't touched anything, neither food nor drink, before bringing the tray to his Dom.

It was not that he wasn't allowed to. Since Dean often forgot to sustain himself when he was engrossed in his writing, Richard even encouraged him to eat whenever he felt an inkling of hunger. Breakfast was a little different, though. It was part of their bonding routine, something that helped them both focus for the day. Not to mention that feeding Dean led to more carnal delights on a regular basis. It wasn't something either of them wanted to miss.

The carnal delights, though, had to wait for another day. As much as Richard wanted things to go back to normal, as much as he wanted to distract Dean, show him how good their life as a couple was, it wasn't what his boy needed right now.

Richard put the mug down and helped Dean climb into bed. They had their breakfast in silence. Only when they had both finished did Richard speak. "So, what is the plan for today?"

Dean fidgeted a little. "I wanted to call Peyton, to see if he can come over. If Emily stays here, she needs a nursery. Then there's all the stuff we're going to need. Clothes, diapers, formula. Perhaps it's a good idea to look for a competent nanny to help us in the beginning. I was also thinking about taking a parenting course, although, if we do find an experienced nanny, that may be unnecessary, since he or she could teach us."

Richard had to admit he was impressed. That sounded suspiciously like a well-thought plan, something that never came easily to Dean. He also noted the tentative use of "we" when Dean spoke.

His boy was unsure.

Given Dean's reaction the other day, Richard knew better than to push him. That didn't mean he couldn't leave him hanging, though. If Dean seriously wanted this, it was better if he found out immediately how stressful having a small child could be.

"Sounds like a solid plan, boy. I'll be out most of the day. I have a few things I need to catch up with. Just text me when the lawyer comes with your niece."

When he saw the defeated expression on Dean's face, Richard felt like a monster. He hadn't said it in so many words, but they had been together long enough that Dean could read between the lines.

Richard didn't want a child, and he was leaving it to Dean. In other words, he was being an insensitive, cruel prick. Richard knew that. He just couldn't help himself. He couldn't stand there and watch Dean try to fit a baby into their life. Richard wasn't sure if he could keep his mouth shut if he stayed, and the last thing he wanted was a fight with Dean. At least not a full-on fight. The passive-aggressive approach would have to do for the moment.

Richard told himself that if Dean had shown signs that he was still too upset about Tricia's death to be left alone this morning, he would have agreed to stay. It sounded like a lame excuse even to his own ears, but he was determined to stick with it. Dean wanted the child; let him deal with the ramifications. And Dean wouldn't be alone, strictly speaking. He would be talking to a lot of people and have Peyton over to look at the future nursery.

It was obvious Dean had put his focus on Emily, which was a good thing concerning his grief about Tricia's death, and rather inconvenient regarding Richard's plans to stop a baby from invading their lives.

Dean just nodded, trying to hide his anguish. "As you wish, Master. I'd better start working, then."

Richard watched Dean leave the bedroom to take the tray with their empty mugs and cereal bowls back to the kitchen. He felt the urge to go after his boy, wrap him in his arms, and make it all right, but he had to stay strong.

To keep their perfect, happy life, Dean had to return to reality. And fast. With a sigh, Richard got up from the bed, showered, and dressed before he left the apartment. He blew a kiss to Dean, who was already talking on the phone, most probably with Peyton. Well, that wasn't his problem, though, was it? He would allow Dean to engage in this foolishness and then be there to catch his boy once he realized the impossibility of raising a child.

FROM THE corner of his eye, Dean saw Richard leave.

He felt like a block of ice was suddenly growing in his stomach. Obviously, his Dom didn't want Emily. Dean felt as if his heart was torn apart. His love for Richard fought with his instinct to protect the little family he still had. Even though he hadn't met her yet, his feelings for Emily won over his need to placate his lover.

Richard would come around. Once he met Emily, he would surely see how much she needed both of them, and then he would do his Dom thing, and they would become a happy little family. Until then, there was enough stuff he had to take care of. Peyton was still bitching about how early he had called him.

"Do you know when I last got up at seven thirty in the morning? No? Because even I can't remember! This is way too early. How can you even dial at such an ungodly hour?"

Dean felt a smile tug at the corner of his mouth. Despite everything that had happened, Peyton's easygoing banter managed to lighten his mood. When his friend paused to take in some much-needed oxygen, Dean intercepted smoothly.

"I'm terribly sorry for inconveniencing you. A lot has happened, and I really need your help."

"What's going on?"

And that was the other thing about Peyton. When his friends were in need, he dropped everything to help them out.

Dean quickly told him about Tricia's death, which caused Peyton to sob. He and Tricia had known each other. When Dean came to the part about being the guardian of a three-month-old now, Peyton couldn't decide whether to keep on crying or start laughing. He did both, and Dean had to hold his phone at arm's length to prevent his eardrums from exploding. When the snorting sounds finally ceased, he deemed it safe to put it back to his ear.

"Are you done?"

"Not quite, but I'm working on it. I mean, you have to admit, it *is* an interesting idea. Do you think Richard's going to buy leather rattles? Is there such a thing as a black pacifier?"

Dean winced. "Richard is not yet on board with the idea."

"Of course not. Richard loves his freedom, and children are like lead weights on your ankles."

Peyton sounded matter-of-fact. He was usually dead-on when it came to judging people, and Dean wondered if his estimate of Richard bode well for their future with Emily. A little annoyed with himself, he shoved that disturbing thought to the back of his mind. He did not have time for speculation.

"Lead weight or not, I still need you to plan and furnish the nursery for me."

"You—what? Dean, honey, you're aware I don't do icky family stuff, aren't you? I'm a prize-winning interior designer and sought-after *adult* playroom genius. The total amount of nurseries I've done is zero."

Dean chuckled. "I know how good you are with playrooms for grown-ups. This could be a new experience for you. Something to add to your list of achievements. Designer of children's rooms."

Dean was only half joking. For one, because Peyton was right about himself. He was a damn genius when it came to interior design and BDSM playrooms. Even though he wasn't into the lifestyle himself, he just knew how to build the perfect room for pain. And second, because he desperately needed somebody to help him with the nursery.

"Peyton, please. I give you free rein. Just make it so that an official from the Child Welfare office can't find anything to object to. Please!"

A huff at the other end of the line told Dean he had won.

"Fine. I'll see it as a challenge. That second guest room next to your bathroom is still free, isn't it? I'll get the blueprints and start planning. I bet there are tons of things to take into consideration when designing for a child, so give me a few hours."

"Thank you so much, Peyton! You are a lifesaver."

Another huff, already distracted. Once Peyton got going, he was almost impossible to stop. "You owe me, honey. Big-time. 'Bye."

Dean breathed a sigh of relief. It had felt strange to talk to Peyton about Tricia's death, as if telling his friend somehow made it real. Or more real. When he didn't say it out loud, he could still stash the fact away in some corner of his brain and pretend the accident hadn't happened. Talking about it meant acknowledging a truth he wasn't prepared for. Dean closed his eyes and tried to get back the numb feeling that had permeated his entire body and shut down his thoughts since he'd first heard about Tricia's death. He couldn't wallow in pain; he had things to do. Emily needed him. Dean was an intelligent man, and he recognized a stalling technique when he saw one. He just didn't know what else he could do. His only hope was that once the business with Emily was taken care of, enough time would have passed for him to no longer feel the terrible sting in his heart whenever he thought of his sister.

There was no way he could face the truth in his current state, and so he threw himself into work.

The nursery was taken care of. What he needed now was professional help regarding the proper care of a child. He fired up his laptop and typed in "nanny service."

Disregarding the obviously adult-related sites, he scrolled until he found one that appealed to him. Precious Care operated nationwide. According to their site, the nannies they employed all had experience as either children's nurses or preschool teachers. All of them were at least bilingual, and they were encouraged to further perfect their skills by taking various courses throughout the year. There were no fees mentioned on the site, but a small, unobtrusive text guaranteed absolute discretion. Being with a billionaire and having quite an impressive amount of money himself, Dean knew how important that was. That the company offered a nondisclosure agreement on all their contracts showed how well they knew their well-off customers.

Dean dialed the number listed on the site and waited for somebody to pick up. After two rings, a woman with a friendly and youthful voice answered. "Precious Care, the place to pick your perfect nanny. This is Cindy. How can I help you?"

"Hi, I'm Dean Connelly. I've been recently appointed guardian for a baby. Unfortunately, I don't have the slightest clue about handling children. I need somebody to teach me, help me and, if possible, move in with me for the first couple of months."

"Where are you located, Mr. Connelly?"

"In Miami." Dean rattled off the address to the furiously typing Cindy.

"Do you prefer a male or female nanny?"

"To be honest, I don't care. If the nanny is good with Emily, I don't give a damn about gender, skin color, or age. I'm gay, by the way, and I live with my partner."

"That is good to know, Mr. Connelly. Information like that helps us find the perfect match for you. What second language would you prefer?"

"Again, I don't really care. To be honest, I'm so new to all this, I haven't even considered that a bilingual upbringing could be a good thing."

"Don't worry, Mr. Connelly. You will grow into this, I promise. Don't let people convince you otherwise. I can see how this is all overwhelming for you, so I'm going to set you up with one of our most experienced nannies. Julio O'Dell has worked for years as head nurse in the children's wing of several hospitals. He gives courses for young parents and can even teach you first aid for children. As you may have guessed from his first name, his second language is Spanish. He can come visit you tomorrow since he lives in the area. If you feel comfortable around him, we can arrange the contract and the living conditions."

"That sounds like a dream. Thank you so much. When will he come by?"

"At your earliest convenience. How about eight thirty in the morning? That would give you plenty of time to get to know each other."

"Eight thirty sounds fine to me." Dean quickly went over his mental list of things he shouldn't forget to ask. There was only one question left. "How much do you charge?"

"That depends on the arrangement. Since you want a live-in nanny for the time being, we would ask for the full fee, which we can talk about once you have met Julio, plus accommodation and living expenses. The nanny is available 24-7 with one day off every ten days. Would that be acceptable for you?"

Dean had no idea what kind of fee would be acceptable. He only knew that even five-figure sums per month were no problem for either him or Richard, and if that money got him the help he needed, he wasn't going to negotiate.

"Sounds fine to me."

"Very good. After your meeting with Julio, we can talk about the contract. Thank you for contacting us. It was a pleasure talking to you."

Cindy waited for Dean's reply before she disconnected the call. Of course, she would be pleased with a customer as easy to handle as Dean. If it had been Richard, she would have had a lot more trouble.

At the moment she was probably running a full background check on him. Once she verified that he was indeed loaded enough to be worth her time, she would go out of her way to make him happy. Dean had seen it happen often enough to know how things worked. Sometimes it made him a little sad, especially when he thought about all the children who could benefit from such excellent care as provided by Precious Care if only their parents had the money to buy it for them. Perhaps he should go and find a charity that dealt with such problems.

Relived that two of his most pressing problems were more or less solved, Dean returned to his laptop to find out more about the art of taking care of children.

CHAPTER 10

IT WAS already noon when Dean's phone rang. "Hello, Mr. Connelly, this is Elisa Connor. I've talked to the Child Welfare Program office, and they have agreed to send somebody over with Emily. Would 3:00 p.m. be fine with you?"

Dean's grip on the phone tightened. He was going to see Emily! "Of course. Whenever it is convenient for you."

"Then we'll see you at three."

Dean had just put the phone aside when the doorbell rang.

He hurried to open. It was Peyton with two men in tow Dean recognized as Peyton's favorite carpenter, Jeff, and his brother, Mike, who owned a construction company. Both men had done practically all the work in their apartment, so Dean knew they were probably the best in their respective fields. He greeted them with an open smile.

Peyton sauntered past him in the direction of the guest room.

"Since I got the impression that you don't have time to waste, I brought these two over as soon as possible. I did some research, but, honey, most of the things I found were simply awful. We have to do this from scratch, following our instincts."

Dean grinned broadly. This was exactly what he had hoped for. When Peyton followed his instincts, the outcome was fabulous. "I leave it completely to you."

"You're a smart one, aren't you?" Peyton patted Dean's cheek before he opened the door to the guest room. He then started talking to Mike and Jeff. Dean knew from experience that he was invited to listen but not to interfere.

"This is going to be a child's room, so it has to be stripped completely. I'm already positive on the color scheme and what kind of furniture I want. Since Emily is so small, we need only the best and healthiest options for wall paint, carpet, and, of course, the wood for the furniture. No nasty poisonous stuff in here."

Mike inspected the room and whistled. "This is one spacious place. Almost three hundred square feet, you said?" He looked at Peyton, who nodded in affirmation. Dean felt a smile tugging on his lips. They only called this place the guest room because they hadn't found another use for it. Compared to the rest of the apartment, there wasn't much inside. A double bed, a wardrobe, a TV. A door at the far side of the room led into a bathroom with a shower and a tub. Both rooms were rarely used, and it showed. Peyton clucked his tongue in disapproval. "I want this to be light and friendly. As long as Emily's so small, she'll be sleeping in a crib, but later I want her to have a real princess bed, right there." Peyton pointed toward one of the walls. "The diaper-changing table is another temporary item, but that doesn't mean it can't have class. All the ones I've found so far are either butt ugly or a far cry from functional. As you know, I'm greedy. I want both. Massive wood, of course. Spruce, I think, all natural, the surface just oiled. Several drawers for clothing, shelves for the baby-care stuff like diapers and…."

On and on Peyton went, evoking a detailed picture of a child's room that would be the envy of the town. Mike and Jeff trailed behind Peyton, taking notes and sometimes making suggestions. Dean went into the kitchen to prepare coffee for the three. While he waited for the machine to come to life, he texted Richard about the appointment.

Emily will be here at three.

The reply was immediate, which Dean thought was a good thing.

I'll be there.

AT QUARTER to three, Richard entered the apartment. He still wasn't sure if he wanted to be there when Dean met his niece for the first time. The entire day he had pondered the pros and cons of staying away under the guise of work. What had tipped the scales in favor of attending this appointment was the fact that he and Dean had never fought before. They were of one mind most of the time, and if they weren't, they always talked it out. What had happened this morning was practically a heated argument, and as much as Richard loved to fight with his partners and opponents in business, he couldn't stand the thought of arguing with Dean.

That, and he needed to regain control. If he was present, he had a much better chance of interfering immediately when things got out of hand.

Dean greeted him in the living room, clearly nervous. He had problems making eye contact, and his hands were fidgeting with the hem of his shirt. Richard opened his arms. It was an automatic reaction to seeing his boy so flustered. With a sigh of relief, Dean fell into Richard's embrace. "Hello, Master."

"Hello to you too, boy. How was your day?"

Dean snuggled even closer. "Exhausting. Peyton left only a few minutes ago. The good news is, the nursery is all sorted out. I also contacted a nanny service, and I'm going to meet with the potential nanny tomorrow. I researched the company. It's going to cost us, but they provide a full-time service."

Richard frowned at all the things Dean had already organized. He was used to his boy relying on him for practically everything that had to do with their daily lives. Seeing him act so independently unsettled Richard more than he cared to admit. He wanted to say something but was interrupted by the doorbell. Dean practically flew to the door.

"They're here!"

He sounded both excited and terrified. With his hand resting on the frame, Dean exhaled deeply before opening the door. "Welcome."

He took a step aside to let two women in, one of whom carried a small bundle. Richard watched both women closely. The one who had first entered was obviously the lawyer. She gave off that special vibe, and along with her business dress, the unobtrusive, yet definitely expensive, pearl necklace, the tight no-nonsense bun on the back of her head, and the confident look in her pale blue eyes, it was not that hard to guess.

When Richard glanced over at the other woman who was holding the baby, he instinctively got his defenses up. Being an out gay man had become easier during the last few years, but there were still those out there who outright hated everybody different. Richard had honed his senses to recognize those people instantly. The look of disapproval in the strange woman's eyes was more than obvious. She was about fifty, with a pixie cut that was more practical than stylish, large, coke-bottle glasses that made her look like an owl, thin lips that gave her face a perpetual look of disdain, and a body that surely had once been curvy but now suggested she wasn't getting enough exercise.

Dean didn't see any of that. His gaze was locked onto the little bundle in the woman's arms, making him oblivious to everything else.

The lawyer stepped forward, her hand outstretched. She and Richard shook. "Hello, I'm Elisa Connor, from Connor and Partners, and this is Meredith Denton from the Child Welfare Program. She's taking care of Emily until you decide whether you want to take her in."

Elisa stepped aside, motioning Dean toward Meredith. "And this is Emily."

Dean approached Meredith slowly. To her credit, she held the baby out to him without hesitation or any show of negative emotion.

Dean looked down at the tiny, heart-shaped face with so much awe and love in his eyes, Richard felt a sting in his heart. He was actually jealous of a baby!

"Can… can I hold her?" Dean's voice shook. Meredith regarded him for a moment, as if she was seriously contemplating his request; then she smiled.

"Yes, of course. Why don't you sit down over there"—she indicated the couch—"and I'll show you how to do it."

Together they went into the living room. Dean sat down, his arms outstretched. Meredith placed Emily in his arms, showing him how to support her head. The baby was awake, staring at the grown-ups with incredibly blue eyes from under a shock of blond hair.

"Look, Richard! She has my hair color." Dean said it as if this alone was reason enough to keep her. Looking at the eager, awed look in his boy's eyes, Richard realized he was in trouble. Until now, Dean had only gotten so emotional with him. Seeing his boy's focus on somebody else, even if that somebody was an infant, made Richard grit his teeth in anger. He had always known he was a jealous bastard, but the depth of his emotion surprised and shocked him. He decided it was time to learn more about his tiny opponent.

"So how does this work? I was given to understand that Tricia appointed Dean guardian in her will. As you can see, neither of us has any experience with babies. Are you just going to leave her here?"

Meredith frowned. "Of course not, Mr. Miller. That would be irresponsible. Today we're here so that you can get to know each other and to talk about certain details. I need to check where you intend to set up the nursery and to help you with all the necessities."

"I already organized a few things." Dean was still busy staring at his niece. His voice had a faraway quality. "I can show you the nursery. Or rather, the room where it's going to be. Our interior designer said it can be set up in less than two weeks. All the furniture will be made of solid wood, the colors for the walls are especially for nurseries and children's rooms, and all the cloth comes from organic sources. I also contacted a nanny service, Precious Care, and one of their staff is coming over tomorrow morning. If we get along, he's going to move in here for the first couple of months to help us get settled."

Richard saw Meredith nodding in approval. His gay-hater radar still pinged when he looked at her, but she seemed to be genuinely interested in ensuring Emily's well-being. Richard caught himself staring again at his tiny rival. The utter devotion on Dean's face was usually reserved for him, and the little intruder had no right to steal it from him. Dean was his. As were his heart, body, and soul. Always. Richard clenched his fists. He had to get a grip on himself. With a faked smile, he zoned in on the conversation.

"You have done a lot of work already, Mr. Connelly. And Precious Care is an excellent choice. There are not many who can afford their services, but I can assure you, they are the best in their field. If your meeting with their staff goes well, we can schedule another visit tomorrow afternoon."

Dean beamed at Meredith. "That sounds fantastic! Shall I call you?"

Meredith handed him her card. "Around noon would be a good time. Then we can see when we'll meet."

She held out her hands. "I need to take her back." Her words came out gently yet firmly. Dean's grip on Emily tightened for a moment. He leaned in on her, his lips touching her forehead in a light, loving kiss.

"I'm going to miss you, princess. See you tomorrow."

Emily made a soft mewling sound. Her eyes were trained on Dean as if she knew who he was. With pure longing in his eyes, Dean handed her back to Meredith, who cradled her close. Then she held out her free hand to Dean. "It was a pleasure meeting you, Mr. Connelly. I'll wait for your call tomorrow."

"It was my pleasure as well, Ms. Denton. Thank you."

The women shook hands with Richard as well before taking their leave. Richard was still stunned by his inability to take charge of the situation. He was always in control, always. But one look at Dean with Emily in his arms and Richard had been so overcome by jealousy and anger, his brain had ceased to function.

"I think it went quite well, don't you?" Dean was standing halfway between the door and the living room, an insecure look on his face. At that moment he was seeking out his Dom for reassurance. Richard was glad that he could still do something for his boy, that Dean still needed him. There was no doubt things were going to change. Richard had a sinking feeling about talking Dean out of taking Emily in. He was too determined, too much in love with the baby already.

If Richard wanted this to work, he had to take back control. Not just over the situation but also over their relationship. He had to be there. For his boy and for himself.

With new determination, he opened his arms. Dean practically flew into his embrace. When Richard held his boy tightly, he could feel the shivers running down Dean's spine.

"It's fine, boy. It went really well. Ms. Denton was impressed. Everything will be okay."

Dean suppressed a sob. "This is all so damn much. Tricia's death. Emily. I feel like I'm drowning."

Richard felt a twinge of self-loathing. Dean had suffered and he hadn't been there. What kind of Dom put their own petty feelings over the well-being of their collared sub? "I have you, boy. Always. Let me take care of you."

Chapter 11

DEAN WOKE in the warm embrace of Richard's arms. It was his favorite place to be. They hadn't done a scene the previous night; Dean had been too mentally exhausted for that. Instead Richard had made love to him like they were some plain vanilla couple. Dean had loved every second of it. He could sense how much Richard resented the way their life had changed in the course of a single day. Not having the full backup of the person Dean loved more than anything or anybody in the world was an added blow to all the bad stuff that had gone down on him, but he had no idea how to fix it. There was no way he could force Richard into this. He had to come around on his own. Waiting for his lover and Dom to accept the new reality unsettled Dean beyond words.

He was devastated by losing Tricia and terrified of the responsibility he now had for Emily. Fate had decided to throw him into the deep end where the sharks were waiting, and the man who could pull him through it all was hesitant. For the first time in their five years together, Dean felt alone.

Deciding self-pity wouldn't get him anywhere, he got up to follow his morning routine. First he went to the bathroom to have a shower and brush his teeth. Then he put his yoga mat down in the living room and did half an hour's worth of routines. The smoother his muscles moved, the more relaxed he became. After he felt settled, Dean prepared his and Richard's breakfast, which he then brought to the bedroom. Waiting on his knees next to the bed had been awkward in the beginning, but as their relationship progressed, Dean had learned to appreciate the quiet moments before his Dom woke. Quite a few good books had come to him while he was on his knees.

When Richard woke, he pulled Dean next to him so they could have their breakfast together. He didn't attempt to feed Dean, though. It was Richard's subtle way of telling his boy how sorry he was about the previous day and that he wasn't quite sure how to fix it. Dean snuggled closer to Richard's bulky frame, pleading with his eyes for a spoonful of the yogurt Richard was eating. Dean was too afraid of all the things he'd have to deal with over the coming days to hold a grudge over something as petty as his Dom's initial reaction to the bombshell that had been dropped on him.

When Richard scooped up a generous amount of yogurt and strawberry to feed to him, Dean moaned happily. At least on the D/s front, things seemed to be back to normal.

DEAN HAD just finished clearing breakfast when the doorbell rang. He hurried to open it. A man in his forties, with sleek, shoulder-length black hair tamed in a ponytail, almond-shaped hazel eyes surrounded by a web of lines that deepened when he smiled, and blinding white teeth held out his hand. "Hello, I'm Julio O'Dell, from Precious Care."

Dean took the hand and returned the smile. Julio was smaller than him, about five foot six, with a stocky build. He radiated confidence. "Nice to meet you, Mr. O'Dell."

Julio must have heard the puzzlement in Dean's voice. His smile broadened. "My mother is Mexican, my father Irish. Makes for an interesting genetic mix and an even more interesting name."

Dean blushed. "I'm sorry. I didn't mean to… it's just, the combination…."

"I know. You might think parents would take such things into consideration when naming their offspring, but, no. All parents are selfish. My middle name is Andrew, by the way."

Julio winked and Dean couldn't help but laugh. He already felt at ease with this man, which was a good thing, since he would be spending a lot of time there. Dean realized that Julio was looking over his shoulder and turned. Richard had come out of the bathroom. He was dressed in one of his expensive, *no nonsense or I'm going to eat you alive and still look sophisticated* business suits and stared at Julio as if he was still deciding what to do with him. Dean knew that tactic. He had seen Richard use it countless times on unsuspecting business opponents and even on him. Dean secretly called it the "scary Dom face." In combination with a stern command, that expression terrified those who wanted to make business deals with Richard and sent Dean directly into his submissive headspace while his cock instantly perked up at the idea of playing. Julio, though, appeared completely unfazed by this display of alpha manliness. His smile deepened, revealing two cute dimples.

"Hello. I'm Julio, the new nanny."

Richard gave Julio his most scary stare before he took the man's hand. "I'm Richard Miller, and if you are the new nanny has yet to be seen."

Julio didn't seem to take offense. His voice stayed smooth, professional. Every bit a man who was used to dealing with intimidating rich people. "Of course, Mr. Miller. The decision whether you wish to employ my services is entirely up to you."

Richard's lips twitched. He had a soft spot for people with courage. "You're pretty good at handling difficult customers, aren't you?"

Julio grinned broadly. "Ever tried to reason with a new mom so high on hormones she's laughing one moment and crying the next without even a change of subject? It's impossible, believe me. Straightforward, cocky males are kind of a relief now and then."

Richard guffawed. Julio had managed to win him over, which made Dean breathe a little easier. "I'm glad I made your day. I must go to work now. Dean will fill you in on everything. Goodbye."

Julio waved. "Have a nice day." It almost sounded sincere, and Richard flipped him off as if they had been friends for years. He gave Dean a kiss on the mouth.

"I'll be back early. Promise."

Dean smiled into the kiss. He appreciated the effort Richard was making. "Thank you. See you then. I love you, Master."

"And I love you, boy."

Then Richard was gone. Dean felt a little awkward but didn't know how to get over it. Luckily Julio had mercy on him. "So, why don't you show me the nursery for a start?"

"Of course. I have to warn you, though. The interior designer was here yesterday and he kind of tore the place down. The workers will arrive in about two hours and start renovating it."

Dean led Julio through the apartment toward the former guest room. When he opened the door, Julio whistled. "Wow. That's quite spacious. A good place."

"You think? Peyton says he can make it the perfect nursery. He has some very distinct ideas."

"If you feel better, I can talk to him. He's coming over too?"

"Yes. He's always there when Mike and Jeff start a new project. For last-minute changes."

"Then let's start shopping online for the basics you're going to need. At the same time, tell me about your situation."

For a moment, Dean felt tears gathering in his eyes. He fought them back. Now was not the time to ponder on his grief. While he fired his laptop up, he quickly explained what had happened in the last twenty-four hours and why he needed professional help. Julio listened with just the right number of sympathetic comments to not send Dean into crying again. He definitely knew what he was doing. When Dean finished his story, Julio summed it up in regard to Emily. "You're stuck with a three-month-old baby you didn't even know existed a day ago. You have no clue how to handle her or the situation, but you want to keep her because she's all the family you have left."

Dean heaved a sigh. "That's it. As you can see, I need you badly."

"Your worries are over, *cariño*. Money has bought you the best help you can find, and I'll make sure you get to keep your princess. First we're going on a little shopping spree. If you don't mind, there's a pretty good shop not far from here. We can order everything online and it will be delivered today. Let's start with the clothes."

Julio rattled off the address of a website and for the next two hours, they were busy shopping baby stuff. Just when they had narrowed the choice of strollers down to three, the doorbell rang again.

When Dean opened, Peyton strode past him with Mike, Jeff, and three workers in tow who were carrying all the items necessary to turn the guest room into a child's wonderland. They made two more trips back to their cars before they had everything stacked in the hallway. Peyton grabbed Julio to discuss some of the details of the room. When he finally released Julio from his grasp, the man was grateful for the coffee Dean offered him.

"Your friend is very energetic. He has some good ideas, though. I can't wait to see the room when it's finished."

"Peyton is a genius. Not that I would tell him that to his face—he's already too fond of himself—but when it comes to interior design, there's nobody who can rival him."

Julio chuckled. "That's the impression I got. Let's get back to the laptop. We still have to decide on a stroller. And didn't you say the Child Welfare lady is bringing Emily over later?"

"Yes! I can't wait to see her again."

RICHARD ARRIVED in time with the delivery from the children's store and only half an hour before Meredith Denton brought Emily. After she had quizzed Julio about childcare until she was satisfied about his proficiency, she agreed to let Emily stay overnight if he spent the night as well. She handed the baby to Dean, who took her with an awed smile on his face, and then left the apartment. The three men were alone with the baby.

CHAPTER 12

RICHARD DIDN'T know what to think. Meredith had really left them alone with the little intruder, as he thought of Emily. How could she do that? He turned away from the door to see Dean cooing over the baby, his face almost splitting in half from his grin. Richard felt jealousy wash over him in an all-consuming wave. That look of pure adoration was reserved solely for him! Dean had no right showing it to anybody else. The knowledge that it was utterly ridiculous for him to feel threatened by an infant did nothing to improve his mood.

Julio beckoned him closer. "Come here, Mr. Miller. I know it's scary in the beginning, but she doesn't bite, and even if she did, she has no teeth yet."

Richard clamped down on his sharp answer and forced a smile on his lips. It was better if Julio thought he was just shy. He came close enough to show willingness but kept enough distance that he could bolt as soon as things became unpleasant. Dean was holding Emily close to his chest with an expression Richard had never seen before. It was a mixture of pure love, awe, and underlying panic.

Julio leaned in to fuss with the blanket Emily was wrapped in. "How about I show you how to bathe her? Then you can feed her and hopefully, she'll sleep afterward."

"What do you mean, hopefully?" Richard couldn't ban the dread from his voice.

Julio grinned at him. "Babies are on a different schedule than us adults. They usually can't sleep for more than five or six hours in a row. This ability builds slowly. Because Emily's stomach is so small, she gets hungry after a while. You have to get used to having your night interrupted at least once."

"How long does it take until she sleeps through the night?" Richard had a sinking feeling.

"Depends. Some babies do it as early as six months, others take until after their second birthday. You never know. You can introduce them to a certain rhythm, though. It probably still won't come close to your normal sleeping patterns, but at least you can sort of program her. That way you can plan your schedule a little more efficiently."

When he saw Richard's expression, Julio quickly went on. "I promise, you'll get used to it. I know it's overwhelming in the beginning, and the lack of sleep is going to wear you down. Adding the fact that you haven't expected to be responsible for a child doesn't make it easier. I'm not going to lie to you, the coming weeks are going to be hard. You basically have to reshape your life to accommodate the needs of a baby. For the next two years, at least, Emily's going to dictate your entire schedule. And every time you think things are finally settled, something will happen. Teething, various child illnesses, and growth spurts that mess everything up."

"This sounds like hell. If you're trying to sell me on having a baby, you're doing a poor job."

Julio chuckled. "I'm just trying to be honest. This way you can't sue me for lying to you."

Dean looked up with a horrified expression. "Who would do such a thing?"

"I'm only joking, Dean." Julio winked at him. "Mostly, at least. As I said, hormones are a scary thing."

"I'm still not sold on this whole staying the night idea. Shouldn't we get to know her better before jumping right in?" Richard tried not to sound too desperate. The baby freight train was taking on speed, and he felt helpless to stop it.

Julio's soothing tone didn't help at all. "That might be a good idea if Emily were older, but with her three months, the only real connection she had was with her mother, and that was based mostly on scent. Of course, she has to get used to you. That will happen more quickly if you spend as much time as possible together. Don't worry. I'm here to help you with this. Now let me show you how to bathe Emily."

Unable to find another reason why they should hand Emily back to Meredith for the night, Richard followed an eager Dean and Julio to the bathroom. Julio showed them how to hold Emily while she was floating in the small baby tub that was among the things Dean had ordered from the baby shop. Soon the room was filled with Emily's happy coos as she thrashed her arms and legs in the warm water.

Richard had to admit, it sounded kind of cute and looked adorable. That gummy grin, the thin, wet strands of baby hair clinging to the round skull, and the look of pure wonder in Emily's eyes when Dean trickled water down on her belly were nice. Richard almost felt something warm spreading in his belly. Almost.

Unfortunately Emily didn't like leaving the tub. Her wails of protest rang loud and clear, and for somebody so small, she had a powerful voice. As well as perfectly functioning lungs. On and on she wailed while Julio helped Dean to towel her dry, put some soothing baby lotion on her skin, adjust the diaper, and put on fresh clothes.

She only stopped her crying when Julio offered her a baby bottle with her dinner. The preparation of the damn thing had been accompanied by a whirlwind of instructions, starting with how the bottles had to be kept clean—apparently, it was enough to put them in the dishwasher—that the recipe of the formula had to be followed exactly, and how to determine the temperature of the milk by putting some drops on the back of your hand between thumb and index finger where the skin was most sensitive. Julio mentioned a fancy thing called a bottle warmer, and Richard could tell by Dean's exasperated look that it was going on the to-buy list. All that information came to the background of endless wailing. All three men breathed a sigh of relief when Emily latched on to the bottle and silence descended.

Dean had the baby in the crook of his left arm, supporting the bottle with his right hand, Emily grabbing it with her small hands as best as she could. He looked exhausted. "Will she always be so persistent?"

Julio shook his head. "No. Sometimes it will be worse. At this age she's driven purely by instinct. When she's uncomfortable for a reason, she will announce it. As she grows older, you'll find that she will also start reacting to other things despite her basic needs. That's when the horrible monster called upbringing comes into play. How much she will be able to manipulate you is entirely up to you."

Richard made a snorting sound. "Just swell. Can we get her to bed before you have any more happy news for us?"

Julio chuckled. "As soon as she's done with her bottle. After a hot bath, they usually fall asleep fast."

Just like Julio had predicted, Emily's eyes started to droop while she was still sucking the last drops of formula. After an impressive burp over Dean's shoulder, she was out like a light. They took her to the small crib Dean had bought as a substitute until Mike finished her new bed. For the time being, Emily would sleep in the master bedroom until Peyton's fancy version of a children's room was done. Richard resented it but couldn't do anything about. Once Emily was settled, they returned to the living room.

"For your first evening, that went quite well. You'll get used to everything in no time at all."

Julio sounded like a motivational trainer. Richard looked at Dean, who didn't seem to mind. In fact, his boy glowed from the praise. Again, the green-eyed monster reared its ugly head. Dean wasn't supposed to be so happy about another man's encouraging words. Only Richard should matter to him. Neither Julio nor Dean seemed to be aware of Richard's sentiment, though. Dean took Julio's small overnight bag, which he had brought just in case he was to stay.

"Let me show you to the guest room."

"I thought the guest room was Emily's new room?" Julio raised a brow in question.

Dean grinned. "That's just the one we never use. We have another one. It's a lot nicer. Please, follow me."

"Thank you, Dean." Julio looked at Richard. "My last advice for you today is that you try to get some sleep right now. You never know how long Emily's going to sleep."

Richard cursed in his head. He needed to let off some steam after this trying afternoon. Spanking Dean's ass and then fucking him senseless would have helped. Unfortunately, one glance at his boy told him there wouldn't be any such activities tonight. Richard mustered all the patience he had left, promising himself a steamy night in the near future for this day's hardships.

DESPITE BEING so wound up, Richard fell asleep surprisingly fast. It had probably to do with the fact that he didn't dare move at all in the bed for fear Emily would wake up. Dean obviously felt the same, lying stock-still next to him. Except for a whispered "Good night," neither of them dared to talk.

Then, suddenly, a wail tore Richard from his sleep. A bleary glance at the bedside clock told him it was only quarter past midnight. Dean was already out of bed and at Emily's side, trying to soothe her. When that didn't help, he picked her up, looking around with wild eyes. His hair was tousled, and his pajama pants hung low on his hips. If it hadn't been for Emily's crying that grew stronger every second, Richard would have definitely taken advantage of the situation. Instead, he sprinted for the door to get Julio. The man was actually worth the ridiculous sum they were paying him, because he was already halfway down the hall. He brushed past Richard to where Dean held Emily, whose face had turned an interesting shade of dark purple.

"What's the matter with her?"

Dean was close to panicking. Julio took the baby and started for the kitchen. "She's just hungry. Nothing bad."

"Just hungry? But we fed her only a few hours ago!"

Richard knew he sounded exasperated. Julio flashed him a knowing grin. "I told you, her stomach is small. She gets hungry more quickly. You didn't hear her when she woke up because you're not yet used to listening for the telltale sounds. Otherwise she'd be fed and back to sleep by now."

While he was talking, Julio prepared another bottle of formula. The moment he offered it to Emily, the wailing abruptly stopped. Instead, the sound of greedy swallowing resounded in the kitchen. They watched as Emily downed the bottle, finishing it with a satisfied burp. As soon as she was done, Julio motioned them back to the bedroom.

"When you have a little more experience, you'll be able to catch her sooner and feed her in semidarkness. Full-on light is always bad. Chances are she's awake now. If you keep the lighting low and, ideally, the baby next to the bed, she will not even fully wake when you feed her. That's for advanced parents, though."

He grinned a tiny bit evilly. Richard looked down on Emily, who didn't give the impression of a baby on the verge of falling asleep. "How long will this take?"

Julio shrugged. "I don't know. A while, I guess?"

Richard looked from Julio to Dean to Emily to his wonderful bed and back. His decision made, he took his pillow and headed for the door. "I leave this to you. There's a lot of work tomorrow, so I need my sleep. Have a good night!"

Dean stared after him as if he wanted to say something but kept his mouth shut. Good for him. Just when Richard left the bedroom, the crying started again. Not as loud and angry as before, but he could hear Emily working her way up to it. While the sound increased in volume, Richard hurried down the hall to the only place in the apartment where he wouldn't hear a thing: the playroom. It was soundproof, and the bed was the same as in their bedroom. Richard snuggled under the satin covers, let his eyes roam swiftly over the assembled implements for pain, switched off the bedside lamp, and started to fantasize about all the things he would do to Dean in here as punishment for bringing this menace into his life.

CHAPTER 13

WHEN DEAN woke the next morning, he was curled around Emily on the bed. He checked the clock and found he had slept about five hours in total the previous night. After her bottle, Emily had suffered from bellyaches that kept them up for almost two hours before she finally fell asleep. Then she had woken once more because she was hungry, but this time Dean had heard her sooner, and she had gone back to sleep quite quickly. When he looked at her now, she seemed like an angel. Her face was completely relaxed, her hands open, flexing slightly when she dreamed. Dean couldn't help himself. He felt a surge of love well up inside him. This was Tricia's little girl, now his to take care of. Dean made a silent vow to his sister that he would always be there for Emily.

While he watched, her tiny lips opened. She made a strained expression and then Dean heard a gurgling noise, followed by a stench that made his toes curl. Emily smiled. Dean hurried to get out of the bed. The sudden movement woke Emily. She looked around for a bit before her gaze focused on him. Dean leaned over to take her in his arms. Another waft of whatever Emily had just produced hit him.

"You, my little lady, need a fresh diaper ASAP. Let's see if we can do this on our own, shall we?"

He carried her into the living room where they had set up a temporary diaper-changing station, and got to work. Everything was fine until he reached the baby's sleeper. Apparently, the diaper had lost against the full assault of Emily's bowel activities and leaked a good amount down her legs and up her back. It was all one stinking, sticky, yucky mess. For a split second, Dean contemplated dealing with this task alone before he let his pride slip and yelled for Julio. This was just too much on an empty stomach.

Julio appeared only moments later, already dressed and seemingly unruffled by the short night and Dean's despair.

"What's the problem? Oh, I see. Well, at least, the stomach trouble should be done with now."

"How can you be so cheerful first thing in the morning?"

Julio flashed Dean a wide smile. "I've been doing this job for quite some time. This was not close to the worst night I've ever had. Plus, every time I feel like getting cranky, I remind myself of the check I'm going to get at the end of the month. Somehow that thought cheers me up anytime."

"You're an evil man, aren't you? I like it."

Both men chuckled before they returned to the problem at hand. Julio assessed the damage with an expert's eye. "The wisest course of action is to clean out as much of the poo as possible with the wet wipes, then free her from the sleeper. After that, it's the bath again."

Dean sighed. "There will be more wailing, won't there?"

"That's the fun of having children."

WHEN EMILY was clean again and the ruined sleeper put into the sink to soak in soapy water, they sat down in the kitchen for breakfast. First they fed Emily; then Dean and Julio enjoyed a cup of hot coffee and some yogurt while Emily sat in a little baby swing and watched the light patterns created by the sun filtering through the high windows.

"So, Richard doesn't seem to be too invested in the baby stuff."

Julio phrased his words carefully, as if giving Dean the chance to tell him off. There was silence for a couple of minutes before Dean answered.

"It all happened very fast. We weren't prepared for it at all. Richard is used to being in control. He'll come around. He just needs time to adjust."

"I'm sure he will. Having a baby is an overwhelming experience. It pushes your limits in ways you never thought possible. Although I think the pushing part, you're used to."

There was a knowing twinkle in Julio's eyes that made Dean blush.

"How do you know?"

Julio shrugged. "I've seen a lot in my time. You and Richard give off a very strong vibe, and if I hadn't guessed by the way you two interact, the cuffs and ropes attached to your bed would have been an obvious hint."

When Dean blushed even deeper, Julio winked at him. "Don't worry. What you do in your bedroom is your decision. I'm only judging you by the way you treat Emily, and in that regard, you've already won me over. Any idiot could see that you've established a connection with her and that you care about her deeply. That's all that matters to me."

"You're very open. That's rare."

"I know. I wish it wasn't. My motto is 'Live and let live.' I don't want people treating me differently because of my preferences, so I try not to judge in return. It's hard sometimes, though."

Dean stared at the ceiling. "As with BDSM?"

Julio took another sip from his coffee. "No. That I can actually understand. The need to control or being controlled. The freedom it can give you. When I first learned about the lifestyle, I wasn't turned on by the sex or the leather, but by the trust built between D/s couples. It made me jealous. The idea of giving yourself completely, knowing you are safe—it intrigues me. Must be hard, though?"

Dean smiled. Julio's words reassured him enough to share some of his insights with the man.

"It was, in the beginning. When I first met Richard, I had just come to terms with the fact that I'm gay and proud of it. I didn't know anything about BDSM, and my sexual experience was limited to jacking off to gay porn. Richard already had tons of experience, but he was very patient. He introduced me to the lifestyle slowly, until I was able to fully embrace it. We're very happy now, although there are still times when I struggle. Placing all my troubles at his feet is not always easy. Sometimes I'm afraid to appear weak."

Julio nodded. "As far as I understand, the sub in a D/s relationship is anything but weak. I got the distinct impression they are the strong ones."

Dean giggled. "Don't let the Doms hear that. In a way, you're right. But it's also about balance. The Dom would be pretty lost without a sub to control, without the sub's permission to work on his limits. The sub, on the other hand, would be equally lost without somebody prepared to take him places he's too afraid to visit on his own. If it's just for a scene, the lines are clear, but the more intense a relationship gets, the blurrier they become. The better you get to know each other, the more layers you can put on the D/s exchange. I'm at a point in my relationship with Richard where I think the kinky sex and the pain are just a yummy by-product of the real deal. Thing is, you don't get the real deal without starting on the sex and pain. So there's a roundabout again."

Julio looked thoughtful. "I've never looked at it like that. In the end, I guess, we all want the same out of a relationship. We just use different means to get it."

"Amen to that!" Dean rose from his chair to take the cups and bowls away. Emily chose that moment to make a little gurgling noise.

"Seems like she agrees with you. Why don't you get a quick shower and then we'll take Emily out on a little stroll?"

"That's a good idea, Julio. You have to show me how to handle that stroller. It's still in the box they delivered it in yesterday. To be honest, I'm a little intimidated."

"No need to be. They may look complicated at first, but once you get the hang of it, it's smooth sailing. After all, they are designed to be used by people with their brains shut down because of hormone overload and sleep deprivation."

"You make it sound so wonderful. Remind me, why did I choose you as my nanny again?"

Julio patted Dean's shoulder in a slightly patronizing manner. "Because I'm the best and my wonderful personality appeals to your masochist heart."

Dean flipped Julio off. "No, I don't think that's it. Must be another reason. Just can't remember it right now."

"Get your ass in the shower before Emily decides to throw another tantrum. When she's screaming her lungs out, we want to be outside so other people have to suffer through it as well."

"You *are* a born sadist. You sure you don't want to embrace the lifestyle?"

Julio grinned like a madman. "No. As you can see, it's not badass enough for me. I want my victims to suffer."

Laughing despite his exhaustion, Dean hurried to get his shower.

IT WAS late afternoon when Richard finally made it to Whisper. He went straight into his office, slumped down in the luxurious leather chair behind his desk, and buried his head in his hands. His three-day emergency trip to New York had done nothing to decrease his workload in Miami. To make things worse, he had trouble concentrating because his mind kept wandering back to Dean and how fucked-up their situation was. Richard was torn between his desire to take care of his boy and his annoyance about Dean's infatuation with Emily. Richard still hadn't figured out what to think or do. He had liked Tricia, and he understood why she wanted her only brother to be her child's guardian. He also had nothing against babies in general. Emily was kind of cute, in a very loud way. No, the problem was the change in his relationship with Dean.

Until now, Richard had never spared a second thought as to how he wanted to progress with Dean. Things had just happened naturally. It was all perfect in a carefree world where their money and status took care of any inconveniences they might come across. That was, until fate had decided to drop a baby in their peaceful, perfect BDSM bubble. It just wasn't fair.

Richard looked up when he heard a knock on the door. Before he could say anything, the handle turned and Martin walked in. He took one look at Richard's face and flopped down on the designer sofa with a sympathetic look in his eyes.

"Man, you look terrible. Like something the cat dragged in after a rainy night. Trouble at work?"

Richard leaned back in his chair. Perhaps it would do him good to talk to another Dom. "Yes and no. The trouble at work has already been taken care of."

"So there's something else?" Martin raised a brow. "Don't tell me this has to do with the ominous phone call Dean got three days ago?"

Now it was Richard's turn to do some brow gymnastics. "What do you know about that?"

Martin shrugged. "Not much. Dean called me when he couldn't reach you. He was close to a panic, so I tried to reassure him. I also told him to call me again should he need anything. Since that didn't happen, I assumed everything was fine, but looking at you, I can tell something's horribly wrong."

Richard sighed. "You could say so. That phone call was from a lawyer. Dean's sister died six days ago. She left a baby behind and appointed Dean guardian. It's one big, ugly mess."

Martin was stunned into silence for a moment, which was rare for him. "Were they close?" There was a rasp in Martin's voice that told Richard how deeply his friend felt for Dean.

"Yes. She was all the family he had left. After his parents kicked him out for being gay, Tricia was the one who helped Dean with money and a place to live. She supported him when he wrote his first book. I hate to admit it, but there were times when I was jealous of her."

"He must be devastated." Martin was no doubt thinking about his twin sister, Olivia. "If anything happened to Oli, I'd go nuts."

"Well, Tricia's death had a great impact on him. He just doesn't have the time to process it because Emily, her daughter, is living with us. Or will be, once the Child Welfare Program decides we're suitable to be parents."

"That's a lot to deal with, man. How are you holding up?"

Richard met Martin's gaze full-on. "Badly. I don't think taking Emily in is a good idea. Unfortunately, Dean doesn't share my view of things. We almost had a fight when I suggested we find a different place for her. He's clinging to that baby because Emily is all he has left of Tricia. He doesn't grieve, at least not openly, which is unhealthy, as we both know. As his Dom, I should take care of matters, see to it that Emily gets a good place and then help him through his emotional pain. But how can I take Emily away from him? You should see the way he looks at her. At the moment she's the only thing that keeps him from falling apart."

"Don't tell me you're jealous of the baby?"

Richard glared at Martin. The man was too empathic for his own good sometimes. Of course, that was also why he was such a good Dom.

"I *am* jealous. There, I admit it. Dean looks at Emily in a way that was reserved for me until now. What makes things worse, our entire life is changing because of her. I had to sleep in the playroom last night to get at least some rest."

Martin snorted with a mixture of amusement and pity in his eyes. He sobered up when he met Richard's angry stare. "Not funny, I know. Well, at least not yet. Give it a few months. Or maybe a year," he added hastily when Richard's expression darkened. "What I mean is, you're both under emotional stress right now. While change in itself is not a bad thing, too much of it can be challenging, especially when it's so drastic. I know I sound like an old man, but you have to give it some time. Show patience. From where I'm standing, I don't think you have much of a choice anyway. And who knows, maybe something good will come out of it. Right now your boy needs you, so focus on that and let everything else fall into place."

"Easier said than done, but thanks for the advice." Richard huffed. "I do feel a little better, though."

"I aim to please." Martin bowed mockingly. "And on that note, we do have some new applications for the club. If you have the time, it would be good to read them."

Richard frowned. Normally, Martin didn't consult him over new applicants. Since he was in the security business, there was no need. "Is there something wrong?"

"No. The background checks were okay. It's just that I have a strange feeling about one of them. I want to know if you agree. If not, we can put it down to me being paranoid. If yes, he's out."

"If he pings your weirdo radar, I'd say he's out no matter what I think. You're never wrong in that respect."

Martin acknowledged the praise with a slight nod. They had been friends and partners for so long, they rarely complimented each other.

"The files are in my office. I'll get them, and you tell me your impression."

"Fine. Get on with it. When we're done, I have to get home and face another night from hell."

Martin grinned. "You'll get used to it."

"That's what the nanny said as well. Somehow, I doubt it."

CHAPTER 14

Three weeks later.

"PEYTON. WHY am I looking at a bill of almost fifteen hundred dollars for a few square yards of curtain fabric?" Richard tried very hard to keep the outrage from his voice and failed.

There was a prolonged silence at the other end of the line before Peyton finally spoke. "If I said those numbers were just a figment of your imagination, would you believe me?" His tone already suggested he didn't think so.

"Try again."

"Weelll, it's superorganic, no-dangerous-stuff-added, hand-dyed cloth especially for environments where children and people prone to allergies live. Plus, the colors I chose were not in their repertoire, so they had some experimenting to do, and you know how it is, once the costs start to rise, it's kind of an upward spiral...." Peyton's voice trailed off. He had clearly run out of excuses.

Richard rolled his eyes. The problem with Peyton was, he sucked at negotiation. He was a genius when it came to interior design, but the monetary part of the business was like an alien planet to him. Come to think of it, he was a lot like Dean in that respect.

"Peyton, did they overcharge?"

"Um, yes. They did. And I'm sorry, Richard. I was just so glad when the color scheme finally worked out, I didn't care about the numbers anymore."

"You never care about the numbers. Are there any other bills I should worry about?"

"No. Mike and Jeff took care of the rest."

"Then I'm going to make a call. Perhaps you should reconsider working with that particular company. Obviously, they don't have any respect for you."

Peyton huffed. "I know I'm bad at this. You don't have to rub it in."

Richard chuckled. "I have to. It's payback for the extra work you're causing me even though I'm paying you."

"Fine, I get it. Rant all you want. I'm going to disconnect now because there are people out there who appreciate my work enough not to make me feel bad about it."

"Goodbye, Peyton."

Putting the phone aside, Richard grinned. Riling up Peyton was one of his favorite pastimes. Unfortunately, it was also his only pastime at the moment, since his D/s relationship with Dean was more or less on hold. When he wasn't fussing over Emily, Dean was usually too tired for anything remotely kinky. The closest they had gotten to sex during the past three weeks had been when Richard walked into the kitchen one evening to find Dean on his knees, swiping up spilled formula from the floor. As compelling as Dean's beautiful butt had looked, the wailing sounds from Emily, not to mention Julio, who had been trying to distract her, dampened Richard's mood instantly.

He was truly grateful for Julio's presence. The man was a solid rock in this time of prolonged crisis, although Richard could have done without his attempts at trying to get him to accept Emily. She was cute in a very pink sort of way, but Richard had no idea what to do with her and no intention of learning. He admitted readily, at least to himself, that he was jealous of her and also angry at her for having ruined his until then peaceful life. Now that it was over, Richard had learned to appreciate just how lucky he had been. Having sex pretty much whenever he wanted with the man of his dreams, going on trips when the mood struck them, spending nights at the club, exploring Dean's limits—all those things seemed like a dream now.

Richard sighed as he pulled into the driveway of his father's house. Aaron Miller, the retired Marine general, had refused to let Richard buy him a grander building in a better part of the city but decided to stay in the house he and his wife had bought before Richard was born. And even though Richard would never admit it openly, he was glad about it. He loved the small house that held so many sweet memories of a very happy childhood. His mother had been the warmest, most caring person in the world, and when she died of cancer, Richard and his father had been devastated. On the day after her funeral, a man from the animal shelter had come to them and handed his father a basket with two adorable little puppies and an envelope. It hadn't said much, just two lines that showed how well Delilah Miller knew her husband. *Keep on living. I love you. D.*

The puppies had successfully pried Aaron from his grief and allowed Richard to breathe a little easier where his father was concerned.

Richard looked up. The adorable little puppies had grown into ferocious-looking mongrels whose coat and facial structure suggested rottweiler and German shepherd in their genetic makeup. They were sitting on the front porch, tails wagging furiously at the sight of him. He smiled and opened his arms. "Come here, boys!" That was all it took, and two bodies, each about a hundred and twenty pounds, slammed into Richard, bringing him down, where he was licked and sniffed, accompanied by the happy yelping of the two dogs. Then the front door opened, and a deep voice boomed across the small lawn. "Thor! Donar! Would you stop it?"

The dogs retreated to Aaron Miller's side and sat down obediently. Richard got to his feet and looked at the man who had raised him. His father's gaze turned from inquisitive to worried before he turned around and went back into the house. "You better come in, son."

CHAPTER 15

INSIDE THE house, Richard followed his father through the living room into the kitchen, where the general was already busy preparing tea and setting out a plate with chocolate chip cookies. Richard took one, realized that they were homemade, not bought, and shot his father a questioning look. The general chuckled. "Don't worry, son, I haven't made them myself. Nancy, my neighbor, baked them for me as a thank-you for helping her out with the kids a few days ago."

Reassured, Richard bit into the cookie. His father was even more inept in the kitchen than he. After he had eaten three of the delicious bits, the tea was done steeping and so was his father waiting. "Are you going to tell me what's wrong, or do I have to wrestle it from you?"

Richard grinned, but only briefly. Despite his MMA training and the black belts he called his own, he wasn't entirely sure if he stood a chance against his father. The man was a Marine, after all. "No, Dad, no need. I had a busy month, and I doubt it'll get better any time soon." He paused, patted Thor, who had snuck up next to his chair, and then kept on speaking. "Dean's sister died about four weeks ago."

"Richard!" His father was clearly upset by this news. Even though he hadn't known Tricia personally, he adored Dean. "Why are you telling me this only now? I could have been there for you two!"

Richard averted his eyes. Despite having a very close relationship with his father, they didn't talk on the phone or meet in person on a regular basis. Neither of them was the type to be clingy, and they both led fulfilling lives. In times of crisis, though, they did rely on each other. Not going immediately to his father when his life had taken such a drastic turn for the worse was close to being an offense.

The only reason Richard hadn't done it was because he had been too distracted by what was happening. Since his father was the only man who could intimidate him, he tried to placate him. "I'm sorry, Dad, but a lot has happened. Tricia had a little girl, Emily, and she appointed Dean as her guardian. Between getting used to a baby in the house, our normal work, and sorting out all the details of Tricia's will, we were barely able to breathe."

His father nodded. He still wasn't happy, but he understood. "So how is Dean doing?"

"He's tired most of the time. Having a baby in the house is terribly exhausting. He's trying his best, though, and we have a live-in nanny to help. He's so focused on Emily, he doesn't have time to grieve for Tricia, although I'm not entirely sure if that's a good thing or not."

"There's more, though, I guess?" It wasn't a question, not really. His father just knew him too well.

"I never wanted children. Hell, I didn't even consider having one. I'm not the type. My life was perfect, and then Emily was dropped in our laps, and now nothing is as it was before. Dean is tired all the time, and just when I think I have him for myself, Emily starts crying or he remembers something he still needs to do for her, and then he's gone again. I have lost my sub and lover and got a wailing, stinking little menace instead."

Richard had talked himself into a rage, not realizing how much the whole situation was dragging him down until he spoke the words aloud. His father's reaction didn't help one bit. The general stared at him for a moment wide-eyed, then he shook his head in disappointment. "You are aware that you sound like a whiny little three-year-old, aren't you? So your life isn't going the way you had planned at the moment. Boo-fucking-hoo and a few tears to spare. You're an adult, a successful businessman, and you have the most perfect partner anybody could wish for, and yet you sit here complaining to me when you should be at home learning everything you can about taking care of a child, not to mention helping Dean with this situation. I can't imagine he's doing so well without his Dom guiding him."

Richard snapped back without thinking. "He's doing just fine. Turns out he doesn't need a Dom when he can have a baby."

His father narrowed his eyes. "I see. You're jealous of Emily. And that makes you blind. As far as I know Dean, he needs you now more than ever, but you are just too busy having a pity party to realize it."

Richard opened his mouth for another sharp reply and closed it again when he caught the look in his father's eyes. His dad was right and he knew it. He had been less than supportive toward Dean, using his work as an excuse to stay away from home so he didn't have to deal with Emily and the changes that had come over his perfect world. Richard was many things, but not a coward. He could own up to his mistakes.

"I behaved like a complete idiot."

"Yes, you did." His father sounded almost cheerful. "But now you see reason again and can go back to your man and make it all right."

"Thanks, Dad. I really needed that."

The general patted the back of Richard's hand. "Always, son. And when you've settled things with your boy, I expect you to introduce me to my granddaughter."

Richard's head reared up. For the first time in six weeks, he saw Emily as more than just an intruder. "Has it bothered you? That I never wanted kids?"

His father smiled a bit sadly. "I'd be lying if I said no, but I always knew you weren't the type, as you have put it yourself." He brightened up. "So Emily is a nice and unexpected surprise as far as I'm concerned. Now go home and make things right with Dean. I expect to hear from you soon."

Richard got up. "Tomorrow, Dad. I'll call you tomorrow, and then you can meet your grandchild."

When he left his father's house, Richard felt a lot better. He knew he had to thank the heavens above for the most understanding and accepting parents in the world. Delilah and Aaron Miller hadn't batted an eyelash when their son had come out to them; if anything, his mother had been a bit too supportive at times, even trying to hook him up with "nice young men," as she always called them.

His only regret was that he had met Dean only after she passed on. When his relationship with Dean had become serious, his father had found out that Richard needed his men to be submissive and that he preferred his sex with a bit of pain. Again, his father had been more than understanding. He had sat down and researched everything about BDSM he could find. A very embarrassing conversation later, one no child should ever have with their parent, the general had known how Richard's relationship with Dean worked and, to Richard's never-ending surprise, it had strengthened not only his bond with his father, but also the bond between Dean and Aaron.

He truly was blessed in more than one way, and it was high time he reminded his boy just how much he meant to him.

CHAPTER 16

WHEN RICHARD entered his home, Dean was sitting on the big couch, feet up and a cup of something hot in his hands. His eyes were half-closed, and he appeared to be dozing. Richard approached, and Dean's eyes snapped open. He wanted to put the cup away and get to his feet, but Richard stopped him with a gesture. "It's okay, Dean." Richard leaned in to claim Dean's lips in a gentle kiss. "Hard day?"

Dean groaned. "I just finished the manuscript for the next Laura Ashbourne book. Julio has taken Emily out so I can work, and now that I have a few quiet minutes, I realize how exhausted I am."

Richard cursed inwardly. His father had been right. His boy needed him, and he hadn't been there. Well, that would change now. "It's fine, boy. Just relax and lean back. I'm going to give you a foot rub, and then we can take a nice hot bath together. What do you think?"

The insecurity and disbelief in Dean's eyes tore at Richard's heart. He had done this. He had made his boy unsure of a relationship that had lasted five years and should have been his pillar of support. "I'm sorry, Dean. I behaved like an asshole. I'm not going to make any excuses. You needed me, and I wasn't there because I was too afraid of the change in our life. Can you forgive me?"

A wide, radiant smile appeared on Dean's lips and made his face shine the way Richard loved best. "Of course I can. It's a lot." He frowned. "The offer about the foot rub is still standing, though, isn't it?"

Richard chuckled in delight. Dean truly was one of a kind. "Of course, boy. Just don't get too used to it. I'm not sure how many of those services my fragile Dom ego can put up with."

Dean snorted. "Fragile, my ass. You can bend horseshoes on that ego of yours. But if it makes you feel better, I can promise you a back massage in return. And if you're a really good Dom, I might even provide you with a happy ending."

"Cheeky boy. I like it." Richard waggled his eyebrows. "That doesn't mean you're not going to be punished, though."

Dean grinned in return. "I like how that sounds."

Richard scooted a little away from Dean and leaned back against the couch, taking Dean's feet in his lap. Just when he was about to take Dean's socks off, Dean's phone started to ring. Both men groaned in frustration. Dean grabbed his cell from the low table in front of the couch and was just about to hit Accept when he realized that there was no caller ID. He frowned and showed Richard the display.

Richard thought about it for a moment. It could be Elisa, although he doubted it. He had told the woman in no uncertain terms that she wasn't allowed to call this number. So whoever was calling had probably acquired it illegally. He had to find out who it was, how they had done it, and then he had to get Dean a new phone—again. "Take the call, but put it on speaker."

Dean nodded and slid the green symbol across the screen. "Dean Connelly speaking."

The voice at the other end of the line was female, a pleasing alto with a hint of steel in it. "Hello, Dean. It's me, Faith."

Dean made a choking sound in the back of his throat and almost dropped the phone. Richard caught it in a swift movement, worried about the ghastly color of Dean's face. "What do you want, Mother?"

Now it was Richard's turn to almost drop the phone. All he knew about Dean's parents was that they were conservative, stuck-up assholes of the highest order. Dean had never told him their names, and the only time they had talked about Dean's childhood and fallout with his parents, he had become so upset that Richard avoided the topic from then on. Hearing from them now came as a shock. And Faith Connelly wasted no time with pleasantries.

"We were informed about Tricia's death by that horrible lawyer woman from Connor and Partners. Since her death was almost six weeks ago, I assume her ashes are already with you. Is that right, Dean?"

Dean was obviously still stunned because he just nodded and whispered, "Yes." Richard winced. Dean's grief over Tricia's death was still raw, and he didn't need the reminder, especially not from somebody as cold and uncaring as Faith Connelly. Oblivious to the hurt in her son's voice, the woman ranted on. "Your father and I have decided to host a memorial ceremony at our country club to give people a chance to pay their condolences. You know the address, so please send Tricia's urn there before next week. We will scatter her ashes over the lake afterward. Don't bother to come yourself. We wouldn't appreciate it."

Dean just sat there, tears streaming down his face as he listened to the cold voice of the woman who should have loved him more than her own life.

Richard had enough. He grabbed the phone, muted the speaker, and put it to his ear. "Hello, Mrs. Connelly. I am Richard Miller, Dean's partner. I would like to know how you got this phone number. It's private."

There was a disgusted huff at the other end of the line. "I really don't see why that should concern you, but if you must know, I called those lawyers. That Elisa woman refused to give me the number, but one of her secretaries saw reason when I explained matters to her."

Richard bit back an angry growl. Connor and Partners were in trouble. He forced a calm he didn't feel into his voice. "I have to ask you not to use this number again"—not that it would be in service for much longer—"and while we're at it, I also have to tell you that we won't send Tricia's ashes to you. She has been very specific in her will, and you not getting her remains was one of her main concerns. If you want to hold that little memorial ceremony, do it, but without involving your children."

Richard listened to the outraged sputtering for a moment, then disconnected the call. He had a nagging feeling this wouldn't be the last time he'd have the displeasure of interacting with Dean's parents. For the time being, though, he couldn't do much about them, so he concentrated on the things he could influence. To make sure Faith Connelly, or anybody else, for that matter, wouldn't interrupt their time together again, Richard shut the phone down. Then he turned back to Dean. His arms opened automatically when he saw the shaken look on his boy's face. With a sob, Dean threw himself into Richard's embrace, and then the tears started to fall. Richard knew how important this was for Dean, finally realizing that his beloved sister was truly gone and letting all his anguish and sorrow out. They had been together long enough for Richard to tell that this was finally happening. That Dean was facing the truth.

Richard held his boy until the sobs stopped and turned into a gentle snore.

As soon as Richard could be sure Dean was fast asleep, he called Connor and Partners to make his anger about the leak known. Elisa did her best to placate him and promised that the secretary who had given away Dean's phone number would be fired. Richard didn't bother telling Elisa that the number would be out of service soon. If she didn't conclude that, the money she had spent on her degree had been wasted. Satisfied with the outcome of his call, Richard settled back on the couch next to Dean and watched his boy sleep.

Only an hour later, Julio returned with Emily. He glanced briefly at Dean, then gestured to Richard that he would take care of her for the rest of the day, including the night. Richard shot him a grateful look. The man was worth every penny they paid him and had just earned himself a generous tip. Even though Richard still wasn't entirely on board with the whole Emily situation, he was glad they had contracted Julio, despite the fact that Precious Care knew how to take from the living.

Around midnight, Dean startled from his deep slumber. Blearily, he stared at Richard. "Master?"

Richard gently stroked Dean's back. "It's fine, boy. Do you want to take a bath or go sleep in the bed?"

Dean actually thought about that for a moment before he snuggled back into Richard's embrace. "Let's go to the bed. Can you fuck me?"

Richard was a little surprised by the request, but not enough not to waste this opportunity. "Of course I can." He lifted Dean up and carried him to their bedroom. Richard still spent most of his nights in the playroom, due to Emily's nightly activities, and when he laid Dean down on their king-size bed, he finally realized how much he missed sleeping next to his boy. Richard knew Dean was too tired to do a scene, but he could still spice things up a bit. He undressed quickly and then leaned over Dean, who was watching him with lust-filled eyes. "Time to get you naked, boy."

Dean shuddered at the predatory tone in Richard's voice. Obediently he lifted first his arms, so Richard could take off the shirt, and then his hips when Richard tugged at his jeans and boxers. Once he was bare, Richard feasted his eyes on Dean's lean body, beautifully sculpted muscles, and his hard cock jutting proudly from his groin.

"My beautiful boy. So eager. I love it." He treated Dean to a lazy, predatory smile. "Lift your hands over your head. Grab the headboard and don't let go. If you do, I will punish you. Understood?"

Dean licked his lips while he obeyed. Precum already leaked from his twitching cock in reaction to Richard's stern voice. Richard's smile grew evil. His boy reacted beautifully to the command. So sensual, so delicious.

Richard bent over Dean and took his lips in a searing kiss, delving in deep with his tongue while his fingers fondled Dean's balls. Richard's own need was riding him hard. There was no way either of them would last. Richard reached for the lube in the drawer, squirted a generous amount on his fingers, and went right for Dean's hole. They had known each other long enough to have had their share of hasty couplings. Richard pressed two of his slicked fingers into Dean, quickly followed by a third. Dean moaned deep in his throat when Richard found his sweet spot and started rubbing it.

"Master! I can't…. Please!"

Richard chuckled despite his own raging hard-on and kissed Dean again while he lubed his cock. As soon as he was done, he sank into Dean's tight hole and started moving. Dean cried out, jerking his hips upward to give Richard better access, but his hands never left the headboard. He was too well trained to disobey. Richard's thrusts grew more frantic; he was already close. When he felt the familiar tingling starting in his balls, he grabbed Dean's cock and tugged it roughly.

"Come, boy. Now!"

Dean cried out, his whole body stiffened, and hot cum poured over Richard's fingers. The sight of his boy in the throes of passion sent Richard over the edge as well. He slammed into Dean one more time before he coated Dean's inside with his seed. His. Claimed and marked.

They lay still for a while. When Richard sensed that Dean was close to falling asleep again, he pulled out of him, went to the bathroom to get a washcloth, and wiped his boy clean. Dean mumbled "Thank you" and closed his eyes.

When Richard came back from the bathroom, Dean was already fast asleep. With a soft smile on his face, Richard cuddled Dean close to his chest, covered them both with the blanket, and enjoyed the feeling of having his boy in his arms again.

CHAPTER 17

THE NEXT morning, Richard woke to the alluring scent of freshly brewed coffee and to the sight of his boy kneeling next to the bed, waiting for him. Richard couldn't help the smile that threatened to split his face in half. It had been too damn long. The past weeks, Dean had simply been too tired to serve him breakfast. And after a night spent apart, it also felt strange to have Dean bring it to him. Another aspect of their previously perfect relationship that had been disturbed by Emily's arrival. Richard firmly stomped on that treacherous thought. He wanted to reconcile with Dean, not make things worse.

"Good morning, boy. Did you sleep well?"

Dean blushed adoringly. "Yes, Master. Very well." He hesitated. "I missed this, Master."

Richard sighed and held out his hand. Dean took it, cuddling in next to him. "I missed it too, boy. And I'm aware that it is my fault. I wasn't as supportive as I should have been. I'm sorry."

Dean stared at him. "Are you now? Supportive, I mean."

Richard met Dean's gaze. "I'd lie if I said I can embrace this situation wholeheartedly. There's a lot going on, and I'm not looking forward to having a child in my life." Richard saw the hurt in Dean's eyes, but part of their contract was to be always honest with each other. So far, the agreement had worked in their favor. "But I promise to try. I know how much Emily means to you, so I guess I have to learn to live with her. Just don't expect me to become prime father material. That's just not me."

Dean smiled a little sadly. "I know. Thank you for trying. I really don't want to lose you."

Richard pulled Dean closer and kissed him gently, ignoring the little sting the implication behind Dean's last words brought to his chest. "You won't. We'll find a way, I promise. And now, let's eat. I talked to my father yesterday, and he wants to meet his grandchild."

Dean slapped a hand in front of his mouth. "Damn. We never told him. Is he very angry?"

"Easy, boy. It's fine. He was a little miffed, but I think he's distracted by the fact that he has a grandchild. With some luck, he'll forget about reaming us a new one when he sees Emily." Richard shuddered slightly. His father could be quite intimidating. "In fact, I'm counting on it."

Dean gave him a wobbly smile. "Then I better dress her in her cutest."

"Do that. But after breakfast. I want to savor the moment."

At ten, Richard's father arrived with Thor and Donar in tow. Luckily, Richard's prediction had been right. As soon as the former general laid eyes on Emily, he forgot about his grudge and started cooing over the infant. The two dogs kept on yapping excitedly until his father lowered down to let them sniff the baby. All three men held their breath when Emily stared at the two huge dogs with wide eyes. Then she started to giggle, grabbed Donar's ear with her tiny fingers, and pulled him closer. The dog obeyed and started licking her face. The happy sounds from Emily grew louder as she enjoyed the attention of her grandfather and the dogs.

Richard gave Dean a quick kiss. "I have work, but I'll be back at six. Can you order something from Mamma's?"

"Of course. It's a date."

"Mmmm, I love dates."

Dean grinned. "Me too." His face fell. "Don't expect too much. Julio has taken the day off, what with your father dropping by and everything. We're on full duty today."

Richard felt a twang of annoyance deep inside but reminded himself that he had to get used to this. Their carefree days were definitely over. "It's fine, boy. We'll just see what happens, okay? Have a nice day "

"You too. I love you."

"I love you." Richard waved goodbye to his father and left.

Dean sighed when the door closed. This was going to be harder than he had thought.

"He'll come around, you know? He just needs some time to adjust."

Dean turned to Aaron, who was sitting on the floor with Emily on his lap and the dogs sniffing around. She was by now pretty good at rolling from her stomach to her back, as well as lifting her head. Thor and Donar watched attentively as she demonstrated her skills after Aaron put her on the carpet. And if she used Thor's front paws for leverage, neither of the dogs would comment on it.

"She's really sweet." Aaron's voice had a dreamy quality Dean had never heard from the usually commanding man before.

"Yes, she is. A real joy." He sat next to Aaron, and they both watched as Emily fingered the dogs' coats.

After a few moments of silence, Aaron spoke again. "I'm sorry about your sister. I didn't know her, but Richard said she was a great person."

Dean felt tears threatening to fall. "She was the best sister I could have wished for." He had to stop talking or he would start crying again.

Aaron put his arms around Dean's shoulder. "It's okay to cry, you know? When my Delilah died, I cried a lot. Let it happen. It's no good to suppress your sorrow. You have to let it out, or it eats you from the inside. The more you allow yourself to grieve, the sooner you will learn to live with the loss."

Dean felt the sobs bubbling up in his throat. "But... but... what about Emily?"

"It's fine. She's fine. We don't know how much a baby of her age can comprehend, but even if it's more than what we think, she will sense your sincerity. Just like animals, children can tell the truth between real and fake emotions. As long as you stay true to yourself, you don't have to worry about her. Letting your feelings out is much better than the tension of suppressing them. Believe me."

Dean looked at Aaron, not trying to keep the tears from streaming down his cheeks. "Do you still miss her?"

"Delilah? Yes. Every day I wake up, I regret losing her." Aaron started rubbing soothing circles on Dean's back. "And then I remember all the happy moments I shared with her. Richard's birth. The day we first met. The first meal she cooked me." Aaron made a face. "It tasted like cardboard, but I ate the entire plate and even asked for seconds, just to please her. The next day, she invited me to dinner at a small restaurant and promised not to force her cooking on me before she had finished her cooking class. She was such a great person with a unique sense of humor. I won't lie to you, Dean. Losing Delilah almost broke me. But even in death, she watched out for me. She sent me these two rascals"—he pointed at Thor and Donar—"knowing they would help me find my way back."

Dean leaned into Aaron, craving the warmth and comfort of the older man's body. Since the relationship with his own parents was nonexistent, he took every scrap of fatherly love he could get. As if he had read his thoughts, Aaron murmured into Dean's hair, "You know you can always come to me, don't you, son?"

"Yes. Thank you. That helps a lot."

Aaron patted his back. "It's a beautiful day outside. Shall we go for a stroll with Emily?"

At the mention of a stroll, Donar and Thor started wagging their tails. They didn't move, though, because Emily was now lying between them, pulling their fur and making happy crooning noises. Dean smiled wistfully at the peaceful picture. He only hoped Tricia, wherever she might be now, could see it as well.

Then he squared his shoulders, got up, and started packing the diaper bag.

CHAPTER 18

RICHARD WHISTLED happily while he climbed the stairs to his home. He and his boy would be going on a date tonight. And not only a vanilla date—they would do a scene at Whisper. He couldn't wait. A week had passed since the conversation with his father, and Richard had not been idle. He still avoided Emily whenever possible, even though Dean had officially filed for temporary custody by now and it looked as if Emily would become a fixture in their lives. But he had taken charge of their daily lives again. Together with Julio and Aaron, he had worked out a schedule that would allow him and Dean to spend some much-needed time together every week. As of today, his father would be on babysitting duty every Friday or Saturday, depending on his own plans, which gave Richard the chance to take his boy out.

When he entered the apartment, he saw Dean sitting on the floor together with his father and the dogs. All four were watching Emily who was propped up on her hands, seesawing back and forth, obviously trying to move forward and failing. How two grown men could be so fascinated by the clumsy and futile efforts of a baby eluded Richard, but he was in too good a mood to make a sarcastic comment. Instead, he leaned down to press a kiss on Dean's lips, nodded to his father in greeting, and then proceeded into the bedroom to get ready for the night.

He knew he didn't have to dress up, since they would both change into their leathers once they arrived at the club. Richard took a quick shower, put on his jeans, a soft silken shirt that was as black as his trousers, and equally black leather loafers. He checked himself in the mirror and then went out to collect his boy.

It took him almost ten minutes until he got Dean through the front door, his boy giving his father last-minute instructions the man had probably already heard, given the way his lips parted in a knowing smile. Then they were in the car, and Richard breathed a sigh of relief. Their evening could begin.

They hadn't discussed when the scene would officially start, but when he looked at Dean's nervously clenched jaw and the way his boy's hands were kneading the hem of his shirt, Richard decided to dive right in. While he steered the car through the traffic, he took a deep breath and settled firmly in his Dom headspace before he started giving his orders.

"Sit straight, boy. Eyes on the road."

Startled by the commanding tone, Dean did as he was told. Richard noticed that his boy was already relaxing. They always were at their best when they embraced their D/s relationship dynamics fully.

"Open your trousers. Get your cock out."

A quick glance reassured Richard that his boy was not only following his orders, but that he was also starting to get hard. Good.

"I want you to play with yourself. Left hand on your balls, right hand on your cock. Get yourself as close to orgasm as possible. You're not allowed to come, though."

When he heard the small whimper escape from his boy's lips, he couldn't suppress an evil smile. "I'm going to push you today, boy. Make you work for it. How does that sound?"

Another whimper resounded before Dean managed to answer. His hands were still playing with his balls and working on his now fully erect shaft. "Sounds good, Master."

Richard risked another glance and saw precum oozing from Dean's slit. "Very good, boy. But I want you a little closer. You can do that, I know it. I want you all hot and horny for me, for my big, fat prick. Can you imagine how good it will feel, having my cock deep inside your body, your hole and ass burning from the whipping I'm going to give you? I'm going to put a cock ring on you, maybe even plug your slit, and then I'm going to pound your ass and you won't be allowed to come."

Dean moaned deep in his throat, his right hand working furiously on his hard shaft. His hands were slick with precum, his entire body tensed as his orgasm approached. At the very last moment, he took his hand away, his cock jutting, hips fucking the empty air, frustration apparent in his face. Richard put a soothing hand on Dean's thigh.

"Very good, boy. I'm proud of you."

Dean moaned. "Master."

Richard chuckled. "As much as I would love to see you edging again, we're already at Whisper. Tuck yourself in and then let's get inside."

Dean hurried to obey. They left their car in the parking lot, proceeded through security, and split at the locker rooms. Richard gave Dean a searing kiss and some additional instructions. "Except for your collar, you will be naked, boy. Once you are undressed, go directly to my private table and assume the position. And, boy, I want to see you all hard and bothered for me, understand?"

"Yes, Master."

"Good. Then off you go." Richard slapped Dean's ass playfully, hinting at what was still to come this night. Dean moaned softly and hurried into the subs' locker room.

Unlike the Doms' locker room, where subs were never allowed, the room of the subs was open for Doms. When Dean hurried to his locker, he saw another sub bent over one of the benches, his master inserting a huge butt plug into his ass. The sub had his eyes closed, trying hard to accept the toy while the Dom slid it in and out, widening his boy's hole, pushing the toy deeper with every thrust. Dean watched them for a moment longer before he went to his locker. He had been a bit worried about staying hard for Richard, but that little show helped greatly.

Dean felt ecstatic about doing a scene with his master tonight; if only he wasn't so damn tired. The night before, Emily had woken three times, and he hadn't had a chance for a nap the entire day. The prospect of getting to bed late today, and after strenuous action to boot, only to be woken tomorrow at six, dampened Dean's mood. He started undressing, determined to enjoy this evening. It had been too long since they had last shared a scene, and Dean missed his Dom. They both needed this, needed it badly. When he was naked, he stroked himself until he was hard again. The thoughts about his lack of sleep hadn't helped his erection.

Dean walked out into the club's main area, his body as straight as possible, hands clasped behind his back, eyes on the floor.

Since it was a Friday night, the dance floor was packed, and the sight of all the hot, sweating male bodies in various stages of nudity helped him maintain his hard-on until he reached the quieter back area with the bar and tables. He went straight for Richard's booth and knelt next to his Dom's preferred seat, his knees spread, hands now clasped behind his head to display the muscles in his arms and upper body, his cock jutting out proudly from his groin. Just when he was settled, Richard appeared.

Dean could only see his master's black leather boots, since he hadn't been allowed to raise his eyes yet. Richard stood there for a moment, not saying anything. Then he patted Dean's head. "Get up, boy. I need to prepare you."

Dean rose gracefully to his feet, waiting for further instructions. Now he could see Richard's bare chest and the black leather chaps he wore. His rigid cock was barely contained by a jockstrap. Dean gulped. His master was a very fine man. Richard produced a leather cock ring and put it on tight, trussing Dean's balls and cock up into an obscene package.

Richard gave Dean's leaking prick a teasing rub that made Dean's legs buckle. Then he pulled out a little package of lube and a plug with three orbs made of metal. Dean knew that plug, knew it would be hard to keep inside because of its weight. Richard was going all out, and it made Dean feel bad, because even though he knew it was his fault that they hadn't had a scene in more than seven weeks, he was too exhausted to greet this toy with his usual enthusiasm.

If Richard picked up on his discomfort, he didn't show it. He bent Dean over the table, slicked his hole and the toy with the lube, and then pressed the first orb against Dean's entrance. Dean gripped the edges of the table to steady himself while Richard worked the toy inside his body, sliding it in and out, wiggling it around, letting the orbs stretch his entrance muscles. Dean couldn't help but beg. "Please, Master."

A hard smack on his ass reminded him that he hadn't gotten permission to speak. Dean suspected it was the lack of sleep that made him forget the most basic rules Richard had installed. "No talking until I say so, boy. Screams are allowed."

Dean shuddered and heard Richard's deep, amused chuckle. His Dom was definitely enjoying himself. The last of the orbs slid into Dean's body. Richard moved them around a bit more until he had grazed Dean's gland several times.

"Resume the position, boy. Our drinks are coming."

Dean obeyed, carefully clenching his inner muscles to keep the orbs from sliding out of his body. He had to bite his lip to prevent the cry when one of the orbs rubbed against his gland, sending shivers up and down his spine. Richard patted his head. "You're doing well, boy."

RICHARD HATED to admit it, but he was feeling giddy. Being with his boy, there at his club, doing a scene, preparing for one hell of a night—this was how their life was supposed to be. He offered Dean the glass with water, trying to get a generous amount of liquid into his boy. The things he had planned were going to push Dean, and he needed him at his best. When both their drinks were empty, Richard stood. Dean did the same, following two steps behind him in perfect sync without the need for a leash. Richard loved that connection he shared with Dean, one he knew quite a lot of Doms and subs in the club envied.

Again they ended up in his favorite playroom, the St. Andrew's cross displayed by two strategically placed lights. Tonight Richard wanted to catch every last detail on his boy's body. He led Dean toward the cross. Obediently, his boy raised his arms so Richard could fasten the leather cuffs around them. Once Dean was tightly bound to the cross, Richard stepped back and admired his work.

His boy was a work of art. So beautiful, so perfect in his submission. He let his fingers trail over Dean's back, marveling at the silky-smooth skin, the way the muscles under that skin quivered from his touch.

"I'm going to whip you, boy. Good and hard. And when I'm done whipping you, I'll get out the tawse, just for your delectable ass."

Dean moaned, his hips jerking helplessly. "All that time, I'll keep you plugged and you're not allowed to lose it. Once I have your back and ass all red and tender, I'm going to fuck you, impale you on my thick cock, make you dance for me, boy, fill you with my spunk."

Dean groaned, wriggling in his restraints. Richard pressed a soft kiss on Dean's shoulder and turned toward the cabinet with the whips. His eyes scanned briefly over the assortment before he selected a cat-o-nine-tails. He let the leather straps caress Dean's skin once, twice, then he let the whip fly.

DEAN CRIED out when the straps bit into him the first time. Apparently, about seven weeks was enough time to let him forget the sting. He grunted at the next two blows, trying to find the pleasure behind the pain, his subspace.

Only it didn't work this time. Under normal circumstances, Dean would have already been halfway into his subspace by the time Richard cuffed him to the cross. He never had a problem with the pain. It always brought him pleasure. But today it was just pain, and not the good kind. Dean blamed it on his exhaustion. He just couldn't focus. But he had to. Richard would be beyond disappointed if he ruined this scene. Dean gritted his teeth and tried his best to lean into the next blow, to accept the pain as his Dom's will.

RICHARD COULD tell things weren't working out. By now, Dean should have been begging for the permission to come, not trying to evade every single blow. His boy wasn't focused, wasn't in the moment as he should be. Richard tried changing the angle of his blows, but all that got him were more pained grunts. One quick look into the mirror on the wall behind the cross showed him that Dean was not only trying very hard to accept the pain and failing, but that he had also lost his hard-on, despite the cock ring.

Richard cast the whip aside. If he wanted this scene to work, he had to change his plans. Perhaps Dean needed a gentler approach today, although his earlier reactions had hinted at the opposite. He covered his boy's body with his own, embraced Dean, and started caressing Dean's flanks and abdomen in an attempt to soothe him.

A sob escaped from Dean's lips, desperate and dejected. Richard made a cooing noise. "Shh. It's fine, boy. Everything is all right. You're doing great. Just relax, leave everything to me."

He wanted to say more, wanted to keep on whispering sweet words into his boy's ear, when he felt Dean take a deep breath. Dean turned his head, tears glistening on his cheeks. "I'm sorry, Richard. Graphic novel."

Richard reared back from Dean as if he had just burned himself. With two little words, Dean had ended their first scene in what felt like ages. Richard felt anger and bitterness overwhelm him. He knew then that he was in no condition to deal with Dean in his current emotional state. Still, his boy needed aftercare, especially since the scene had gone wrong. Richard hurried to loosen Dean's restraints and then carried the sobbing man over to the big bed. He made sure Dean was covered and had a bottle of water standing close by. Then he turned to leave. "I'm sending somebody in to look after you. I'm too agitated right now."

Dean only nodded, his eyes half-closed, a sad, hurt look on his face. It made Richard even angrier, and he hurried to get out of the room before he said something he wouldn't be able to take back. Why did Dean have to look like a beaten puppy? It wasn't Richard who had ruined their scene, their night. He stormed outside toward the bar. Leeland was on duty tonight, and he also happened to be a friend of Dean's. Richard tossed him his membership card.

"Please go and take care of Dean. He's in the red room."

Leeland opened his mouth to ask a question or perhaps to protest, caught sight of Richard's thunderous expression, and settled for "Yes, Master Richard" instead. Richard watched as the slim, beautiful man took off. At least Dean would be in good hands.

"Geez, what's gotten your panties in a knot?"

Richard turned around to face Jonathan White, the burly owner of a garage that specialized in restoring vintage cars and motorbikes as well as customizing high-class rides. Jonathan had worked on Richard's BMW, and that was how they had met. They had both smelled the Dom on the other and taken an immediate liking to each other. Jonathan was one of the few men Richard considered a friend. He slumped onto the barstool next to Jonathan and signaled the other sub manning the bar to bring him a drink. When the whiskey was placed in front of him, Richard held out his wrist so that the boy could put the black stamp with the crossed-out whip on it. Nobody was allowed to do a scene under the influence in the club, and even one drink was considered one drink too many.

Richard raised the glass in silent salute before he took a deep swig. Jonathan watched him intently. The man's burning gaze reminded Richard of how wrong this evening had gone. Perhaps it was a good idea to share his anger.

"Dean just safeworded during our first scene in seven goddamn weeks! That's what's gotten my panties in a knot."

Jonathan merely lifted an eyebrow at Richard's furious tone. "Subs safeword. That's why we have them. It's hardly the end of the world. Or a reason to react so strongly."

Another thing Richard liked about Jonathan, despite the fact that he couldn't be easily intimidated, was his refusal to be bullshitted. Only, at the moment, he wished the man was a bit less perceptive and more on Richard's side.

"For me it is. It's the first time ever that Dean has used his safeword. And tonight, of all nights!"

"What's so special about tonight? I thought your anniversary was a couple of months ago?"

"It was. We haven't done a scene since then. A lot has happened. Dean's sister died and left him in custody of a three-month-old baby. Well, almost five months old by now. I have an infant in my home, sleep most of the nights in the playroom because it's soundproof, and I haven't gotten any action to speak of for seven weeks. Tonight was all about reconnecting with my boy, of getting our old life back, and he *safeworded*!"

Jonathan looked at Richard as if he had grown a second head. "Your boy has just gone through such traumatic changes in his life and you're upset because he didn't act out a scene?"

Richard buried his head in his hands. Put like that, he sounded like a total jerk. "He didn't even give me a chance to make it right. I could sense that the scene wasn't going well and I tried to steer it in another direction, but then he suddenly safeworded. I got so angry. I still am. This is just not how we work. Dean never safewords! He doesn't have to. I have him covered. He can trust me."

Jonathan patted Richard's shoulder. "So, are you upset because Dean ended the scene before you both could get your rocks off, or because you think he has betrayed you by not trusting you?"

"Both. Although, I have to admit, the second reason hurts more."

"You are aware that using a safeword is not a personal insult? Despite what you seem to think, you are only human, Richard. All Doms are, even though we don't like to admit it. Yes, you are really good at gauging your boy's mood and reactions, but you are not your boy. Whatever reason Dean had to use his safeword, it was a valid one. You have to respect that."

Richard stared at Jonathan long and hard. Then he reached for his glass and downed the whiskey, gesturing for the boy behind the bar to bring him another. Of course, Jonathan was right. From a purely BDSM point of view, there was nothing wrong with using a safeword. It was a good thing indeed, the way a Dom and his sub could still communicate when things got out of hand. The problem was, Richard wasn't sure if Dean's use of the safeword was entirely motivated by a scene that had become too intense.

"Dean and I have been together for five years. I introduced him to BDSM. I was the first and only to teach him the joy you can find in pain. I'm his keeper, his Dom, his lover. He has always trusted me, and I have never once disappointed him. I feel like I've been dismissed, like Dean has betrayed me on more than one level, like he has somehow made a mockery of what we have together. And I know how stupid that is."

"Man, listening to you, I'm glad I'm not into the whole commitment thing. I just do scenes with clear rules, written down for everybody involved to comprehend, no strings attached. This whole being in love business seems to fuck with the straightforwardness I like about BDSM."

Richard sighed. "It does. When you're with a stranger, or even a play buddy, it's easier concerning the rules. The power exchange is clear, no shades and hidden depths. With the man you love, on the other hand…. The scenes are more intense. You discover layers, deeper emotions. Sometimes it's scary, but I can't say I regret playing only with Dean. I get so much more out of a scene than before I met him."

Jonathan lifted his beer. "Now I'm a little jealous. Also makes me wonder why you're not with your boy at the moment, trying to figure out what went wrong. I mean, dude, he's lost his sister and is now responsible for raising a child. I'm not sure if that is something you can figure out in just seven weeks."

Richard sighed once more. Jonathan's words made sense. They were also true. That didn't mean he had to like them. All he wanted right now was to get drunk enough to forget about this whole disaster. And if that made him a selfish asshole, so be it. "Are you going to help me drown my sorrows?"

Jonathan seemed to weigh his options. If their roles were reversed, Richard would have insisted that Jonathan went back to his boy and tried to make things right. But as things were, Jonathan knew him well enough not to try to push Richard. He needed time to process the events of the evening, and alcohol was the way to go. Jonathan sighed and then gave Richard a crooked smile. "That's what friends are for."

CHAPTER 19

Three weeks later.

DEAN MANEUVERED the stroller between two tables at the café where Leeland was waiting for him. Emily was fast asleep and hopefully wouldn't wake until Dean and Leeland had enjoyed their lunch. His little niece had by now adopted a schedule that would allow Dean to plan a little bit ahead, even though those plans got thwarted half the time. Dean usually spent Emily's lunch nap sleeping himself, because his nights were still interrupted at least once and ended at five o'clock. Emily was an early riser. The initial two months during which Julio had lived with them were up, and Dean was now on his own, at least during the night. Julio still watched Emily three days a week so Dean could get some work done, and Aaron also helped out a lot. Nevertheless, Dean bore the brunt of taking care of Emily, and he couldn't remember when he had last felt fully awake.

After the disastrous scene at Whisper, Richard and Dean had a talk about what had gone wrong, but all Dean had taken from that discussion was how frustrated Richard was about the changes in their relationship and a strong feeling that Richard did not completely understand him. It made his heart constrict with a mixture of guilt and anger.

He loved Richard from the bottom of his heart, but he hated what was happening between them. Why couldn't Richard be a little bit more understanding? All Dean needed was time to get this whole caring-for-a-child business sorted out. It wasn't like their life was over now that they had Emily. Richard sure made it sound like it.

Dean reached the table where Leeland was sitting and went for a hug. His regular meetings with the other sub had helped him keep his sanity during the last three weeks. Leeland looked him over, concern apparent in his almond-shaped brown eyes.

"You don't look very good. Still trouble in paradise?"

Dean slumped into the chair next to Leeland after making sure the stroller's brakes were on. "You could say so. Richard's on a business trip. Before I had Emily, it was hell when he was gone. I just felt so helpless. Now I'm almost glad that I have a few days where I don't have to tiptoe around, bending over to please him, and keeping Emily out of his hair. I'm starting to fear that…." Dean stopped, tears threatening to fall. Again. He was a mess and he knew it.

Leeland patted his hand. "Oh, honey, don't even think about that! You have to stay positive. You and Richard—you're one. Everybody knows that. He loves you to distraction. He just needs time."

Dean sighed. "I know. It's just—as my Dom and my partner, he should be there for me. But he isn't. He's leaving me alone, and I'm no good on my own. That's why I needed a Dom in the first place."

"Not to mention he's also your lover. I can only imagine how that must hurt."

There was a wistful tone in Leeland's voice that startled Dean out of his self-pity. He knew Leeland's life wasn't perfect either. "I'm sorry, Leeland. I've only been thinking of myself. How are you doing?"

Leeland started to answer and then shut his mouth again when the server came to take their orders. Once that was done, he started speaking again. "I'm doing fine, mostly. I still seem to attract only the Doms who see me as a nice toy for inflicting pain and not as an equal partner, but I haven't given up hope yet."

Dean made some sympathetic noises. He knew how much Leeland suffered from his looks. The man was the very definition of a gorgeous twink. At five foot six, with a slim, yet perfectly toned body, a beautiful face with large dark brown eyes, a pert little nose, a sensual mouth, and a mass of black, silky hair that went down to his waist, Leeland was like a walking wet dream for most men, especially Doms who liked their subs to be meek and obedient. Unfortunately, Leeland was neither, even though he looked like it. Both his parents were detectives, and they had seen to it that their son would always be able to defend himself. Leeland was an excellent shot, had black belts in judo, tae kwon do, and jujitsu, and knew how to handle and throw a knife. When he was out, he always carried at least two with him. He was still looking for a Dom who respected him enough to treat him as an equal and not some fragile flower.

"There has to be one out there just for you. Perhaps we should go looking together? It would give me something else to think about, and we might get lucky."

Leeland huffed. Then he smiled at the server who brought their lunch. Leeland liked food. "I already have a candidate. Unfortunately, he's not interested in something permanent. I have yet to convince him to meet me outside the club."

"You mean Jonathan? You do realize that he's the very definition of a caveman Dom who needs to dominate with his sheer body mass."

Again Leeland blew out his breath. "I know. But the scenes we do together are so nice. He doesn't just whip and fuck me. He's surprisingly playful and has amazing skills when it comes to sensual torture. I enjoy the scenes with him."

"He's also a no-strings-attached guy. Leeland, I'm not even sure Jonathan knows how the word commitment is spelled."

"You don't have to rub it in. I'm not dumb."

"But desperate."

Leeland threw his hands up. "Fine, I'm desperate. Very much so. There's just nothing I can do about it."

Dean smiled grimly. "Neither can I. So, are we going to be miserable together?"

Leeland grinned. "Being miserable means we're entitled to huge amounts of chocolate. And I just happen to know a shop where they sell all the good stuff."

"What are we waiting for? Let's finish lunch and then dig in. I have a lot of things I need to compensate for with chocolate."

WHEN DEAN returned home that afternoon, he had a definite spring to his steps. Most of it was the sugar coursing through his system from way too much chocolate. The shop Leeland had taken him to was more than great, and Dean felt giddy just thinking about all the different treats he hadn't even tried yet. After talking to Leeland, he had also decided to take the initiative concerning his troubles with Richard. Dean longed for their relationship to be whole again, and he would do anything for it.

He put Emily down on her play blanket in the middle of the living room, took out his brand-new cell, and typed a message for Richard.

Hello, Master. How about a romantic dinner when you come home tomorrow? I can ask Aaron to babysit and make a reservation at Mamma's. Love you.

The reply came immediately.

I would love to, boy. Make the reservation for 8.

Dean grinned as he typed again. *Done.*

He called Mamma's to make the reservation, and Aaron to invite him over for babysitting. Aaron was thrilled. He and Emily had hit it right off.

The little girl loved spending time with her granddaddy and his two dogs, all three of which she had wrapped around her tiny little finger.

"Granddad is coming tomorrow, princess. He'll look after you while your daddies have a big boys' night out."

Emily stared at him with her huge blue eyes for a moment before she decided her toys were more interesting. She held a limp little teddy bear out to Dean, who took it and winced at the wetness. Emily had started salivating like crazy the day before. Everything was drenched despite the cute and thickly woven bibs he had bought for her. Julio had assured him that this was normal at her age, but Dean still found it gross. Emily didn't seem to mind, though, and so they spent the rest of the day playing peacefully on the floor.

Chapter 20

Richard hadn't even opened the door to his home when the sinking feeling in his stomach started. From inside the apartment, he could hear Emily wailing and Dean trying to hush her. Past experience had taught Richard that this was not an angry or tired cry, which both were tedious, but could be handled. No, this was a full-on "it really hurts and you better do something about it" wail. Richard just knew that Dean would cancel their dinner date, and he felt anger welling up inside him. Once again Emily had managed to come between him and his boy, his lover. Determined not to make this easy for Dean, Richard entered the apartment.

The noise level rose to almost intolerable heights when he reached the living room. Dean was pacing around with Emily in his arms, alternating shushing sounds with out-of-tune lullabies. Emily's face had taken on a beet-red color, her little fists drawn close to her body as if that would help her scream even louder. Dean shot Richard an apologetic look that told him all he needed to know. Their dinner was off.

"She's been crying for two hours. I don't know what to do. I tried to call Julio, but he didn't answer."

Seeing his boy so helpless and desperate struck every protective chord in Richard. Yet instead of offering his help, he clung to his wounded pride about being rejected once more in favor of this squealing menace in Dean's arms and simply shrugged. "Then I guess you have to deal with this on your own. I'll tell my father that he doesn't have to come over."

"Richard, please…."

Richard shook his head. "No, Dean. I understand. I'm taking a shower now, and then I'll go and have dinner on my own. Again. Have a nice evening."

He ignored Dean's pleading eyes and stomped to the bedroom. That should teach his boy a lesson! He had told him right from the beginning that Dean wasn't fit to take care of a child, but he hadn't listened. A nagging little voice told Richard that he was being an absolute ass. He ignored it in favor of his outrage. After texting the general that his services weren't needed tonight, he got under the shower, quickly cleaned himself, got dressed, and then walked out the door without sparing Dean or the raging little monster in his arms another glance.

WITH TEARS in his eyes Dean watched Richard leave him—again. He felt so numb inside, even Emily's screams seemed muffled. Mechanically he stroked her head, not knowing what to do. Just when he was ready to fold under the pressure, his phone rang. Dean sent a prayer to the gods above. It was Julio.

"Julio?"

"Yes, Dean. What's the matter? Wait, don't tell me—I can hear it."

Julio's attempt to lighten the mood almost sent Dean over the edge. He had trouble suppressing his own sobs.

"Emily—she's been like this for more than two hours. I don't know what to do. I already gave her some fennel tea, but that didn't help."

"Are you sure she's having stomach cramps?"

"No. Not anymore. She started screaming after I fed her. That's why…."

"Okay, first of all, calm down. Go and take her temperature."

Dean did as he was told, glad Julio had taught him how to do that when he lived with them. When he saw the number on the thermometer, his knees went weak.

"Oh God, Julio, she's at 100.3! I need to go to the hospital!"

"Calm down, Dean. Don't rush this. Feel around in her mouth. Are her gums swollen?"

Again, Dean did as instructed. When his fingers slid over the flesh in the front of Emily's lower gum, he could feel it pulsing under his fingertips. Oddly enough, the contact seemed to be comfortable for Emily, because she stopped crying for the first time in what felt like forever. On the other end of the line, Julio chuckled.

"Guess you found the spot."

"Seems so. She likes it when I rub it."

"Congratulations, Dean. She's getting her first tooth. No need to go to the hospital. Here is what you do: use the chamomile gel from the small tube and rub it into her gums. It numbs the pain. Do you remember the teething ring we bought? Put it in the freezer for fifteen minutes and then give it to her. If she hasn't fallen asleep by then. She sounds pretty wrung out."

"Thank you, Julio. I wouldn't know what I'd do without you!"

"No problem, Dean. I mean, you're paying me and everything."

The good-humored laughter at the other end of the line told Dean that Julio cared about him and would have helped him anyway.

"Then I'll make sure to add a tip to your next check. Have a good night!"

"I will. See you the day after tomorrow."

After he had disconnected the call, Dean gave Emily the chamomile gel and kept on rubbing her gums until it kicked in. Once it did, Emily immediately fell asleep. Knowing not to question his luck, Dean put her in her crib and went to bed himself. There was no telling what the night would bring.

RICHARD CAME back home at eight the next morning. He had meant to spend the night at the club, only to realize that being there just rubbed in the fact that his boy was back at home. Because of that he had booked a room at the Hilton. The eerie silence greeting him when he entered the apartment made him wary. Just yesterday, Emily had been screaming like she was about to be slaughtered. Now everything seemed just a little bit too peaceful. When he entered the kitchen, he saw Dean sitting at the table, feeding Emily in her high chair. His boy turned around, a happy smile on his lips even though the dark circles under his eyes told of another sleepless night.

"Richard! Look, Emily has her first tooth!"

Emily grinned and showed a small, blindingly white dot on her lower gums. When Richard didn't show the enthusiasm Dean had clearly been expecting, his shoulders slumped. His voice sounded dejected. "I'm so sorry about yesterday, Richard. I just couldn't...."

Annoyed by Dean's defeated tone and posture, which Richard knew he had a part in, he snapped back coldly. "Don't worry. Of course, Emily comes first."

Dean tensed. "Why do you have to be so mean? It's not my fault that she started teething yesterday."

Richard felt his anger boil over. He wanted—he needed a fight. "No, *that's* not your fault."

Dean's eyes narrowed. "Then what is? Since you seem to think I'm at fault for something."

"I told you right from the beginning that taking Emily in was not a good idea. And surprise, surprise, it really wasn't a good idea. Look at yourself. You look like shit. When have you last slept through the night? How is your writing going? When was the last time your—our—life was normal? Wait, I can answer that question. It was before she came here!" He pointed an accusing finger at Emily, who stared with interest at the two arguing men.

Dean paled. A dangerous glint appeared in his eyes, and his voice took on a steely quality, one Richard had never heard before. "Do you think I chose this? Do you think I wanted my sister to die so I can take care of her baby? You feel threatened by Emily because you think I chose her over you. I get that. What I don't get is how such an intelligent man as yourself can't see that I had no choice, that this is not a personal insult to you. Emily is all the family I have left. Tricia trusted me with her care. The sister who supported me when my parents threw me out. I don't know if I would be here, or even still be alive, if it wasn't for Tricia standing up for me, protecting me. It was her dying wish that I take care of her little girl. How can I not do that? How can I not love Emily? She's mine, as much as I am yours."

"So you do choose her over me," Richard snapped back.

"Have you listened to a word I said? No, I don't choose her over you. I could never do that and you know it! And if I had had a choice, I would have wanted Tricia to live and Emily to be my niece whom I could spoil occasionally and then hand back to my sister. But Tricia is gone and now Emily is my daughter, and I'm going to take care of her, which would be a lot easier if my fucking Dom and lover would be more accepting."

Richard had never seen Dean so agitated. It kindled his own anger. "So this whole mess is my fault now? How very convenient for you! 'My Dom doesn't help me, so it's no wonder I fuck up'?"

"Are you even listening to yourself? You're so selfish. I wonder why I haven't seen this sooner. Things are not going as planned, and like a coward, you tuck tail and run. You haven't even tried to make this work. In all the time Emily has been here, you've held her twice. And only because Julio practically forced her into your arms. That was the extent of your participation. Not a whole lot for a man who claims he loves me."

Richard's eyes narrowed down to slits. "You know what? I've had enough of this. If Emily is so much more important than me, why don't you just go ahead and leave with her? It's not like you need me anymore."

The hurt in Dean's eyes felt like a balm to Richard's wounded pride. "You can't be serious." The words were only whispered, desperate.

Richard steeled himself. Perhaps it was for the best, now that it had gone so far. "I am. Maybe it makes me selfish, but I can't stand your 'Emily first in everything' attitude. I think it's better if we end things now."

For a moment it seemed as if Dean wanted to plead with Richard, but then he squared his shoulders and stuck out his chin defiantly. "As you wish. It probably is for the best. I'm going to pack a few things for me and Emily. Once I find a place to stay, I'll send for the rest."

Richard watched as his now ex-boyfriend went into the bedroom. When he turned around, he saw Emily staring at him. Richard threw up his arms defensively. "Don't look at me like that! He's leaving me, not the other way round!"

Emily stared a little longer. Suddenly she grabbed the plastic bowl with the porridge and threw it on the floor.

CHAPTER 21

"HEY, DEAN, there you are!"

Leeland opened the door to his small apartment to let Dean in. He helped him park the stroller close to the wall, and then they brought Emily and Dean's luggage inside. Leeland watched his friend with worry. Dean seemed almost eerily calm, not as if his whole world had shattered around him—again.

"Are you sure you're okay?"

Dean smiled weakly at Leeland. "I'm far from okay. In fact, I'm hanging on by a thread. I just don't have the time to freak out. I don't even have a roof over my head I can call my own. Emily needs me now more than ever, and I want to be there for her. The meltdown must wait till I have things sorted out."

A pained expression flitted across Dean's features and made Leeland wish Richard was there so that he could punch him in the face. "With any luck, I'll be so dead inside by then that it will stop hurting so badly. Can you keep an eye on Emily for a while? I have a few phone calls to make."

Leeland nodded and took Emily from Dean's arms. "Has she eaten yet?"

"No. Her bottle and the formula are in the diaper bag."

"I'm on it. You go and make your calls."

Dean waited until Leeland had disappeared into the kitchen before he took out his cell. First he called Julio to give him the new address. Then he called Aaron, telling him he was no longer dating his son. The general sounded devastated.

"Oh, Dean. I'm so sorry! Is there anything I can do for you?"

Dean took a shaky breath. "If you still want anything to do with me…."

"Dean, don't go there. I'm well aware of my son's misgivings. I don't blame you for breaking up. What do you need?"

"Do you think you could still babysit Emily? In the coming weeks, I'm going to be busy with finding us a home and getting everything sorted out. I still have Julio booked for three days a week, but he has another child to take care of as well, and I don't want Emily to have to adjust to somebody new at a time like this."

"Do you even have to ask? I'd love spending time with my cute little princess. Things at the youth center are slow, so you can call me anytime."

Dean breathed a sigh of relief. "Thank you so much. Can you please get her on Friday? I'll text you the address."

"Sure, Dean. I'll see you on Friday at nine."

The general hung up, and Dean dialed the last person he had to talk to. Peyton answered after just one ring.

"Hi, Dean! How are you doing? Do you need an addition to the nursery?"

Dean felt the tears starting to slide down his cheeks. Somehow he managed to keep his voice steady. "No. In fact, Richard is probably going to call you soon about removing it again. We broke up."

"Honey, no! That's impossible! You and Richard, you're an item. You were so happy. I can't believe this!"

"I can't believe it either, but it's the truth. You don't happen to know about a nice place for me and Emily? Perhaps with a yard?"

In addition to designing, Peyton staged houses, so he often had an inside track on real estate, and he knew Dean very well. Asking him was the quickest way for Dean to find a suitable home. There was silence for a moment, as if Peyton was contemplating his next words. When he spoke, he sounded almost cheerful. "It just happens that I have the perfect place. It's a house in the Keys. Nothing too fancy, nice neighborhood, very quiet. There's a huge yard as well. The couple who are living there want to move to Texas, of all places, and they're looking for a buyer. Since they want this done as soon as possible, I'm sure we can negotiate a great price. Shouldn't cost you more than half a million. I can call them right away and make an appointment for tomorrow. We can go house shopping together."

"That would be great, Peyton. Can you text me the details later?"

"As soon as I have them. See you tomorrow."

The line went dead. Dean stared into nothing for a while, wondering why his life had suddenly turned into such a mess. About two months ago, his biggest concern in the world had been how to handle a few days without Richard by his side. Those problems seemed petty now in comparison.

His sister was dead. He was now in charge of an almost six-month-old baby. And the man Dean had wanted to spend the rest of his life with had just kicked him out. Or he had left him. He still wasn't entirely sure who was to blame for the fallout.

Dean sighed. If this were a novel, he'd also be broke and would meet the man of his dreams in the next twenty-four hours. Only the man of his dreams didn't want him anymore. And he wasn't broke. Dean chuckled. One had to be grateful for small favors.

He headed back to the kitchen to fill Leeland in on everything and find out how long he could stay with him. Dean had no desire to go to a hotel with Emily.

Two weeks later.

"HOW IS he doing today?"

Aaron looked at Leeland, who had opened the door for him. Since the breakup with Richard, the two of them took turns watching over Dean. The man was simply too calm. No angry outbursts, no breakdown, no snide remarks about his ex. Nothing. As if Dean had gone completely numb inside. Aaron and Leeland were waiting anxiously for the eruption.

"Focused, as always. He was working late yesterday, and then he couldn't stop tossing around in his bed for hours. If he's slept more than a couple of hours, I'd be surprised." Leeland sounded like he was trying to keep the worry from his voice.

"This is not good. Is he eating?" Aaron was growing more concerned with Dean's condition every day.

"No. Nothing solid. I managed to get some milkshake with protein powder into him, but that's not exactly a balanced diet."

They both sighed. Aaron stepped inside the small apartment. "Do you know how his house purchase is going?"

Leeland huffed as if that was another problem. "A little too fast, for my liking. Peyton dropped by yesterday and told Dean that it will only take a couple more days, four tops, to get everything wrapped up. I don't like the idea of him being all on his own."

"Me neither. I already talked to Julio, and he would be available to move in with Dean for another two months because the contract for the other child he's taking care of expires in two weeks, but apparently Dean doesn't want that. He says he's got it all covered. If he keeps going like this, I'm afraid he'll break."

Leeland frowned. "What makes you think he hasn't already?"

Aaron shuddered. "Do you think it's that bad?"

"I'm not sure. His reaction isn't normal, though. Perhaps it was too much. All the change in his life in such a short time. He needs solid routines to function."

"Is there a way to break him out of this?" Aaron was used to getting things done, and Dean needed the help.

"If there is, I have yet to find it. Getting him drunk backfired, because he fell asleep and I woke with a headache the next morning." Leeland winced. "He won't go out with me, not even for a quick drink, and since he's stopped eating, I can't even stuff him with chocolate. It's infuriating. Even telling him he has to eat to keep his strength up for Emily didn't work. It's as if he's operating on a different level of reality. I'm waiting for him to either crack or simply collapse, depending on what breaks first, his psyche or his body. Given how stubborn he is, my money is on his body."

Aaron patted the younger man's back. "You're trying. I think that's the most important thing right now. We have to trust that when he's ready, he'll come around. Until then, I do believe you need to go to school?"

Leeland smiled, although the concern was still evident in his eyes. "Yes, I do. I've got work after that, so I won't be home until midnight."

"That's fine. Perhaps I can get Dean to sleep a bit."

Leeland snorted. "Good luck with that. See you later."

"HI, RICHARD. How are you doing tonight?"

Martin sat down next to Richard at the bar, gesturing for the boy on duty to bring him a water. Richard didn't acknowledge his partner and kept staring into his whiskey instead. He wasn't doing well, and he knew it. The first couple of days after Dean left, Richard had found himself wandering through the apartment, looking for his boy—only to realize that he wasn't there anymore. He missed Dean so terribly, it hurt him physically, and wasn't that weird?

Then he had become angry. How could Dean just walk away from him, from their life together? When Richard remembered all the cold, horrible things he had said to Dean, he became even angrier, this time at himself.

All those warring emotions, the hurt over the loss of his boy, his fury about how things could have gone so wrong, his longing to have Dean back, his own stupid pride that prevented him from calling his boy—they chased each other inside his mind, and when it became too much to bear, he came to Whisper, like every night since their breakup, to distract himself. And there he was, sitting at the bar, unable to answer a simple question. He glanced over at Martin, who had just accepted his water from the boy.

The big man smiled at him. "You know it's normal to grieve after a breakup, don't you? I mean, that's a natural reaction, and everybody copes differently. But man, what's wrong with you? You've had eight different subs on as many nights and didn't do so much as a spanking with any of them."

Richard felt himself bristle under Martin's glare. "None of them were compatible." That was the truth.

"Yesterday you went with Alex. He's the definition of the word compatible, and he's been drooling after you for years, just like the others you picked. Don't tell me they weren't accommodating, because I know for sure they'd do anything to get a chance at you."

Richard sighed and took another sip from his whiskey. There was no denying it. He was in deep shit. "You're right. Each of them was eager, wanton, and hell yes, all of them are damn good-looking. But none of them is Dean."

He swished the whiskey around and watched the ice cubes bouncing. "The irony is, I always thought I had trained Dean to my liking, molded him so he met my standards. Turns out all that training went both ways."

Martin stared at Richard with a stunned expression. "And you only realize that now? Man, we all knew from the first time you walked in here with Dean on your leash."

Richard almost choked on his whiskey. Martin slapped his back until he regained his ability to breathe. "Why did you never say anything?"

Martin shrugged. "I thought you knew. Damn, Richard, you two were so deeply in love, it made many of us gag—and jealous as hell. You and Dean, you're magic. I've never seen a D/s pair like you. There are quite a lot of men here who wish for the same perfection."

"So you're telling me I'm making the worst mistake of my life?"

"If you haven't realized that by now, there's no helping you. Look, man, I know how hard this is for you. Your life has been completely shaken up, but when you let Dean go, you lost the one thing worth living for. I know you, Richard. You're a hard man, a ruthless businessman and, yes, I'm aware that you have to be those things in order to keep your business going. I'm fine with that. Hell, I'm like you, and we both know it. Dean balanced you, gave you something else to focus on. He was good for you, and don't you deny it."

Richard buried his face in his hands. "Damn, Martin. How do I fix this? I accused him of choosing Emily over me. I was jealous of a baby!" He paused for a moment. "And to be honest, I'm still not sure if I can handle having Emily in our life now. She has shaken us up, and all I want is to have my boy back."

Martin winked at him. "You just said it yourself. In your life *together*. If you want Dean, you have to accept Emily. They come as a package deal now. Perhaps you should see it like this—if you had met Dean when he already had Emily, would you still have chased after him?"

Richard didn't have to think about that. The answer came straight from the core of his being. "I would have definitely made him mine."

Martin patted his shoulder. "That's all you need to know. Now go and get your boy back."

Richard grinned and emptied his glass. "Thanks, man. I already feel better."

Martin just huffed and turned his attention to the boy behind the bar. He was a gorgeous little twink, and judging by the way the two men were burning holes into each other, Martin was in for an interesting night. Richard went home.

He had some planning to do.

CHAPTER 22

DEAN STARED at the papers Peyton had just brought him, trying to make sense of them and failing miserably. The realtor had explained it to him, but it had been a bad night with Emily, and Dean had felt himself tuning out of the conversation as soon as the word "delay" was uttered. All he understood was that he wasn't going to move in to his new house by the end of the week as he had planned. Some complicated legal issue had come up at the last moment, and now it seemed as if he would be stuck in this purchase forever. He knew he couldn't stay with Leeland much longer. Even though the other sub was more than understanding, his apartment was simply too small to house two grown men and an infant. It was also probably for the best to get out from Leeland's and Aaron's constant watch. As much as he appreciated their concern for him, he felt a bit smothered.

It wasn't as if he would go off the deep end if they took their eyes off him. At the moment, Leeland was out studying and Aaron had taken Emily to the playground. Dean had some much-needed time for himself. If only that didn't scare him so much. He had already cleaned the entire apartment, gotten all the laundry done, and even changed the bedsheets. All that activity had done nothing to release the feverish energy burning inside him ever since he had walked out on Richard.

Dean knew he was a mess. He couldn't sleep. He felt nauseated when he so much as thought about food, and the only thing that kept him upright was the knowledge that Emily needed him.

Tricia had needed him as well, and he had failed her. Dean was aware that his overprotective sister had wanted to spare him and that there was nothing he could have done about it. Still, it stung that Tricia hadn't turned to him when she needed help. Had she thought he wouldn't be able to handle her difficult pregnancy? Had she feared that he would be more of a burden than an actual help? Dean was the first to admit he didn't do well in day-to-day life, and he was always happy when he could shut the world out. But he was a grown man who earned quite a lot of money and who could take care of those he loved. He could be strong if he needed to be, and it made his heart break that Tricia had either not seen that strength or chosen not to rely on it. Either way, she had been alone during her pregnancy and alone when she gave birth.

He didn't know if there had been somebody else in the car when she died and made a mental note to find out once he could cope a little better.

The thought of having to spend the rest of his life without his sister hadn't fully registered with Dean yet. Which made the pain when he was reminded of her death almost unbearable, like a wave crashing over his head and burying him underneath.

The house he would soon own—or maybe not, according to those documents in front of him—had kept him going so far. It was the big project that ate up all the spare time he might have had otherwise to ponder his situation and despair about the drastic changes in his life. Peyton had left pretty quickly after dropping the house bombshell in Dean's lap, and he suspected the designer had been taken advantage of again. Unfortunately, this time it was Dean who had to pay the price.

He tried once more to make sense of the documents in front of him. It had something to do with the current owners not being the owners of the entire house. Or was it the property? He simply didn't understand. The idea of getting a lawyer was more than tempting.

Then again, he didn't like lawyers. Lawyers spoke in a language Dean didn't care to understand, charged gigantic sums just for being available, and when things didn't go as predicted, they always found fault in everybody else, never themselves.

Normally he would go to Richard, and he would take care of all his problems. Dean shivered. Richard. At the thought of that name, a deep ache started spreading from his gut, radiating out through his entire body, making him wince in pain and despair. He felt as if somebody had just ripped the bandage off an open wound. His heart had been shattered into a million pieces that would never be whole again, and he just knew that nothing, nothing and nobody, could ever replace what he had lost.

Silently the tears started falling, dripping down his chin and onto the documents in his trembling hands. Dean took one long, shaking breath and then all his dams broke.

RICHARD WAS busy trying to figure out how to get his boy back. So far he hadn't come up with a suitable plan. Dean was an easygoing man who never held a grudge and was quick to forgive. Richard knew that, but he refused to rely on Dean's good nature. What he had done screamed for some serious groveling, and Richard took pride in the fact that he always owned up to his mistakes.

Dean would not only get a heartfelt apology but also the box of chocolates, the flowers, the jewelry, and the spa trip. Nevertheless, Richard felt as if something was still missing, as if he hadn't thought this through.

He sat back on the couch where he had been plotting his reunion with Dean and forced himself to assess the situation once more. He loved Dean. His boy was his reason for breathing, and he hated himself for having forgotten that. And he had forgotten it because he had been jealous of a baby. He, a grown man, had only seen the inconveniencies forced onto his carefree life instead of realizing how hard it all had been for Dean.

It made Richard wonder with whom he had been in love—his boy, or the fact that there were no problems in their life. How could he have lost his focus? Dean was the man he had planned to spend the rest of his life with. And although they had never openly talked about marriage, Richard had always known that kind of union was in their future.

Richard realized he had been so absorbed in the perfection he and Dean had together, that he forgot what truly made a relationship stronger and kept it growing: the challenges faced side by side. Instead, he had abandoned Dean when he had needed him most. Richard wanted to kick himself. This would be his burden to carry from now on. That and the resolve to never let his boy down again.

Propelled by a feverish energy, Richard activated the tracking app on his cell. He only hoped that Dean had forgotten about this little gimmick on his new phone. Once the app had traced Dean down to an address close to Miami Dade College, Richard got into his car.

RICHARD CLIMBED out of his car and squinted against the sun. The building Dean was supposed to be in was an apartment block that had seen better days. It wasn't shabby yet—for that it was too well maintained and cleaned—but it was on its way. Richard felt anger boiling inside him. This was no place for Dean to live. His boy needed a secure space where he could work without being disturbed. This neighborhood was altogether too loud. Richard checked the doorbells to see if he recognized a name. When he read Leeland Drake, he felt some of the tension in his body releasing. So Dean had been with Leeland, not on his own. Richard tried the door and when it opened, he stepped into the building. Leeland's apartment was on the third floor, and as soon as he reached it, he had to stop for a moment to rein his nerves in.

He would see his boy again. Richard shuddered. He would get Dean back. With trembling fingers, Richard reached for the buzzer and pressed the button. Inside the apartment, he heard a shrill sound and then the shuffling of feet. Richard straightened himself and waited.

When Dean opened the door and Richard got a good look at him for the first time in two weeks, he couldn't suppress a gasp. His boy had lost weight, at least twelve pounds. His skin had an ashen tone, and his eyes were red-rimmed from crying. Dean looked completely and utterly exhausted and so lost Richard wanted to hit himself. They had both worked so hard to make Dean proud of who he was, to make him self-confident and strong. All that seemed to be gone.

"Richard, what are you doing here? If this has anything to do with us, can you come back another time? Now is not good."

Richard felt his heart break at the defeated tone in Dean's voice. He had done this. It was his fault that his beloved boy was so beaten that he didn't even get angry at seeing him. "It has to do with us, Dean. I'm here to tell you that I'm an asshole of the highest order and that I deeply regret the things I said to you. I behaved like an immature five-year-old, and I hurt you so badly, I would understand it if you'd never want to see my face again. Still I'm here, begging your forgiveness for being so insensitive and childish and jealous. I left you alone when you needed me the most, and I swear to you, if you give me one more chance, I'm going to make it up to you. So please, can we try it again?"

Dean just stared at Richard, his eyes wide while a whole slew of different emotions flitted across his face. There was surprise, a hint of anger, sadness, despair, and, underneath it all, an insane longing, one Richard recognized as the same that was driving him.

They looked at each other for what seemed like an eternity but couldn't have been more than a few minutes. Finally Richard simply opened his arms. With a muffled cry, Dean threw himself into his embrace, shaking like a tree in a storm.

Richard lifted him up, carried him into the tiny apartment, and sat down with Dean on the couch in the middle of the living room, stroking Dean's back with soothing motions, trying to reassure him of his presence. His poor boy was all skin and bones and felt so cold it made Richard shiver.

"Shh, boy. It's fine. I'm here. I've got you."

Dean snuggled into Richard as if he wanted to crawl under his skin. He inhaled deeply. "I missed you so much. Everything is falling apart."

"I missed you too, Dean. Missed you like breathing. And I'm terribly sorry about the things I said, how I handled the whole situation. I was a poor excuse for a Dom and a bad lover."

Dean hiccupped, his breath starting to even out. Richard took comfort that his presence had that effect on Dean. "I'm sorry too. I should have tried to include you more, should have been more patient. You barely knew Tricia, and you had no reason to welcome Emily. I never really listened to you because I was so caught up in caring for her."

"You are aware that your apology makes me sound like an even bigger jerk?" Laughter rumbled in Richard's chest and took the sting out of his words. Dean leaned back a bit to look at him.

"You know it wasn't meant like that!"

Richard gave Dean a quick kiss on the nose. "I know. I'm just trying to lighten the mood a bit. You look terribly exhausted."

Dean chuckled. "Breaking up can do that to you." He turned serious again. "Without you, I'm nothing. Being apart only drove that lesson home. I was devastated and so cold inside, I didn't think I'd ever get warm again. And then, when I was at my lowest, you simply turned up at my doorstep and made it all seem like a bad dream. I'm so, so glad you came. So glad."

Richard pulled Dean closer again, enveloped him in his arms. "I'm glad as well, my sweet boy. Let me warm you up and chase away the sadness. And if you allow me, I want to be your Dom again. There's nobody else for me, just you. I need you so much, and I treated you so badly."

Dean slung his arms around Richard's neck. "I know how hard this is. I never wanted to corner you or make you feel like you don't mean the world to me. Because you do."

Richard sighed as he buried his nose in Dean's hair. He had brought this upon himself. Making Dean choose between him and Emily seemed like the single most stupid thing to do. How could he have put his precious lover in such a situation? It was he who had cornered Dean, and then he had been angry about the outcome.

"I guess we both forgot to communicate clearly. I felt so jealous of Emily. She appeared and, all of a sudden, you changed from the Dean I knew to somebody who could run not only his life but that of his little charge as well. I felt left out and no longer needed. That's a terrible thing to do to a Dom, you know?" Richard hated to admit this weakness, but, strangely enough, he also felt better once the words were out.

It also helped to see the look of pure astonishment on Dean's face. "But I do need you. I just… I could tell how much you resented having Emily in the house. I wanted to make it easier for you, to make it less of a burden. As your sub, it's my duty to care for your needs. I know I'm not always good at it, that you do a lot for me, which is why I tried so hard to make Emily a part of our life. My efforts just didn't seem to be enough and instead of asking, I went ahead and assumed the worst."

Richard nuzzled Dean's neck with his nose, pressing little kisses on the soft skin. "Did you safeword because of that? Because you felt as if we had lost our connection?"

"Partly, yes. But the main reason was that I was bone tired. I don't think I would have found my subspace that night. Even if you had changed to sensual play, I would have probably fallen asleep. You really needed that night for us to bond, and I didn't want to ruin it, and then I went ahead and did just that. I felt so, so… useless. Like a failure. As if I had let you down even more."

Richard closed his eyes for a moment. They'd had this conversation before, when their relationship had just started and Dean had picked his safewords. Back then, Richard had explained to Dean—as he had explained to every sub he ever played with—that using his safeword did *not* mean failure. That it wasn't a reflection on his personality but a means for him to communicate with his Dom. Oh yes, they had that conversation, and then, somehow, they both had forgotten about it. He *had* felt as if Dean had let him down. The reasons for his feelings might have been different to the ones Dean had assumed, but the outcome was the same. It wasn't Dean who had failed, but Richard. And as much as it hurt, he owed Dean honesty.

"Oh, Dean. I'm not going to lie to you and tell you I wouldn't have been angry if you had fallen asleep, but I'd rather have had you sleeping than safewording. We both know how important safewords are and that you had every right to use yours. Nevertheless, I felt as if you had betrayed me somehow."

When he saw the pain in Dean's eyes, Richard rephrased his sentence. "Not in the way you may think. We've been together for five years, and I don't think I exaggerate when I say that our relationship is unique, even for BDSM standards. You had never safeworded before, because I always anticipated your needs and emotions. We were perfectly in tune, a fact I took great pride in. When you ended our scene, it made me realize that I'm not as perfect a Dom as I thought, which stung. All I cared about was my wounded pride."

A little insecure, Richard looked at Dean. Admitting his faults cost him.

Dean pressed a gentle kiss on Richard's cheek. "You are a perfect Dom. My perfect Dom. You sensed that I couldn't reach my subspace and instantly tried to change the scene, to give me another chance. It wasn't your fault that I was just too tired and that I hadn't told you that. To be honest, I hated using it. I know safewording is nothing to be ashamed of, that it's vitally important for the games we play, but, like you, I took pride in the fact that I never had to use mine. I always thought 'my Dom knows me so well and I trust him so implicitly that there's no need for it.' And because I thought like that, I was devastated when I had to use it. I guess that was pretty stupid."

"No, it was not. It just shows that the people who thought about safe, sane, and consensual in the first place knew exactly what they were doing. There's always the possibility of a scene going wrong, and I would have hated myself if you had wanted to end the scene but couldn't. It's better like this." Richard smiled wistfully. "I just wish we had that conversation right after the scene, not only now. Well, better late than never. I just hope you still trust me, at least on the Dom front?"

Dean looked at Richard as if he had lost his mind. "Why wouldn't I trust you? You respected my safeword although you were really angry. What more could I ask for?"

A grin of pure relief blossomed on Richard's face. "A lot. You have the right to ask for everything from me. At any time." He turned serious again. "Now that we have talked about this, how do you feel about giving me another chance at being your Dom and lover? I swear, this time I won't let you down."

"There's nothing I would love more!" Dean slung his arms around Richard's neck. After a few moments of blissful, happy silence, he checked the clock on the wall. "Aaron should be back with Emily soon. Perhaps we can ask him to keep her for the night."

Richard caressed Dean's forehead with his fingertips. "That's a good idea. And if he doesn't have time, you can teach me how to prepare Emily for bed."

When he saw the look of pure astonishment on Dean's face, Richard shrugged. "I'm aware that you and Emily are a package deal."

"And you're fine with that?"

Richard thought about it for a moment. "Martin had an interesting question for me the other night. He wanted to know if I would have gone after you if you already had Emily before we met. The answer was a solid, unconditional yes. So I'm going to learn how to take care of her, because there's no way I can live without you."

Tears pooled in Dean's eyes. He wiped them away and took Richard's lips for a deep, lingering kiss. "I love you so much, Richard Miller. Thank you."

Before Richard could answer that, the front door opened, and Thor and Donar came racing into the room, their tails wagging like crazy as they greeted Dean and Richard. Richard's father followed with a giggling Emily in his arms. He looked at the two men with raised brows. "What are you doing here, son?"

Richard pulled Dean closer and noted how giddy it made him when his boy slung his arms around his neck once again. "Making up with the love of my life. What else?"

His father blew out his breath. "Thank God! I was starting to wonder what took you so long." A scolding tone crept into his voice. "You're normally not that slow."

Richard cringed. "I'm sorry, Dad."

"Don't apologize to me. Apologize to your boy!"

"He already did that." Dean beamed at Aaron. "But he would like to do a bit more than just apologizing tonight…."

Richard's father smiled warmly. "I get it. I'm going to take Emily with me. Shall I tell Leeland?"

"That would be great. Thank you, Aaron. You're the best!"

Dean ignored Richard's glare and started packing his bags. "I guess Leeland is going to be relieved to have his couch back."

Richard went to gather the three bags from behind the door to the kitchen. "We will find a way to thank him adequately, boy. Now hurry up. I want you home and in the playroom as soon as possible."

His father laughed. "Don't overdo it! Dean hasn't slept a lot in the past few weeks."

"I won't. I intend to take good care of my boy."

Richard looked down at the table where the documents about the house purchase were scattered. "Do you need those, Dean?"

Dean nodded. "I was thinking about buying a house for Emily and me to live in. There are complications, and I can probably back out, but I guess I still need those."

Richard just glanced at the papers before he shoved them in the front case of one of the bags. "A house doesn't sound too bad. You can show it to me and then we'll see."

The way Dean's face lit up happily told Richard how much his boy loved the idea. They finished packing, Dean kissed Emily goodbye, his father patted both Richard and Dean on the back, telling them not to mess up again, and then they were on their way back to the apartment.

CHAPTER 23

DURING THE ride, Dean stayed silent. Too much had happened, and he needed time to process everything. When they arrived, they carried the bags upstairs, left them in front of the couch, and proceeded to the bedroom.

Dean felt anticipation building in his stomach. God, how he had missed the scenes! As soon as he was through the door, Richard took his hands and kissed him lightly on the mouth. "Since I can see how tired you are, boy, we're not going to do a strenuous scene. First, let's clean up."

Dean shuddered and followed his master into the bathroom. Richard turned. "Strip."

The sure, commanding tone made Dean's cock twitch expectantly. He started undressing, taking his time, enjoying the look of sheer hunger on his master's face. When he turned his back to Richard and slowly slid his jeans over his hips, bending forward in the process for maximum effect, Richard actually started growling. "Naughty boy."

Dean straightened up and winked at him. With another growl, Richard pulled him close. Their lips met in a searing kiss that stole Dean's breath away.

Nobody kissed like his master.

Groaning, he rubbed his naked skin against Richard's still fully clothed body, enjoying the friction of the cloth. Richard planted his hands firmly on Dean's asscheeks, drawing him to his toes. Dean let his head fall back, exposing his throat to Richard's fevered kisses and bites in the universal gesture of submission.

Richard swiped his tongue along Dean's chin, bit slightly into the soft skin at the juncture between his neck and his shoulders, and then he retreated, panting heavily. "Undress me."

Dean moaned, the tone as well as the command itself driving him crazy. He started undoing the buttons of Richard's silken shirt. When he reached the last one, he let the fabric slide over his master's shoulders to the floor. Then he knelt, his head level with Richard's groin while he undid the belt and opened the fly of his jeans. He pushed them down and helped Richard step out of them, taking off his socks in the process. That left only Richard's briefs, and they went the same way the jeans had taken. Gloriously naked and hard as nails, Richard stood in front of the still kneeling Dean, who started to nuzzle his master's big, fat cock.

RICHARD GRITTED his teeth. The temptation to give in to his urges was almost overwhelming, but he had other plans for tonight, plans that—

He lost his train of thought when Dean closed his soft lips around his cock and started sucking. Perhaps one quick orgasm would allow him to take the edge off? That wasn't unreasonable. Although Richard wasn't sure if he would recognize unreasonable when he saw it right now. All his blood seemed to have congregated in his prick.

Dean kept on sucking, taking him deeper with every swallow, his tongue massaging the underside of Richard's cock. Richard fisted his hands in Dean's hair, giving a firm tug to the left, their silent sign that he was close. If Dean didn't feel like swallowing him, he could back out now. Or he could suck even harder and start to fondle Richard's sack, speeding his orgasm along. With a guttural roar, Richard emptied his balls into Dean's willing mouth, basking in the pure bliss the act brought him. Richard took a few deep breaths to regain his composure while Dean licked him clean, the soft laps of his boy's tongue arousing him anew. Then Richard bent down and lifted Dean up, kissing him deeply, tasting himself on the soft lips. "Thank you, boy. That was real good. Love you."

Dean snuggled closer, his own erection grazing Richard's thighs. "It was my pleasure, Master." He grinned, just a tiny bit challenging. "I love you too."

"Brat." He started leading Dean toward their walk-in shower. "Before we proceed, we need to shower. I would prefer to have a long, hot bath with you, but judging from the circles under your eyes, you'd probably fall asleep." He pressed another kiss on Dean's forehead. "And as much as I want you to get your rest, I need to have you first. It's been too long."

Dean stepped into the shower, his head bent sideways so Richard could see the lust burning in his eyes. "I wouldn't want to fall asleep right now. I want you. I need you."

Richard quickly closed the shower door and turned on the spray. As the warm water from the four showerheads started cascading down their bodies, he took Dean's favorite body wash, squirted a generous amount on his hands, and started soaping his boy. Dean moaned in pure bliss.

Richard let his hands glide over every inch of Dean's body, making sure he was perfectly clean. His fingers drew circles on the sweet asscheeks, coming closer and closer to his target. When he let the tip of his right index finger slip into the taut hole, Dean moaned and bucked his hips, trying to impale himself on Richard. Richard blew his breath into Dean's left ear, tracing the earlobe with his tongue. "Do you like that?" He allowed his finger to slide deeper.

Dean tried pushing back with more force, but Richard held him steady with his left arm. "Don't. You're exhausted, so don't fight me."

Shivering, Dean complied. Richard kept on teasing him, adding a second finger, then a third. With his free hand, he grabbed Dean's weeping cock, stroking it until Dean's knees grew weak and Richard had to steady him.

"Please, Master. Please, take me."

There was so much raw need in Dean's voice that Richard realized they would never make it out of the shower and into the bed. Not with both of them so starved for each other and Dean so tired. He helped Dean to find a comfortable, stable position against the tiles and then breached him without ceremony. Dean pushed back onto him, welcomed him with his perfect heat, with this body that was so undeniably in tune with his own.

Richard thrust deep, establishing a quick rhythm that drove them both to the edge in no time. When Richard felt his own orgasm building, he tugged at Dean's cock, alerting him. "Close, boy. So close."

"Me too, Master. Please. Together. Fill me up."

It didn't take more for Richard. Dean rarely talked dirty. He usually wasn't coherent enough, but on the few occasions he did—it always slew Richard. With two more powerful thrusts, he let his orgasm wash over him and enjoyed the sensation when Dean, too, came and started milking his pulsing prick with his sweet, sweet hole.

Panting, they stood under the warm spray and enjoyed the feeling of being close. When Richard felt his cock soften, he slowly pulled out of Dean, still holding him tight. His boy was even more worn-out than he had thought, and he was determined to get him into bed as quickly as possible.

Richard washed them both down once more; then he toweled Dean dry and carried him to the bed. They snuggled together under the covers, Dean burying his nose in the crook of Richard's neck, inhaling deeply. "I'm sorry, Master. This wasn't much of a scene."

Richard petted Dean's still slightly damp hair. "On the contrary, boy. It was the best scene we've had in a long time. This was us, pure and simple. Sometimes it's good to reconnect like that." He closed his eyes and ran a hand over his face. "God, listen to me, all sappy and soft, nothing like a big bad Dom."

Dean chuckled against his neck, still busy crawling into Richard's skin. "You're the biggest, most badass Dom I've ever had."

"I'm the only Dom you've ever had."

Again a chuckle. "Okay, how about this: you're the biggest, most badass Dom I've ever met. And the best thing is, you're mine."

"That sounds a lot better." Richard hesitated a moment. "I love you so much, Dean. So much."

Dean stopped nuzzling Richard's neck and looked up, his beautiful eyes big and sincere. "And I love you, Richard. You are my world."

Content, Richard kissed Dean on the tip of his nose. "Let's get some sleep. It was a long two weeks."

"Yes, it was." Dean turned around and let Richard spoon him, their favorite position to fall asleep in. It didn't take long until both of them were snoring lightly, both feeling safe and secure in the presence of the other.

CHAPTER 24

THE NEXT morning, Dean woke to the smell of freshly brewed coffee. When he opened his eyes, he caught sight of Richard, who was sitting next to him in bed, the breakfast tray on the nightstand and a cup of steaming coffee in hand. Dean blinked once or twice, because he couldn't remember when Richard had last brought breakfast to bed. That was his job as Richard's sub. "I'm sorry, Master. I didn't wake."

Richard smiled and handed him the second cup before he reached for the tray. "That's fine, boy. After the weeks we've been through, I didn't expect you to make breakfast today. I wanted you to catch as much sleep as possible."

Dean felt himself blush. "Thank you, Master."

Richard pressed a quick kiss on Dean's temple before he handed him his bowl of cereal. "You're welcome. Now eat. We have a lot to discuss."

Dean did as he was told but didn't get far. Suddenly he had Richard's spoon hovering in front of his mouth with a scoop of yogurt and a strawberry on it. Without hesitation, he opened his mouth, accepting the food his Dom was offering.

They often fed each other; the act was so intimate and wonderful. Dean returned the favor by offering Richard a spoonful of his own yogurt and cereal, and between sips of coffee and fruit they hand-fed each other, breakfast was soon finished. They put the bowls and empty mugs on the tray before they set it aside. Then Richard reached for a big brown envelope Dean knew all too well. He gasped.

"Master!"

Richard smiled and ran his free hand soothingly over Dean's upper arm. "Don't worry, boy. It's not what you think. I don't want to cancel our contract." He frowned. "But our circumstances have changed, quite drastically, I may say, so we have to revise the contract. There are some things we have to change, new paragraphs we have to add. Are you ready for that?"

Dean seemed torn for a moment. Then a shy smile started to blossom on his lips. "You really thought this through, didn't you, Master?"

Richard cocked an eyebrow. "What did you expect? As soon as I realized that you're the only one for me, I started planning. So let's go over this."

Richard pulled the documents with their D/s contract out of the envelope and placed them on the sheets before he grabbed a pen.

"I assume it's safe to say that we can leave the section about the sexual practices alone. Or has anything changed?"

Dean grinned and shook his head. There weren't many things he wouldn't be willing to try with Richard, and those few were listed under his hard limits. "Nope. In that department, everything's stellar."

"Glad to hear it." Richard chuckled. "What we do have to talk about is the 24-7 aspect of our relationship. I think this is no longer a possibility. At least not at the moment."

Dean gulped. He knew how important the 24-7 had been for Richard in the past. "I can still try, Master. I don't want you to give this up. You love having me under control all the time."

Richard gently kissed Dean on the mouth. "I do. But this is not something we can achieve right now. Emily takes up too much of your time, and between her and both our work, it wouldn't be fair to either of us."

"But…."

"Remember what I told you about business once? That a good compromise can turn into a victory?"

Dean nodded dazedly. He couldn't see how giving up the 24-7 would be a good thing. Richard kept on talking. "We are no longer as careless as we've been before. And the past weeks have shown that we must find a new balance. So we erase the 24-7 and decide on a set number of scenes we have every month. Scenes where we actually leave the house and go to Whisper. Until we get a better feel for the new dynamics, I'd say two scene dates per month are an achievable goal."

Dean knew he was staring. His mouth was hanging open. Richard smiled, sweetly and full of love. "That doesn't mean we can't have more or that I won't play with you spontaneously when the opportunity presents itself. This is simply a basic guideline, and I'm keeping it simple so we can reach our goals. I also think we should have at least two dates per month. Dates where Emily is included. We could go to the zoo or wherever children her age like to play."

Now it was official. The lack of sleep had caused Dean to hallucinate. Richard had not just suggested to do something together with Emily. "Don't look so startled. I'm not a heartless bastard."

Dean grabbed Richard's hands and kissed the tips of his fingers reverently. "I know," he whispered. "This is just—it's all I've been wishing for, and you're giving it to me just like that. I don't know what to say."

Richard chuckled and kissed Dean on the lips. "Then say nothing and listen to what else I've cooked up. I was thinking we also need another safeword."

"Why?" Dean sounded clearly confused.

"Because, my love, part of what went wrong was a lack of communication. Or, to be more precise, the lack of getting our points across. We did talk, yes, but neither of us was able to convey the meaning of our words. We can't let that happen again."

"What has a safeword got to do with our inability to put our feelings into words?"

Richard grinned. "We choose a word each of us can use at any time when we get the impression that something is not working out right. It's like a time-out card. When we say that particular word, we both know that there is a problem. Then we each go into our corner and think about what is wrong. After that, we try to talk it out. If that doesn't help, we get a referee."

Dean frowned. "A referee?"

"Somebody who listens to both our sides and hopefully helps us see clearer."

"Any particular prey in mind? I'm sure there are tons of people out there who can't wait to listen to our relationship problems."

"I love it when you get all sarcastic and snarly. Makes my hand itch to give you a spanking. And yes, I do have two candidates in mind. My father, for the more domestic situations, and Martin, for anything to do with BDSM. How does that sound?"

"Like a well-thought plan. I'm in on it. So what's the word? Given how you've already worked out everything else, I assume you have one in mind?"

"If you must ask…. How about *taraxacum*?"

"The Latin word for dandelion? Good idea. We're not likely to mention it on accident, and it does have a certain symbolism. Get rid of the weed in our relationship."

Richard pulled Dean close and kissed him. "*Taraxacum* it is. Also, for the record, I would have never thought about that metaphor. I just like the sound of the word."

"You're something and then more. Have I mentioned how much I love you?"

"Only a few times, boy. I'm going to put all the changes in the contract, and then we can sign it anew. I'm looking forward to that."

Richard straightened up, and the Dom tone crept into his voice. "Now tell me everything about that house."

CHAPTER 25

"IT LOOKS nice enough." Richard didn't sound as if "nice enough" was something to be desired. Dean rolled his eyes but was careful to do it when Richard wasn't looking his way. It had been four days since their spectacular reconciliation, and things were almost as perfect as they had been before Emily's arrival.

Richard was trying his best to get to know Emily. He had even started to change her diapers, feed her, and play with her, which she enjoyed a lot. Richard had also discovered, much to his apparent surprise, that he could redirect his constant urge to dominate and care for Dean into looking after the little girl. Not that Emily could be dominated—she was more like a bag of fleas—but Richard had quickly started worrying about her future and planning for every eventuality with the same determination he used for his and Dean's scenes. This redirection of Richard's energy proved healthy for their relationship, even though looking for the perfect house was turning into an odyssey. After reading a bunch of books on childcare, Richard had decided that Emily needed proximity to nature to gain her full potential.

Dean chuckled inwardly. The indifference Richard had shown before was now completely replaced by overcaring. Not that Dean minded. He was so happy, he wanted to scream it from the rooftops.

"Dean? Are you coming?" Richard's voice was a little impatient. This was only the second house they were looking at today, but there were three more on the list, and it didn't seem as if this one would be the winner. It wouldn't even make it into the second round.

Dean smiled. "Coming." When Dean had told Richard about the house he wanted to purchase, Richard hadn't been as averse to the idea as Dean had thought he would be. On the contrary, he had immediately faxed the documents to his lawyers to find out if the purchase could be accelerated, which it could not. But after they had visited the house together, Richard decided it wasn't what they wanted anyway. Dean stepped back from the contract, and now here they were, hunting for the perfect house to raise a little girl.

Dean glanced at the list Richard had printed out for every house they were going to visit. It had two columns, one for positive and one for negative things, as well as differently labeled boxes. "First impression," "Size," "Proximity to educational facilities," "Number of rooms," and so on and so forth. There was no box for the actual price, because that wasn't something Richard bothered with. If they liked it, they would buy it.

Dean glanced around and put a cross in the negative column under "First impression." The house was neat, well-groomed, and obviously prepared for potential buyers, but it was also cold and soulless. When Dean imagined Emily running around on the perfectly manicured lawn, he couldn't suppress a shudder.

"I see we're on the same page concerning this monstrosity." Richard's breath tasted of coffee and cinnamon. Dean accepted the deep kiss and slung his arms around his lover's waist.

"Will we ever find the perfect home?"

Richard sighed. "We will. But it might take us more time than I had assumed."

Dean snuggled closer into Richard's embrace. "I'm not sure if I still want it when it's such a hassle."

"I know what you mean. Looking for something too hard can make it slip away completely." Richard stroked Dean's back. "Let's look at the houses we have scheduled for today. If we don't find one that fits our needs, we'll go back home and wait for our house to come to us. How does that sound?"

"Like a perfect plan."

Dean was about to kiss Richard again when his cell phone rang. With a sigh, Dean pulled it out, recognizing the ringtone as Peyton's.

"Peyton?"

"Hi there, sunshine. Why so grumpy?"

"House hunting."

Dean didn't have to say more. Peyton made a sympathetic noise.

"Aww, poor baby. But rejoice, I have the solution to all your problems. Come to the address I texted you."

"What, now?"

"No, in ten years. Of course now."

Peyton managed to sound indignant, as if Dean had offended him with his moronic question.

"Peyton, you are aware that Richard and I are on a tight schedule to visit three more houses today? We can't just—"

"Trust me, Dean. You can." Peyton hung up. Dean groaned in frustration, knowing that he and Richard would go wherever Peyton wanted them to go because his instincts about everything interior living had yet to fail them.

Richard raised a brow. Dean's cell beeped, announcing an incoming text. When he looked at it, it was an address on the outskirts of the city. Dean showed the screen to Richard.

"Peyton wants to meet us there. He claims to have found our house."

Richard groaned the same way Dean had but climbed into the car nevertheless.

AFTER A forty-minute drive, they pulled up in front of a jungle. Dean looked around as if he couldn't believe his eyes. He and Richard jumped from the car, both completely caught up in what Peyton had found. The interior designer approached them with a smile. "Did I promise too much?"

Dean was still busy staring, so Richard answered for him. "Since I don't know what you promised, I can't tell. What is this, Peyton?"

Richard gestured toward the grand but completely run-down house. It stood on top of a slight incline, looking out over the biggest freaking congregation of trees, weeds, and tall grass one could imagine, complete with a crumbling brick wall surrounding the perimeter. There were no other houses nearby, the closest estate almost half a mile down the road.

Dean was already opening the creaking metal gate, his gaze fixed on the house that was flanked by gigantic oak trees. "It's perfect."

Richard stepped next to his boy and had to admit that Dean was right. They had found their house, even though, at the moment, it was more of a charity case than anything else. "How long will it take to fix all this?" Richard looked expectantly at Peyton.

"Well, the bones of the house are still good. Of course, there's a lot to be done. New plumbing, the roof needs fixing, you have to decide which walls you want to be gone, where you want your playroom, and where the nursery should be. Depending on how much money you want to invest, between three and nine months."

Richard chuckled. "You know my pockets are deep, Peyton. We want to move in as soon as possible."

"Then I better call Mike and Jeff. Good news is, the house itself and all that lovely space are probably the least expensive part of this bill."

Richard waved Peyton off. His boy was tugging him along the weed-covered gravel path toward the house, his excitement radiating off his body like a bonfire. And Richard could understand it, felt it himself. This house was something special. It had character, a gothic charm that called to them both.

They reached the huge entrance door by climbing three partly broken marble steps. The door itself was made of oak that apparently had never seen any paint. Dean trailed his fingertips over the withered wood and brought his nose close enough to inhale the scent. Richard did the same and smiled. He knew what his boy was thinking. "I'd like to keep that door. But I promise, I'll find one just as old and have it commissioned into a spanking bench just for you."

Dean shuddered visibly. His breath hitched. "Oh yes, please." He grinned and pressed a quick kiss on Richard's cheek. "You know me too well."

"That's my pleasure, boy. Shall we?"

They pushed the door open and entered a huge hall with twin stairs leading up to the second floor. The wooden railing had peeling paint and some of the steps were broken, as well as about half the marble tiles on the floor. To their right, a glass door in a withered frame led into a room with a window that looked out into the jungle surrounding the house. To their left was the kitchen, a run-down space with lots of promise.

"It needs some work done, but I think it's perfect for you two, or shall I say three?"

Peyton sounded utterly smug, but Richard decided to let it slip for once. The designer had earned a little smugness.

"We want as much of the old substance preserved as possible. Like the door and the railing. No paint, just the natural wood."

Peyton nodded. "Understood. Mike and Jeff are on their way. Have you decided where the playroom should be?"

Richard shrugged. "We just entered the house. I have no idea of the layout."

As if he had been waiting for that cue, Peyton produced a blueprint of the house and laid it out on a wobbly old table that had apparently been forgotten when the previous owners moved out. "In my opinion, you can either go high or low. I can turn the attic into a playroom, or part of the first floor. It's your choice."

Richard didn't have to look at Dean to know what his boy wanted. "The attic. With huge skylights."

Peyton grinned. "Excellent choice. The master bedroom is here"—he pointed to a spot on the blueprints—"and I can build you a walk-in bathroom right here." He pointed at the squares on the blueprint. "Then we can set up Emily's room here, which leaves two office rooms and a guest room on the first floor. The attic will be the playroom, of course complete with bathroom, Jacuzzi, and a roof garden when you want to get kinky under the night sky."

Richard chuckled. He loved how well Peyton knew their needs.

"What about the yard?" Dean looked through the open door into the wilderness surrounding the house. "I kind of like it the way it is."

Richard put his hand on the small of Dean's back. "It does have a certain charm, but we won't be able to find Emily if she decides to hide out there. It has to be at least a little trimmed."

"Can we keep the trees?"

Richard looked at Peyton. The designer held up his hands. "I'm not a landscaper, but I think it shouldn't be a problem. They'll have to check if the trees are still safe, though. But Jeff knows a very good landscaper who should be able to work out the details with you."

Richard nodded. He trusted Jeff's judgment of people way more than he did Peyton's.

"Then see to it that Jeff brings that landscaper in. I assume I can leave this house in your capable hands?"

Peyton grinned. "Of course. I'll go over the plans and talk to you later about any decisions where you need to be involved."

Richard nodded and patted Peyton's shoulder. Even though the man could be a pain in the ass sometimes, he was also a reliable contractor who always made sure that his clients' wishes were met. "Thank you, Peyton. I appreciate it."

Peyton rolled his eyes and focused on the blueprints again. Richard took Dean's hand, and together, they explored their new home.

CHAPTER 26

Three months later.

DEAN WAS sitting at his computer, trying to figure out how to get Laura Ashbourne out of an ingenious trap her archenemy Sheila, aka the Black Rose, had created, when he heard a happy squeal from the living room.

"Dada!"

Dean smiled, saved the file, and rushed out of his office room to greet his master. As usual, Emily had beaten him to it. At almost ten months, she was like a whirlwind on all fours and already making attempts at standing. Dean watched as Richard picked up a laughing Emily and whirled her around before planting a kiss on her rosy cheeks. Then he settled her against his right hip like a pro and extended his free arm toward Dean. Smiling, Dean approached his master, his lover, sank into his embrace, and accepted the searing kiss.

"Welcome home, Master."

"It's good to be back, boy."

Richard had been on a business trip for the last three days. Dean and Emily had missed him like crazy. Behind them, Julio got up from the floor where he had been playing with Emily.

"Hi, Richard. I'm leaving you three now." He turned to Dean. "You sure you're covered for tomorrow?"

Dean smiled back. "Yeah. Aaron is coming over in the afternoon so Richard and I can have some adult time."

Julio winked knowingly. "Have fun."

"Get out!" Laughing, Dean pushed Julio in the general direction of the door. The nanny managed to press a quick kiss on Emily's forehead before he left the apartment. Richard sat down on the couch with Emily in his lap, tickling her with his fingers. While Dean listened to her happy giggles, he silently thanked the gods for having sent Richard his way. During the last three months, Richard had embraced their new life wholly and had turned into the best father a child could hope for. He even went on night duty now and then, and to both their surprise, their love life was thriving. Of course, there had been changes. Most of the spontaneity of the time before

Emily came to them was gone, and sometimes Dean missed the old days. Then again, both he and Richard had learned to appreciate the predictability of a well-planned and scheduled seduction. Their days had become more structured, with Richard trying to be home at appointed times, which gave Dean a heightened sense of security. Once Richard had realized that the routines Emily forced on them were actually good for their D/s relationship, he had sat down and put out some ground rules.

Another thing they had learned—and which surprised them a lot—was that babies loved routines as well. Thanks to Richard's efforts, Emily was now sleeping a solid ten hours every night without waking up once. Julio had explained to them that most babies thrived on structures and set routines, a knowledge that made it easy for Richard to sink into his new double role as Dom and father.

Dean sat down at Richard's feet, took off his shoes and socks, and gave him a foot rub. Richard groaned in appreciation. "Dean, so good."

"I'm glad you like it. How was your trip, Master?"

Richard groaned some more. "Exhausting but successful. We found the perfect place for the new club in Berlin, and all the contracts are signed. If everything goes as planned, we will open next year."

"That's good news." Dean started working on the other foot. "I'm almost finished with my next Laura book, and I have an idea for a comedy. Oh, and Peyton called. The house is almost finished, and he wants to show us everything."

"Excellent. We can go tomorrow, take Emily with us."

"Then we have to ask Aaron as well."

Richard looked puzzled for a moment before realization dawned. "You're right. We can't inspect the playroom with Emily around."

They both took great pains to keep the kinky side of their relationship from Emily. Although she couldn't understand yet, Dean and Richard thought it better to get used to keeping their sexual preferences from her. Once she was old enough, they would explain everything to her, but until then, the door to the playroom would be secured with not only a lock but also with a handprint identification pad.

They had also talked to Julio about Dean calling Richard Sir or Master and Richard referring to Dean as boy. To their mutual relief, Julio had just shrugged. "It's like other couples calling each other darling and honey. Emily will grow up knowing this is an endearment. Don't worry about it."

Dean put down Richard's foot and smiled happily. Everything was perfect. Richard chuckled. "Such a blissful expression, boy, and I haven't even mentioned anything kinky."

"You don't have to. I'm so happy, I could scream—not that I don't like you getting kinky," Dean added hastily when he saw Richard's eyes light up with predatory intent. His master leaned back, sprawling Emily over his broad chest.

"What do you think, little princess? Shall I make your Daddy pay for his little slip?"

Emily waggled her little fingers and grabbed Richard's nose. "Dada!" she exclaimed proudly. Richard lifted her up to drop a kiss on her forehead.

"Aren't you the cutest thing around, princess?"

"Dada!"

"Come here, boy." Richard held out his hand, and Dean rose gracefully to his feet. He snuggled close to his lover, tickling Emily in the ribs when she reached for him. Richard pulled Dean close, nuzzling his neck. "I've been thinking about getting a kitten. The house is certainly big enough, and it would be nice to have something furry running around."

"Why don't you buy her a pony? The yard is big enough." Dean tried his level best to keep the sarcasm out of his voice and failed miserably. Richard pinched his left nipple through the shirt, rubbing the tip when it grew hard. Dean tried to flinch back but had nowhere to go.

"Ouch!"

"That should teach you to be more respectful toward your Dom. And just for the record, if Emily wants a pony, she'll get one, but I'm aware that she has to be old enough."

"I was just teasing, Master. I think the kitten is a great idea. Do you want to get one from the shelter or from a breeder?"

Richard pinched Dean's nipple again, biting his earlobe at the same time. "Don't think you can distract me, boy. Once Emily is in bed, I'm going to take my sweet time punishing you. I think you need a firm spanking to remind you of who is the boss around here." Richard paused with an evil grin on his face. "And I think we should get a kitten from the shelter."

Dean groaned in anticipation. "You're a cruel man, Master."

Richard bent down and kissed Dean deeply. "I know."

The NEXT day, they met with Aaron at their new house. When they got out of the car, they couldn't stop staring in awe. The crumbling stone wall surrounding the property had been repaired and the formerly rusty metal gate returned to its former glory. On their approach, it swung open to reveal a gravel path now free of weeds and broad enough to let a car through. Thor and Donar went off to explore the huge yard whose wild state had not been tamed, but slightly altered.

The trees still guarded the estate, and in many places, the bougainvillea and high grass had been left untouched. In others, a certain order could be detected. In a clearing, the landscaper had set up a playground with swings, a teeter-totter, a slide, and a sandpit. There was also a stone basin where fresh water welled up in the middle and could be directed through three different openings that all had open pipes attached. With wooden planks of different sizes, the water could be staunched and released. There were buckets and sieves and wooden ladles to move the water around. It was a perfect playground for children.

Richard's father took the spot in and whistled. "Your landscaper is a genius. And he knows what children like."

Richard grinned broadly. "Yes, *she* is pretty good."

His father let the patronization slip, too busy taking the yard and the view of the house in. Emily was squirming in Richard's arms. When he sat her down, she crawled over to the sandpit, looking expectantly at her grandfather. He smiled. "You two go on and inspect the house. Emily and I are here."

"Thanks, Dad."

Richard slung his arm around Dean's shoulders and led him to the front door. When they climbed the marble steps that were still broken but had been set together again like a big puzzle, Richard squeezed Dean's ass. Dean yelped at the sting. "Master!"

Richard grinned, a steely glint in his eyes. "Complaining, boy?"

Dean gulped. "No, Master. Never. Please forgive me."

Richard stepped next to Dean and kissed him on the lips. "I'll think about it."

Before Dean could answer or plead some more, the door opened and Peyton stared at them. "Keep the kinky stuff for after the tour."

"Good day to you too, Peyton." Richard didn't let the interior designer ruffle his feathers. "Show us around."

Peyton huffed, trying to keep up an indignant front, but failed miserably. He radiated excitement as he bounced into the hall in front of them. "Ta-dahh!"

Richard and Dean stood there and stared, the same way they had done in the yard. Richard was the first to get his speech back. "You really are a genius, Peyton."

"I know. And you haven't seen the best parts yet."

If Peyton had sounded more pleased, he would have started purring. "As you can see, Jeff and Mike were able to preserve almost all the original materials." Peyton gestured toward the handrail on the twin stairs and the wooden frames on the doors and windows. "They took off all the old paint and put in new glass so the house is insulated according to the latest standards. It's also burglarproof with a high-tech security system provided by Martin, but you know that. The wood floors have also been cleaned and sanded. That nice smell is from the oil they used."

Peyton led Richard and Dean to the kitchen. "I went with the style of the old kitchen. I know you're probably never going to use it, but the kitchen is the heart of the home and I couldn't do less than the best for you. So top-line appliances all around. I had to bring some new wood in here to get the contrast I wanted."

Richard looked in amazement at the kitchen wonderland Peyton had created. The fronts of the cupboards and drawers were made from old, silver-gray fir with wormholes in it. Richard furrowed a brow.

"When I say new wood, I mean wood we couldn't get from the house. It took me almost a week to hunt those boards down. Luckily, I heard of the demolition of an old house only a few miles outside Miami and was in time to get the boards. They wanted to throw them away, can you imagine that?" Peyton shook his head at the stupidity of humankind in general. "Anyway, with the glass and the steel, it makes for a nice look, don't you think?"

"It's perfect, Peyton. Beautiful." Dean smiled at his friend. The designer had outdone himself this time.

"Then come on, you have to see the second floor and, of course, the attic."

Richard and Dean followed Peyton upstairs to marvel at Emily's nursery/playroom that was both modern and retro style. They gaped at their master bedroom, where one wall was decorated with wooden planks in different states of decay while the others remained bare. The floor had hand-scraped hickory planks, and the bedframe was covered in black leather with discreetly hidden hooks for chains and cuffs at all the right places. The attached bathroom was a symphony in warm earth colors with a grand view of the backyard.

But it was the playroom in the attic that made Richard add another zero to Peyton's tip. Most of the light came through the skylights in the roof. Peyton had used the roof pitch to full advantage, with built-in wardrobes on the low sides of the walls. The St. Andrew's cross, spanking bench, and other furniture for torture were strategically placed around the space, and Richard realized he could have a view of the yard and the sky from each of them. The huge bed stood a little aside, directly under a smaller skylight.

Out on the roof garden, Peyton had installed a Jacuzzi and another bed with a retractable canopy. Dean squeezed Richard's hand, and he could smell his boy's arousal. His need had to be almost as great as his own.

"Peyton, you totally outdid yourself. This is beyond perfect."

Richard looked at the designer who had not only found their home for them, but had also made it perfect. Peyton blushed a little bit. "It was my pleasure." A grin stole over his face. "Besides, it's a good thing you're so overwhelmed. That will make it easier for you to pay the bill."

Richard shrugged. He had no illusions concerning the amount of money he'd have to spend on the place. He also didn't regret even one penny. This place was their home, the place Emily would grow up in. He had more than enough money, and compared to the joy he found with his boy and his daughter, it didn't hold as much allure.

Being rich was nice. Being able to recognize what truly made you rich was even nicer.

"It's fine, Peyton. I didn't expect this to be cheap. You did an excellent job, and you were even faster than I had anticipated. When can we move in?"

"Give me one more week for a few minor tweaks."

"What do you think, boy?" Richard kissed Dean on the cheek. "Can we wait one more week?"

Dean smiled happily. "We can. But I wouldn't waste that week with waiting. I'd say we have a lot of packing to do. And a kitten to find."

"My lovely boy. Let's get started, then."

CHAPTER 27

"WELCOME TO our new home!"

Dean stepped aside to let Leeland enter the house. He was one of the first guests to arrive for their housewarming party, and Dean couldn't wait to show his friend around.

"Dean, this is awesome!"

"Thank you, Leeland." Richard sauntered over from the kitchen where he had checked on the catering. Not that it had been necessary—Mamma knew what she was doing—but he had managed to steal a bite or maybe two, and that made him happy.

Leeland had automatically averted his gaze, used to their interactions at Whisper.

Richard shook his head. "Don't, Leeland. This is a normal party tonight. No Doms and subs, just friends. Speaking of which, can I talk to you for a moment?"

Leeland nodded a bit insecurely and followed Richard into the spacious living room. Richard smiled at the beautiful man. "I wanted to thank you, Leeland. You were there for Dean when I had my head stuck up my ass. I don't know how Dean would have fared without you."

Leeland smiled back. "Dean is my friend. That's what friends are for. There's no need to thank me."

"I'm doing it nevertheless. And I want you to accept this." Richard held out an envelope to Leeland, who took it tentatively. "I know you are a proud man and that you are fully capable of taking care of yourself, but I wanted to express my gratitude by helping you the way you helped my boy."

With furrowed brows, Leeland opened the envelope and gasped when he read the content. He stared for a long time at the deed in his name to a five-room apartment located in the Keys area. When he looked up, his almond-shaped eyes twinkled in amusement. "I'd say you don't have to go to so much trouble and give me something so valuable, but I know that this won't make even the slightest dent in your bank account, which is why I'm going to accept your noble gift with gratitude. Thank you, Richard. This is much appreciated."

He took a deep breath. "Just for the record, I would have helped Dean no matter what. And I will keep on doing so, without expecting thanks in material form, but I might call in a favor in the form of nonmaterial help someday."

Richard slapped Leeland's back. "And you shall have whatever you need. Thank you, again, Leeland."

"No problem, Richard."

"Are you two done in here?" Dean poked his head through the glass door. "The other guests are arriving, and they're asking for you, Master."

Richard went to his boy. "I'm here."

They greeted Julio, Jonathan, Martin and Olivia, Peyton, Mike and Jeff, and Richard's father, who handed them Emily. She had spent the day with her grandfather so that Richard and Dean could prepare for the party. When Richard took her in his arms, she snuggled against his neck, clearly tired. Dean looked at his father-in-law. "What have you done to her?"

The general laughed. "You better ask what she has done to me! We spent the entire day outside. She just didn't want to go in, and she missed her lunch nap. I tried, but she didn't want to sleep at all."

Richard kissed Dean on the temple. "That's a good thing. If we manage to keep her awake for another hour or so, we might get lucky, and she'll sleep till eight tomorrow."

"That would be nice!" Dean beamed.

"Ahem, I don't want to interrupt, but I think the dogs have just killed the kittens." Martin sounded worried and gestured toward the still-open entrance where Donar and Thor stood, both with a limp feline body dangling from their snouts. The other guests looked horrified as well, but Aaron, Richard, and Dean only chuckled.

"Don't worry," Richard said. "They're just playing."

"Bit of rough play, don't you think?" Olivia muttered behind them.

Richard's father winked at her. "Watch."

They all watched as the dogs strode in with the kittens and sauntered to a pile of pillows and blankets under the stairs. They dropped their booty and flopped down next to each other. The kittens shook their little paws and made mewling sounds while they started climbing the two dogs, looking for the perfect spot to lie down. The black kitten with the white dot on the forehead was the first to settle, digging its tiny claws into Donar's thick fur until it curled up in the crook between his shoulder and belly. The tabby took a little longer until it stretched out on Thor's belly, purring loudly. The two dogs didn't move, and when the kittens had settled, they lowered their heads and closed their eyes.

"When those four first met, we thought it would end in tragedy." Richard sounded amused. "The dogs bounced in, saw the kittens, and went straight for them. We had that meeting planned carefully, but the dogs were simply faster than us. Anyway, they approached Wilma and Fred, and we all thought they would eat them then and there. Instead, Wilma and Fred started hissing, puffing out their fur like they were already grown cats, and when the dogs got close enough, they swiped them with their little claws. They didn't hurt them, but I guess their show of bravery impressed Donar and Thor, because from then on, they were as thick as thieves."

They all looked at the serene picture in front of them. "Cozy," Olivia muttered under her breath. Richard flashed her a quick smile before he ushered his guests into the living room. "Make yourself comfortable. The food will be served right away."

As if on cue, the two waiters Mamma had brought with her entered the space and started placing plates laden with antipasti, baskets filled with fresh bruschetta bread, as well as bottles of wine and water on the tables. Everybody inhaled the delicious aroma of the different foods. "Enjoy your meal." Richard spread his arms in an inviting gesture.

After the antipasti, Mamma's waiters served five different pasta dishes, grilled scampi and octopus, and saltimbocca. Dessert consisted of tiramisu, panna cotta, and fruit salad. When Dean put Emily to bed after they had all eaten, Martin met Richard at the little bar Peyton had built into one corner of the living room.

"You look good, Richard. Content."

Richard smiled at his friend and business partner. "I am. Content, I mean. And genuinely happy."

"You sound surprised."

"Well, it's definitely not what I had expected. When Emily came into our life, I was afraid to lose all the freedom and good things I had with Dean. And I'm not going to lie to you, I still miss going spontaneously on trips with my boy."

"I'm sensing a 'but' here." Martin lifted a brow.

Richard poured him some wine and nodded. "There is indeed a 'but.' Before Emily, everything I had with Dean, I took for granted. Going on trips, having sex whenever and wherever and however I pleased. Basically doing what I wanted to do. I never questioned our lifestyle. It was what we did. Now I'm grateful when we have an entire evening to ourselves, and I'm willing to get down on my knees for a night of unrestrained sex where we don't have to keep in mind that we have to get up at six in the morning.

Granted, I don't share as many scenes with Dean as we did before, but they are even more intense now. This feeling that he trusts me not only with his own life but with that of Emily as well—it pushes all my Dom buttons. I'm truly happy."

"Amen to that." Martin emptied his glass. "Listening to you makes my own love life look even sadder."

Richard refilled Martin's glass. "Do you want to talk about it?"

"There's not a lot to talk about." Martin sighed. "It's the same as always. I just can't find a boy who is willing to stay with me, not with my money. I had two dates with a guy called Rufus. He was the perfect little twink, airheaded, a little clumsy, absolutely stunning in the one scene we did together. We sat down to talk about a six-month contract, but when I mentioned that I wanted him to stay at home and let me provide for him, he got downright angry. Told me he would never mooch off a guy no matter how much money he had. I couldn't explain to him that I didn't think he would. He was out the door in under five minutes."

Richard shook his head. "And apparently, he was a good guy with no intention to use you for your money. Perhaps you should rethink that particular hard limit of yours. Would it really be so bad if your boy earned some money for himself?"

"That's not the point and you know it, Richard. I'm not asking them to stop working and keep everything on hold for me. I would pay the monthly amount they would earn in their job into a trust they could use when things don't work out between us. Rufus wasn't impressed. He said he wanted to be more than a burden. That he wants a Dom who is proud of all of his achievements."

"And he's not wrong. Especially if he's as airheaded as you said. Then everything in his job must be an achievement for him. Taking that away—I can see how that would make him feel unappreciated."

"I know. The story of my life. Just pour me another glass."

When Richard lifted a brow, Martin shrugged. "Oli's driving. I can get rip-roaring drunk if I want."

"As you wish, old friend."

"Look at you, handling Emily like a pro."

Julio grinned at Dean when he came out of the nursery and closed the door behind him. The nanny had accompanied Dean upstairs when it was time for Emily to go to bed. Even though Julio still looked after Emily three days a week, he didn't see much interaction between Dean and his niece because those three days, Dean was writing like a madman and rarely came out of his office.

"I learned from the best."

"Oh, *cariño*, you make me blush."

"No, really." Dean turned serious. "I don't think I would have made it without your help."

Julio embraced him, and they stood for a moment in silence. "You look happy, Dean."

"I am. Insanely happy. Richard is my life, and when he turned his back on me, I thought I would die. Having him back is like a miracle."

"No." Julio shook his head firmly. "Seeing him transform into Superdad is a miracle."

They both giggled. "To be honest, I never doubted he would be a good father. Whatever he does, he's perfect in it. Emily is one lucky girl."

Julio thought about that. "You're right. Once he's gotten an idea into his thick head, he pursues it with admirable single-mindedness."

"I'm glad it's you who said that. If it had been me, I wouldn't get out of the playroom for days."

Laughing, the two men went downstairs to join their friends.

LEELAND WAS standing on the veranda, gazing up into the night sky. As spectacular as Dean's new home was, the most remarkable thing was the yard with its wonderful view. He was really happy for his best friend, who had now everything Leeland dreamed of himself.

A partner who truly loved him and a child to take care of. Leeland was in no hurry to become a parent, but he longed for a special someone in his life, somebody who was there for the long run. Leeland heaved a sigh.

Suddenly he felt a hand on his shoulder and reacted without thinking. He grabbed the wrist of the person who had snuck up on him, dug his elbow in the man's abdomen, and threw him over his shoulder. The moment Jonathan landed on the planks of the veranda with a solid *thunk*, Leeland realized what he had done. He paled.

"Jonathan? Are you okay? I'm so sorry. You startled me, and I thought…."

Jonathan groaned and lifted his head. "Man, Leeland, that hurt."

Leeland helped Jonathan to his feet, inwardly cursing. He had already known that his chances with the man were slim to nonexistent, but after this little show, they had certainly evaporated into thin air. Leeland wondered if such a thing as negative chances existed.

Jonathan shook his head like a cat that had gotten wet and then stared at Leeland. "You tossed me."

It sounded like a statement, not like an accusation.

"As I said, I'm sorry, Jonathan. You startled me, and I kind of reacted instinctively."

"You tossed me."

Leeland flinched. He couldn't quite read the look in Jonathan's eyes, but he was sure it didn't bode well for him.

"I didn't know you could do that. It's kind of cool. Do you train? Karate? Judo?"

Taken aback by Jonathan's enthusiastic reaction, Leeland answered truthfully. "My parents are both cops, and they didn't want me to be helpless. I do MMA and knife fighting. I'm also a good shot."

Jonathan stared so intently at Leeland that he started feeling nervous again. "But you're a submissive."

"I am. I mean, with my looks and my build, what else could I be?"

Jonathan shrugged. "Whatever you want, I'd say. Do you have the urge to dominate sometimes?"

Leeland sighed. "I'm not a switch, if that's what you mean. I like to submit. It's just…."

"Just what?"

"Sometimes, just submitting isn't enough. I want more. But the type of guy I fall for—they want what is promised in the advertisement." Leeland gestured along his slim body. "Unfortunately, the wrapping and the content differ greatly."

"Hey, that's okay. I think I like that."

Leeland stared at Jonathan in disbelief. "I've been trying to get you on a date for weeks, and you always turned me down."

"I didn't know you could toss me around back then."

"And that's your reason for suddenly flirting with me?"

Jonathan shrugged. "We have one thing in common. I don't want my submissives to be just submissive. I turned you down because I thought you were just another twink who couldn't stand a chance against me. Now, I want to get to know you better."

"Are you asking me out?"

"Yes, that's exactly what I'm doing." Jonathan grinned. "What do you say?"

Leeland knew he had to be dreaming, but he had no intention of ever waking up. Not when he could have a chance at Jonathan White. And since he had nothing to lose, he decided to be himself. "I'm warning you, I'm high maintenance."

Jonathan winked. "My kind of guy. How about we meet at the gym where I'm working out, do a few rounds, and then have dinner."

"Sounds like a perfect first date."

TWO HOURS later, Richard waved their last guest goodbye before returning to the house. Dean was standing at the bottom of the stairs, ready to go to bed. Richard slung his arm around his boy's shoulders, pressed a kiss on Dean's temple, and led him upstairs.

"Are you happy, boy?"

Dean beamed at him. "Happy is too weak a word to describe how I feel. I have the man of my dreams, a cute little daughter, and a group of close friends. Back when my parents tossed me out, I thought I would never have any of those things. I'm truly blessed."

Richard held Dean closer, partly to prevent his boy from seeing the wet sheen in his eyes. "As am I, Dean. As am I. I love you, boy."

"And I love you, Master."

Chapter 28

"Come on, Emily. You can do it again. Do it for Dada!"

Dean tried to coax his daughter into walking again. She had been trying to walk since the day after the housewarming party and now, two weeks later, she had finally managed her first steps alone. Dean had cheered her on and then gotten his cell to film her. Unfortunately, she didn't seem to be in the mood to repeat her heroic deed. She only stared at Dean with her amazing blue eyes and held out her hand for the cell. Wilma and Fred watched the proceedings from the couch, too lazy to get in on the fun.

"Really, princess, you could try again. Richard would love to see this."

Emily grinned, showing the set of eight tiny teeth in her mouth. Dean wanted to say more when the doorbell rang. He furrowed his brow. They weren't expecting anybody, and Richard would be late today. He had a business meeting with some investors. He got up and checked the screen of the surveillance camera. It looked like some kind of delivery man. Dean pressed the intercom button.

"What do you want?"

The man stared into the camera and held a manila envelope up. "Delivery for Dean Connelly."

Dean gulped. He had a sinking feeling in his stomach. "Come in." He activated the buzzer and then opened the front door. It took the man about five minutes to reach him. He held out the envelope. "Dean Connelly?"

Dean nodded.

He handed the envelope to Dean. "You've been served. Sign here."

His hands shaking, Dean signed the paper that said he had accepted the document and then went inside.

Emily was happily playing with Wilma and Fred, tossing them balls of yarn across the living room. Dean ripped the envelope open and started to read through the papers. When he reached the second page, they fell from his lifeless fingers and he had to sit down. Shaking, he took his cell and pressed speed dial. Richard answered on the second ring.

"Dean? Is everything all right?"

Dean trembled so hard, he had problems holding the phone. When he spoke, his voice shook. "Master."

Richard must have known from his tone of voice that something was terribly wrong. "Boy? I want you to sit down and breathe. In and out. Long, steady breaths. Can you do that for me?"

Dean closed his eyes and did as his master instructed. After a few minutes, he felt calm enough to talk. "I just got some papers from the family court. My parents demand custody for Emily. They claim a gay man is not suitable to raise a child."

"Fucking shit!" Richard cursed. "It's fine, Dean. Everything will be okay. Put those papers aside and go play with Emily. I'll be home in forty minutes."

"Tell me they can't take her away! Please!" Dean was on the verge of a panic attack.

"They can't just take her away. I'll get us the best lawyer, and we will sort this mess out. I promise. Now go to Emily. I'm coming home."

Still frightened but feeling a little better, Dean did as his master had instructed. He sat down on the floor next to Emily and helped her to exhaust Wilma and Fred while his thoughts ran a mile a minute.

RICHARD RUSHED to his car, dialing Martin's number. When the other Dom picked up, he didn't waste any time.

"Martin, I need a full background check on Christopher and Faith Connelly. They are Dean's parents and trying to take Emily from us. I want everything, you hear me? Every dirty little secret, every bank account, every ticket for speeding. I have a feeling we might need all we can get."

"On it" was all Martin replied before he hung up again. Once again Richard was grateful for having such wonderful friends.

He entered his car, started the engine, and made the next call, this time on speaker and to his lawyer.

"Richard, what can I do for you?"

"Seth, I need a lawyer for family matters. Can you recommend someone?" Richard didn't add that the person had to be the best in their field. Seth and he had known each other long enough for it to be obvious.

"Let me see…. The best choice would be Peter Lake, from Lake and Partners. His office is here in Miami, and you can't get a better man. Shall I send you his contact info or put you through?"

"Put me through. This is urgent."

"As you wish."

Seth didn't waste Richard's time, a trait Richard appreciated in all his business partners. While he weaved through traffic, trying to get home to his boy as fast as possible without endangering his life, he listened to the beeping of his phone. After what felt like a million rings, somebody finally picked up.

"Peter Lake."

"Richard Miller. How much has Seth told you?"

The man on the other end of the line chuckled. "Not much. Only that you're in need of a family lawyer and that I shouldn't be intimidated by you."

Richard grinned. He already liked the man. "The problem is as follows. My partner has recently been appointed guardian for his late sister's daughter and is in the process of adopting her. He also controls the trust the daughter will inherit and the legacy of the sister. Today he got papers from court stating that his parents demand custody of the child, saying that a gay man can't take care of her properly. I have already sent a PI to find out everything he can about my partner's parents."

"So you've already done your homework. Very good. I think it would be best if we met in person as soon as possible. Demands for custody can get ugly pretty quickly. Where do you live?"

Richard rattled off the address.

"Would it be acceptable if I dropped by this evening at about six?"

"I would appreciate it. Thank you."

"You're welcome."

They ended the call and ten minutes later, Richard parked in front of his home.

Dean yanked the door open, a troubled expression on his face. Richard approached him, his arms held out. Dean sank into his embrace with a sob.

"Oh, Richard. I can't lose her! I just can't."

"And you won't." Richard spoke with his Dom voice in an attempt to soothe Dean. "Tonight a specialist in family law is going to drop by, and I have already arranged for somebody to go through your parents' lives. No matter what they are hiding, we will know about it and use it to our advantage."

Dean snuggled closer into Richard's embrace. "*If* they have something to hide. I hate to say this, but except for their ultraconservative tendencies, they're model citizens."

"Everybody has something to hide, boy. Trust me. And my gut tells me it has to be something big. You say they are conservative, so why would they want a child their daughter conceived without being married? A child

whose father is unknown? There is more to this, and we will drag it all out
into the open."

"Thank you, Master."

"You're very welcome, boy. Now tell me, where is my little princess?"

PETER LAKE was a friendly looking man in his early fifties with a tiny
paunch and big green eyes that seemed to miss nothing. He wore his hair
short and was dressed in an expensive yet unobtrusive suit. Richard asked
him in and introduced him to Dean.

"It's a pleasure to meet you. Is this the child in question?"

Peter looked over Dean's shoulder to Emily, who was curled up on the
couch with Wilma and Fred. Dean smiled softly.

"Yes, this is Emily."

"She's beautiful. How old is she?"

"Almost a year." Richard couldn't keep the hint of pride from his
voice.

"Ah, that's a wonderful age. When they're not teething." Peter made
a face.

"You have children yourself?" Dean looked at the lawyer with renewed
interest.

"Yes, three. My oldest is already seventeen, the middle fifteen, and
the youngest twelve. They can be a handful, but it's such a joy to see them
grow up."

"Which is our cue, Peter." Richard hated having to bring the topic up,
especially now that Dean seemed to have relaxed a bit, but there was no use
in procrastinating. "I have gathered all the documents concerning Emily
here. If you would follow me."

Richard led the way to the kitchen, where the three men sat down at the
table. They could have gone to the big table in the dining room, but Richard
like the coziness of the kitchen, and he knew Dean would feel better in
here. Peter didn't seem to mind. He read the papers that had been delivered
earlier that day and then glanced at Tricia's will and the documents stating
that Dean had full custody.

"You have no ties to Emily?" Peter looked at Richard.

"Not yet. I was planning to adopt her, though." He squeezed Dean's
hand while saying this. His boy flashed him a weak smile.

"Well, this does not look too bad. Of course, a conservative judge
can always cause problems, and here in Florida, there are still a bunch of

them, but since custody over Emily always includes her trust, which, by the way, is impressive, the court will look very closely at who wants to claim her. The only problem I see at the moment is your D/s relationship. If the Connellys have a good lawyer, he will most certainly use that to emphasize their claim."

A dark red had crept into Dean's cheeks, and Richard stared at the lawyer with narrowed eyes. "How do you know about this?"

Peter raised his hands in a conciliatory gesture. "Don't worry, nobody talked. I'm a sub myself—not 24-7, obviously, but when you're in the scene, you learn to recognize the telltale signs. You two are quite obvious to somebody who knows about the dynamics in a Dom/sub relationship. I don't think outsiders would see more than a couple where one partner is very dominant, but you have to be aware that you're not the only one who can hire a PI."

Richard exhaled, stroking Dean's hand in a soothing motion. "We're not exactly hiding it. I'm a successful businessman, and one of my businesses is BDSM clubs. I'm the owner of Whisper."

Peter cocked an eyebrow. "It's an honor to meet you. Although your club is gays only, its reputation is very good. I have only heard the best."

Richard grinned. "For the annual fees I charge, it had better be the best. I'm working very hard on keeping the club at the top."

"Of course." Peter smiled back but turned serious almost immediately. "Concerning Emily, this can become a problem. Your businesses are no secret, and when things get ugly and Dean's parents don't back off, they might use the club as ammunition against you. I'm sorry to ask this, but do you have a dungeon here in this house?"

Dean tensed again, but Richard stayed calm. He knew the lawyer had to have all the information if they wanted to stand a chance against the Connellys. "Yes, in the attic. It is secured with a handprint scanner and two locks only I have the keys for. Plus there's a door in front of the stairs leading up to the attic, which is also always locked. I take Emily's safety very seriously."

"That's good to know. Depending on what your PI finds out about the Connellys, it may be enough. But you should maybe get used to the idea of not having a dungeon at your home."

Peter cringed when he spoke those last words, clearly expecting an outburst from Richard.

It didn't come. Richard had suspected from the beginning that it might come to this. He placed one hand on Dean's back, his boy a lot more agitated than he was.

"But this is our way of living! We would never allow Emily to witness anything—perverted." Dean was breathing hard.

Peter held up his hands again. "I know that. You know that. But the people who are going to decide whether Emily can stay with you or not will most probably not be in the lifestyle and know nothing about it except for the things they have learned from the media. Perhaps not even that. Or, worse, they have read *Fifty Shades of Grey*."

Dean groaned. "Oh no."

"You understand the problem, don't you, Dean?" Peter was talking in a soft voice now. "You don't have a problem with me working for you, even though I told you that I'm a sub. Because you know very well what being a sub means and that there are a lot of different kinds of subs. How many vanilla people do you think would employ my services if they knew about my preferences in the bedroom?"

Dean lowered his eyes. "I get it. I'm sorry I yelled at you. That was stupid."

"It's fine." Peter winked. "I'm not a Dom, so my ego isn't so fragile that I can't handle a little shouting."

"Ahem." Richard cleared his throat. "Do I have to make a call to your mistress?"

Peter blanched a bit. "No need, Sir. I was just trying to soothe your sub."

"Which you did very well, boy. Good save." Richard winked as well, and Peter started grinning.

"I like your master, Dean."

"Thank you. But he's mine."

Peter laughed. "I prefer having a mistress. And I doubt I could handle somebody as intense as your Sir."

"It's all a question of the right training." Richard had a predatory look in his eyes. "If you want, I can meet with your mistress. Perhaps she's interested in comparing notes?"

"Uh, I guess rather not. But thanks for the offer. Now about the problem at hand, I'm going to prepare all the required forms, and then we'll wait for what your PI finds out."

"An excellent idea. And thank you for your help. We appreciate it."

Richard held out his hand and Peter shook it.

"No problem, it's my pleasure. I'll send you my bill once everything is settled."

Richard opened the door for Peter. "If I had any doubt, your last comment just confirmed that you are indeed a lawyer."

Laughing, Peter got into his car and drove away.

Chapter 29

Richard was going over some documents in his office at Whisper when Martin knocked on the open door. It had been five days since their first meeting with Peter Lake, and things were still tense. He had made sure that Dean was never alone. Either his father or Julio were always with him. The whole situation had his boy on the verge of a breakdown, and Richard was starting to feel nervous as well. He looked expectantly at Martin, who grinned broadly.

"I assume you have good news for me?"

Martin sauntered over, fell into the guest chair, and tossed Richard an envelope. "The PI brought me these today. I already faxed copies to Lake's office, but I thought you'd want to see them as well."

Richard tore the envelope open and stared at the report. One glance at the bank accounts and various columns of numbers told him all he needed to know. A malicious smile tugged at his lips. "So the Connellys are in trouble."

"That's putting it mildly. They have lost a lot of money. In their current situation, the only thing that could save them would be Emily's trust. In combination with Tricia's very explicit will, this should put an end to their attempts."

Richard let out a sigh. "You know things are never that easy, especially not when you have special tastes."

"You mean like you and Dean?"

"Exactly. All it takes is one homophobic or misinformed judge, and the things we do behind closed doors are suddenly a lot more important than Emily's well-being or the obvious financial gain her grandparents are hoping for."

Martin furrowed his brows. "This doesn't sound like you, Richard. You're a fighter."

Richard rubbed his eyes in a tired gesture. "I am. I hate to admit it, but I'm truly afraid. It took me so long to accept Emily, and I almost lost my boy over it. Now that I have them both, I can't imagine losing either. It's like a fist of steel around my heart that makes it hard to breathe. They are my life, Martin. The reason I get up in the morning."

"I know, man. I know. And that's exactly why you have to stay strong. They need you, Richard. Besides"—a grin appeared on Martin's lips—"you are not alone. You have friends who will do everything to help you. Not to mention all your money that pays for one of the best lawyers in the country."

Richard sat up straight. "You're right. I can have my meltdown when this is over."

"Or you can go spank the shit out of your boy to celebrate."

A wolfish grin appeared on Richard's face. "Now that's an interesting idea. Maybe I should do that now too. Just to release some of the tension…." Richard adjusted his hard-on none too subtly.

Martin laughed out loud. "Come on, go home to your boy. Perhaps he can do with a little relief as well."

Richard got up quickly, grabbed the documents, and gave Martin a pat on the shoulder when he brushed past him out of the office. "Thanks, man. I really needed to hear that."

"You're always welcome."

IN THE car, Richard dialed Peter's number. The lawyer answered after the second ring. "Hello, Richard. I gather you want to talk about the PI's report?"

Richard chuckled. "You gather right, Peter. What do you think?"

"That it looks a lot better than when I accepted this case. I'm not going to lie to you, there's still a chance that they will be successful simply because there are people out there who think it's worse to have a sexual kink than to be greedy, unloving assholes. But with their finances in such a pinch, they're going to have a hard time pretending they only want the best for Emily. If things start to look bad for us, I can even use Tricia's will to keep the trust under Dean's control. I wonder how eager the Connellys would be to get custody if the money stays with you."

"You are downright evil, Peter." Richard laughed. "I like it."

Peter's answering chuckle sounded malicious. "That's one of the reasons why I'm a sub. To keep the balance. Otherwise I'd go on a rampage."

"I really need to speak to your mistress one of these days. She must be an interesting woman."

"She's the best."

Pure love laced those words, and Richard smiled softly. "So you think we're good?"

"Yes. I have a meeting with the Connellys' lawyer tonight. Trent Colby is an asshole of the highest order, but he's also good at what he does, so we have to be careful."

"Does he know about the lifestyle?"

Peter let out a huff. "Enough to be dangerous. I'll see what he has to say today and call you tomorrow."

"Thank you. Goodbye."

Richard ended the call just before he drove into the garage of his home. When he got out, Aaron was already waiting for him, a worried frown on his face. Richard regarded his father closely. "Bad day?"

His father sighed. "I think Dean needs you badly today. He got some writing done in the morning, but when he came down to have lunch with me and Emily, he broke down and started crying. I took him outside for the afternoon to distract him, but with meager success. I'm not a pro at this, so I'm not telling you what to do, but he seems to need a good spanking or something along those lines."

Richard quirked an eyebrow. "You're the second person today to suggest spanking. Who am I to ignore the signs?"

His father grinned. "I'm going to take care of Emily. It's bedtime for her anyway, and I can stay the night."

Never was Richard gladder that they had given his father a permanent room in their new home. "Thank you, Dad. I'd better take care of my boy, then."

"Do that, son. I'll handle the rest."

CHAPTER 30

WHEN RICHARD entered the kitchen, he saw immediately that his father had been right. Dean was oozing despair. The way his shoulders hunched and how he hung his head, barely acknowledging Richard, reminded him of the first time he had had to go on a business trip and leave Dean alone for four days. Their relationship had been fresh then, Dean needing Richard like a lifeline. Now it looked the same.

"Come here, boy."

Richard opened his arms, and Dean slipped into his embrace, pressing his lean body against Richard's hard bulk as if he wanted to crawl into his master. "Everything's fine, boy. I'm going to take care of you."

"Master." Dean started sobbing, deep, raw cries on the verge of becoming hysterical.

Richard's eyes hardened as he slipped into Dom mode. It was high time he saw to this boy's needs. "Get upstairs. Take a shower and clean yourself thoroughly. I'm going to check. Then go to the playroom. Kneel on the mat in the middle of the room, presentation position."

Dean inhaled deeply and stepped back. "Yes, Master."

Richard watched his boy retreat and then hurried upstairs to open the playroom. He calculated that Dean would need about forty minutes to get himself ready, which gave Richard the time to kiss Emily good night.

Then he changed into a set of black leather trousers and heavy combat boots. Geared up like that, Richard went to the playroom. Dean was waiting for him with perfect posture, his knees spread to present his cock and balls, back ramrod straight, eyes cast downward, hands clasped behind his head, highlighting his biceps. Richard felt his cock swell and licked his lips in anticipation.

"Very good posture, boy."

"Thank you, Master."

Richard walked around Dean, looking at him from every angle. "I know how hard everything is for you at the moment, boy. Tonight I'm going to make you fly, make you forget all your troubles. Tomorrow we'll talk."

A shudder ran down Dean's spine. "Thank you, Master."

"Your safewords?"

Dean hesitated for a moment, and Richard knew why. The mention of safewords still reminded them both of their breakup, something they wanted to forget. But Richard would not jeopardize Dean's well-being and safety during a scene just because they'd had a rough spot before.

"Manga chick for slow down, graphic novel for stop, epic for go on."

"Very good, boy. I'm going to spank you now. You are not allowed to come, do you hear me?"

"Yes, Master."

A note of dread had crept into Dean's voice. He loved being spanked and could shoot just from the feel of Richard's hand on his ass. Richard smiled. He sat down on the padded bench next to the big four-poster and patted his thighs. "Assume the position, boy."

Gracefully, Dean draped himself over Richard's lap, his legs dangling down on one side, his head on the other, his already thickening cock wedged between Richard's thighs. Richard drew some lazy circles on the soft white skin before he brought down his palm quick and hard. Dean grunted, and Richard decided to push his boy a bit more. "Count them, boy. And thank me for giving you what you need."

Dean moaned. "One, Master. Thank you."

"Good boy."

Richard kept on raining blows on Dean's quickly reddening cheeks, just waiting long enough for his boy to scream out the count and his thank-you. When they reached twenty, Dean was squirming in Richard's lap, his cock leaking precum, his hips gyrating helplessly.

"Master, please."

Richard stopped the blows, waiting till Dean had calmed down a bit. "Another ten, boy. Can you do that for me?"

Dean sobbed. "Yes, Master. For you."

Richard smiled. "I won't go easy on you, boy. Those ten are going to hurt."

"Whatever pleases you, Master."

That was all Richard needed to hear. He could tell from Dean's body language, from his labored breathing and the way his rock-hard cock pressed against Richard's thighs, that his boy was completely in the scene and well on his way to find his subspace.

The first five swats came quick and hard, leaving Dean no time to prepare for the next ones. Then Richard took a short break, rubbing the glowing skin with his thumbs, pinching it until Dean cried out. "Five more, boy. Brace yourself."

Richard didn't wait for a reply, just let his hand fall down with even more force. Fascinated, he watched as the skin whitened in the form of his handprint before the blood rushed back. Richard drew it out, giving the swats slowly, carefully, aiming for maximum impact. When the last one fell, Dean cried out, and Richard felt him tensing, desperately trying to rein his orgasm in. It took a while, but finally Dean stilled in his lap.

"Thank you, Master."

"You took that spanking so beautifully, boy. You do me proud."

He caressed the hot, red cheeks, dipping his finger in the crease, searching for the wrinkled hole. Dean groaned.

"Don't worry, boy. Before we continue, I'll give you a nice cock ring to help you with your task. Get up."

Dean obeyed. He got to his feet, and Richard steadied him until he was sure his sub could stand on his own. Then he went over to the drawer where he kept all the toys. He selected a leather cock ring and a metal plug with four heavy spheres. Grabbing a bottle of lube, Richard went back to his boy. Again, Dean was in perfect display position, which made it easy for Richard to attach the cock ring that drew Dean's balls up in one breathtaking, obscene package. Unable to resist temptation, Richard bent down and licked the precum from the leaking tip. Dean groaned, his hips snapping forward in an involuntary movement. Richard slapped his boy's hard prick.

"Keep still."

"I'm sorry, Master." Dean whimpered and kept still, his thigh muscles shivering from the effort. Richard straightened and gestured toward the spanking bench. "Bend over."

Dean obeyed immediately, spreading his legs in invitation. Richard stepped closer, his eyes fastened on the twitching hole between the glowing, pulsing cheeks. He squirted a generous amount of lube on his fingers and then started to breach the tiny hole. Dean moaned, pushing his hips back. For a moment, Richard contemplated ordering Dean to stay still, but then he decided it would be more fun if his boy could get some workout. He corkscrewed his fingers inside Dean's tight channel, searching for the sweet spot. When he found it and Dean started pumping his hips, Richard purred. "That's it, boy. Fuck yourself on my fingers. Show me how much you want me. How much you need me."

"God, Master. Please." Dean had lost coherent speech. He was mumbling single words, begging his master while he fucked himself on Richard's fingers. When Richard felt Dean's insides constrict, he knew it was time to end the fun. He pulled his fingers out and watched his boy's hole twitch in frustration. "Remember, boy, no coming until I say so."

"Master, please."

"No. You can do this, I know it."

Dean whimpered in frustration, but he stilled. When Richard was sure his boy was under control again, he slicked the plug up and pushed it inside Dean's body. Every time one of the spheres breached the sweet hole to the maximum, Richard paused, twisted it a bit, slid it back and forth, and then let it sink into Dean's tight heat. Once the plug was seated, Richard stepped back. The teasing had made him so hard, he decided he needed some relief. He grabbed Dean's hair and pulled him up.

"Get down on your knees and show me what a good cocksucker you are, boy."

Dean groaned. He knelt in front of Richard, waiting for his master to open his fly and pull his hard prick out. When the dark meat brushed Dean's lips, he opened his mouth and let his tongue swirl around the bulbous head. Richard closed his eyes. "That's it, boy. Suck me hard."

Dean complied willingly, sucking and licking Richard's fat cock with enthusiasm. Way too soon Richard felt the tingling in his spine. He grabbed Dean's head to keep him in place and thrust his cock into the hot mouth with increasing speed. Dean swallowed around him, creating suction, and with a guttural scream, Richard emptied his balls into Dean's throat. His boy drank him down eagerly, licking and lapping at his still erect cock until it was clean. With a sigh, Richard slipped from Dean's wonderful mouth and tugged his aching erection back into his trousers.

"You're a wonderful cocksucker, boy. A real talent."

"Thank you, Master."

Richard smiled. "You deserve a reward for your service. Bend over the bench again. I'm going to put some stripes on your back, and then I'm going to paddle that hot red ass of yours."

Again Dean obeyed immediately, his eyes already slightly glazed over, a sure sign that he was headed for subspace. Richard selected a riding crop from the drawer, took position behind Dean, and rolled his shoulders. "Ready, boy?"

"Yes, Master."

"Ten with the crop. You don't have to count. Then I'll get the paddle to tenderize your ass."

Without additional warning, Richard let the crop fly through the air. The swishing sound was almost as good as the sight and feel when it connected with the flesh on Dean's back. His boy's sweet cry was like the icing on the cake.

Richard set the ten marks unhurriedly. When he was done, he took a moment to admire his handiwork before he reached for the paddle. It was wooden and slightly curved for maximum impact. Richard let it land on the fleshiest parts of Dean's ass a few times before he moved to the junction between his ass and thighs. Every time he hit there, he also drove the plug deeper. The first three hits, Dean tried to evade the paddle, but then he started leaning into the blows and Richard knew he had to speed things along. The paddle connected with Dean's ass five more times before Richard cast it aside and pulled the plug out. He then lubed his leaking cock and lined it up with Dean's quivering hole. When he sank into the tight heat, they both groaned.

Richard started an unrelenting rhythm, and thanks to the blow job earlier, he was able to keep it up for a while. Beneath him, Dean was moaning and whimpering, begging him for permission to come. When Richard felt his own orgasm approaching, he bent forward, reached for the cock ring, and unsnapped it. "Come now, boy."

His booming Dom voice did the trick. Dean's channel tightened around Richard's cock like a vise as his boy sprayed cum all over the spanking bench. Richard roared as his own orgasm was torn from him. He pumped his seed deep into his boy's body, reveling in the tightness and the beauty of Dean's red and abused ass.

It took Richard a few moments to come down from his high, and then he waited patiently for Dean to return from subspace. Once he was sure his boy was aware of his surroundings again, Richard got up, pulling Dean with him, and carried him over to the bed. There they lay down, snuggling together. Richard used some of the wet wipes from the bedside table to clean Dean. His boy fell asleep quickly, and Richard closed his eyes as well.

AN HOUR later they were ready to go down to their bedroom. Richard smiled at Dean. "You were very brave today, boy. I'm so proud of you."

Dean blushed a little at these words. "Thank you, Master. And thank you for giving me what I needed. I feel a lot better now."

"I'm glad. Now let's get down, take a shower, and then let's sleep. We can talk tomorrow."

Dean snuggled happily into Richard's arm as they went down the stairs together.

CHAPTER 31

"SO, WHAT'S going on, Master?"

Richard looked into Dean's worried face and sighed, unsure how much he should tell his beloved sub. This morning Dean had woken him with coffee in bed, and now he obviously wanted to use the time until Emily got up to talk. As if he had read Richard's thoughts, Dean reached for his hands and squeezed them.

"Please, don't lie to me. I know you think you have to carry all my burdens, and normally I would agree with you, but this—this is too big to be shouldered by just one person. I want to be there for you, Richard. Just like you are there for me. I promise, I won't fold under the pressure."

Richard pulled Dean close and kissed him on the mouth. "I know, baby. Old habits just die hard. Before Emily, you wouldn't even have been aware of the situation. I would have kept you safe and sheltered. Then again, before Emily, nothing seemed as pressing or bad. At least not in hindsight."

"I know what you mean."

"The gist is that your parents are broke, and that's why they want custody. Not because they care for Emily, but because they need her trust. Which gives Peter a lot of leverage. We're not out of the woods yet, though, because bigots are everywhere and your parents are desperate enough to press the matter. But our chances are definitely better now. Peter had a meeting with the lawyer working for your parents yesterday, and he wanted to phone me today."

Richard took Dean's face in both hands and looked at him with a hint of worry. "If the judge accepts their claim and we have to go to court, things are bound to become ugly. Your parents will dig up anything they can find to prove that we're unfit to take care of Emily. I want you to be aware of how tough it could be."

Dean smiled weakly. "I know. But I have you and Emily and Aaron and Julio and all our friends. It's just… I feel bad, you know. About you having to take care of this when you didn't want Emily in the first place."

Richard winced, knowing Dean wasn't trying to be mean, but voicing a fear he would have had as well, had he been in Dean's shoes. He hugged his beautiful lover.

"Thank you for sharing that fear with me. I know how hard that must be for you. And don't worry. I may not have been enthusiastic about Emily in our life in the beginning, but that has changed. Now I can't imagine not having her with us. And everybody who goes against her, goes against me as well. I love you both, Dean. Never doubt that."

With a sob, Dean buried himself in Richard's arms. "And I love you. More than anything else. More than my own life. For you to accept Emily— that makes me so happy."

Richard smiled and held his boy close.

HALF AN hour later, they sat together with Aaron and Emily at the breakfast table. Emily had a bowl with yogurt and strawberries, which she attacked with enthusiasm. At almost twelve months, she wasn't an expert with the spoon yet, more like a novice, but it was fun watching her battle it out. Under the table, Donar, Thor, Wilma, and Fred were waiting patiently for their share. Experience had already taught them that sticking close to Emily's high chair was a surefire method to get some scraps from the table.

Richard watched the scene with fondness. He felt content and happy with his family around him. This feeling was new to him, and he knew he had Emily to thank for that. Before her, his father would have never spent the night at his house or stayed for breakfast. It just wasn't something grown men did. But for the little princess, staying over and sharing meals felt natural.

Emily had just finished her yogurt when Richard's cell rang. One glance and his heart started beating faster in his chest. Peter.

His father realized this was important and took Emily and the zoo outside. Richard accepted the call and put Peter on speaker while Dean slipped into his lap, seeking and giving comfort at the same time. With one hand wrapped tightly around his boy's waist, Richard placed the phone on the table.

"Good morning, Peter. You're on speaker and Dean is here with me."

"Good morning to you two as well. I have interesting news."

"Spill." Richard was too nervous to bother with common courtesy.

Peter seemed to pick up on his crankiness, because he cut to the chase without making a comment about his rude behavior. "My meeting with Trent was as unpleasant as could be expected. I really don't know how that man manages to keep his clients. His people skills are simply horrible."

"Peter."

"Sorry. I got sidetracked for a moment. I mean, he really is an ass. I know, I know, not the most important thing at the moment. So, our meeting was the usual trying to get as much information from the other party as possible without revealing too much of your own dance, and unfortunately, I think he does have something substantial. He was a little too confident for my liking, and he didn't try very hard to find out what I managed to dig up on his clients. Which means he either doesn't know about their financial troubles or he doesn't care, which, frankly, would be the less preferable scenario. Anyway, he suggested a meeting this afternoon at his office with both parties involved to find an amicable solution that doesn't involve going to court."

Richard furrowed his brows. Something was wrong; he felt it in his gut. "If he was as confident as you claim, why would he suggest something like that? He doesn't strike me as the type of man who would settle for an amicable arrangement with less glory and money for him when he can have an all-out battle and write a bill for double the sum."

"Exactly. That's what made me hesitate as well. Either his clients don't want to go to court, which is understandable given their monetary situation, or there is something else. Unfortunately, we don't know, and this is too important to rely on guesswork."

"You think we should meet with them?" Richard asked matter-of-factly.

Peter sighed. "Yes. Don't get your hopes up—it will most probably be in vain—but this way we can find out what kind of ammunition they have. Perhaps we can even scare them off, although Trent is not the kind of man to run with his tail between his legs."

"When does he want to meet?"

"At four o'clock at his office."

"We'll be there. Let's meet at half past three. If I remember correctly, there's a coffee shop around the corner from Trent's office."

"How do you know where his office is?" Peter sounded surprised.

Dean snorted, which made Richard cock an eyebrow. "I like to be prepared, Peter. Always. As soon as I knew who the other lawyer would be, I had him checked out. It always pays to know the enemy."

"Now I'm afraid. Are you sure you need me?" There was only a hint of mockery in Peter's voice.

"Yes, definitely. I may be a good general when it comes to open slaughter, but for the finer aspects of stabbing people in the back without leaving evidence behind, I need professional help."

"I'm not quite sure if I should feel flattered or offended."

Now Dean laughed out loud. "Go with flattered and bask in the knowledge that the ruthless Richard Miller needs your help."

"Feeling flattered it is. I'll see you at half past three."

"Goodbye, Peter." Richard disconnected the call and looked expectantly at Dean. "How do you feel, boy?"

Dean sighed and reached for Richard's hands as if to reassure himself through the connection. "Nervous. Frightened. Angry. All mixed in one. Even a bit sad, although that is the weakest emotion. I guess I still feel some attachment to my parents, even though they made it more than clear what they think about me."

"They're idiots. Look at the wonderful son they've lost. But their loss is my gain. And my father is more than happy to call you son, you know that."

"I do. Which makes it easier and harder at the same time. Knowing there are parents out there who love their children unconditionally, who support them in everything they do, makes me sometimes wonder why I drew a short straw in the parent department."

Richard placed a gentle kiss on Dean's forehead. "I think it was so that my father got to have two sons instead of one. My parents always wanted more children, and now he even has a granddaughter."

Dean felt tears springing to his eyes. "How do you do that?"

"What?"

"Always telling me what I need to hear?" He paused for a moment, seemingly lost in thought. "You know, if my mockery of a happy childhood is the price I had to pay for having you in my life, I would do it again in a heartbeat."

Richard smiled broadly. "Now you're doing it. Telling me what I need to hear. You make me complete, Dean. Out of the two of us, I'm the lucky one."

Dean buried his head in the crook of Richard's neck, and they sat in silence for a few minutes. When they heard a happy squeal from outside, Richard pried Dean's arms from around his chest. "Let's spend the morning with our daughter." His eyes hardened. "And then we're going to slay some dragons."

CHAPTER 32

DEAN GLANCED around Trent Colby's office and couldn't suppress a shudder. The place was immaculate, perfectly designed with lots of chrome and white and polished marble, and also cold and impersonal. The people working there looked as if they had jumped right out of some manager magazine, the men in expensive, tailored suits, the women in costumes and high heels. All the smiles were perfect, with blinding white teeth, and not one reached the eyes. *A pool of sharks*, Dean thought.

The Great White was approaching them, and Dean had to suppress the urge to hide behind Richard. Trent Colby was a good-looking man in his forties, with short blond hair, a cut, sharp face where the gray eyes were dull and dead, and a body that screamed of hours spent in the gym. Trent had a half smile plastered to his lips that showed clearly how little he thought of his guests.

Dean no longer wondered why Peter didn't like the man. He shared the sentiment without having talked to him once. Peter had the same half smile when he greeted Trent and then introduced Richard and Dean. Trent shook Dean's hand first, clearly trying to rattle Richard by questioning his alpha status.

But Richard was used to the games powerful men played, and since there was no doubt who the most potent male present was, he simply smiled and greeted Trent as if they were old acquaintances. Now it was Trent who seemed rattled, but he shook it off quickly and led them to a small meeting room that didn't look any different from the rest of the office building, except for the presence of Dean's parents.

Christopher and Faith Connelly didn't rise to greet their son and his partner but stayed glued to their chairs, barely acknowledging Dean. In a way, their behavior made it easier for Dean. He had been afraid that he would be overcome by emotion when he saw his parents after such a long time, but the way they treated him, like he was some stranger, helped him do the same. He felt a small pain in his heart at the realization that he really didn't have a family anymore, but then Richard squeezed his hand, silently reminding him of the family he had found instead. Grateful, Dean squeezed back and sat down next to his Dom and lover, opposite his mother.

Trent sat down next to Christopher and shuffled some documents before he started to speak. "Since we all know the reason why we're here, I guess we can leave the pleasantries aside."

"Since you wouldn't know how to exchange those anyway, I agree to your suggestions." Peter shot Trent a syrupy smile with a hint of steel underneath.

Dean hid his own smile. Peter might not be an openly aggressive alpha type like Richard and Trent, but he had his methods and they worked. Trent shot Peter an annoyed look, losing his composure for a moment. *Score one for Peter.* Dean regretted that he couldn't cheer their lawyer on.

Trent caught himself and opened one of the files in front of him. "Since there is no question that my clients will win if we bring this case to court, let's start talking about the terms for which they would abandon the lawsuit."

Peter raised a brow. "Your clients wish to abandon the lawsuit?"

"They have no real interest in raising a child at their age. They simply feel that it wouldn't be right for a little girl to grow up in a household with two men whose sexual—let's call it *preferences*—are more than questionable."

"But they would be willing to forget about their worries for certain—let's call it *favors*?" Peter had no problem imitating Trent's condescending tone. "I don't know about you, but where I got my degree, that's called blackmailing, and it's forbidden."

"No, no, no. Blackmailing is such a harsh term. Let's just say my clients had some time to think things through and have come to the conclusion that their views of the world might be a bit—outdated. Still, they want to make sure that their little granddaughter is safe. Nobody can argue with that." Trent spoke smoothly, full of self-confidence, but Dean saw him sneak glances at Richard's impassive face, and suddenly it hit Dean: Trent was afraid of Richard.

He felt relief wash through him. The situation was still far from being solved, but if this cutthroat lawyer was wary of Richard, then they had a chance. If Peter had picked up on that as well, Dean couldn't tell. He just followed Trent's none too subtle lead.

"And what would those conditions be? Not that we agree to anything. We just want to know what you are up to."

Trent opened another file. "I drew up a preliminary contract, although I have to say that the points are nonnegotiable." He glanced at Christopher and Faith, who sat there with smug expressions on their faces. "To ensure Emily's mental well-being, Richard Miller is not allowed to adopt her as his daughter. She has to remain as Dean Connelly's charge. Also, Richard Miller has to sell his BDSM clubs, so that Emily won't come in contact with that kind of perversion. Richard Miller and Dean Connelly have to live apart. Two men under one roof are not a healthy environment for a child. There are some other points, but those are the most important ones."

Dean couldn't believe it. He couldn't believe the audacity of the conditions, or the hatred being spilled. He couldn't even look at his parents, or he would have done something he would probably regret later. Or perhaps not. Dean straightened his back. He had promised himself to be a pillar of support for Richard. The last thing anybody needed right now was him throwing a tantrum or having a breakdown.

Peter opened his mouth to answer, but Richard stopped him simply by leaning a bit forward in his chair. His voice was cold and low.

"In other words, you wish to dictate how we lead our lives. I'm just surprised that you haven't asked for any money yet."

Trent gulped. He squirmed under Richard's glare. "That's among the minor points of the contract."

Richard smiled coldly. "Since you have been so straightforward with us, let me return the favor. You don't want me to adopt Emily, because then I get a say about her trust. A trust your clients would love to get their hands on, given their financial predicament. As for me selling my clubs, I won't let anybody dictate my business decisions. Dean and I are living together in a house that is paradise for a child. And if you thought you could extract money from me by threatening my family, I have to disappoint you. I protect what is mine. Now, do you have any other proposals, or are we done here?"

This time it was Christopher Connelly who spoke. "How dare you! We were giving you a chance to spare yourself the embarrassment of a court trial."

He reached for one of Trent's files, opened it, and started pulling photographs out of it. "We have evidence of your depraved lifestyle! We know what is going on in those pits you call clubs. In a trial, we would make all those compromising photos public. We can squash you, you arrogant fuck."

Dean was still waiting for foam to form on his father's mouth when Richard took some of the pictures, glanced at them, and then put them down. "All of those pictures were taken at official functions for the clubs. None of them shows me or Dean in anything other than stunning leather clothes. There is not one compromising picture in here. So far, I have yet to be impressed by your threats."

Richard eyed Trent and his clients for a moment before he continued. "Your financial status, on the other hand, is a problem. You can't afford going to court. Especially since your prospects of winning are fleeting at best. Any judge who sees the documents we have found on you will deduce quickly that you are not interested in Emily's well-being, but her impressive trust. Add to that Tricia's very explicit will, and you have no chance at all. And even if you should be lucky enough to find a homophobic judge who will rule against us simply because of our sexual orientation, I have the financial resources to take this through to the Supreme Court. And believe me, I will do it. You have an empty hand, and I'm calling your bluff."

Richard leaned back, glaring at Trent and the Connellys. Faith had started to gasp, Christopher was squashing one of the pictures he had thrown at Richard, and Trent just sat there openmouthed. Dean was so proud of his Dom, he thought he would explode.

It was Peter who ended the silence. "I think with that, we don't have anything else to discuss. Or is there something, Trent?"

The other lawyer shook his head. A condescending smile appeared on Peter's lips. "It's of course still up to you, if you want to take this to court, although I wouldn't recommend it. Richard's pockets are deep enough to see this through, while I doubt that your clients will even be able to pay your fees. Let's just forget about this whole mess and call it a day. Richard, Dean? I think Mr. Colby wants to be alone with his clients."

They all rose from their chairs and exited the office while the Connellys stared daggers at them.

Once they had left the building, Peter turned to Richard. "If you weren't a Dom and bigger than me, I would punch you right now. That was a risky thing to do, cornering and threatening them like that."

Richard shrugged. "It worked."

Peter sighed. "Yes, it did. But only because it was harebrained from the beginning. I don't know what came over Trent to even take them on. He's normally more calculating."

Richard slung an arm around Dean. "You probably won't believe it, but I have seen people do even stupider things for money. And I have quite a lot of it. My guess is that he thought I would do anything for Emily. Which is true. He just didn't anticipate that this 'anything' doesn't include me rolling over and letting others take the lead but, on the contrary, me eliminating any threat I see for my family."

Peter nodded. "I can see how that makes sense."

"But why would they ask for such insane conditions?" That was the part Dean didn't understand.

Peter smiled sadly at him. "It's an old tactic. They presented us with conditions that seemed to have Emily's best interest in mind. Those were also the terms they knew you would never consent to. If we had agreed to enter negotiations, we would have eventually come to the point where they would have settled for money. Sorry, Dean, but that's how the world works."

Dean shuddered and snuggled closer to Richard. "They just wanted the money?"

"Yes, boy. That's all they ever wanted. After reading the report on their financial problems, I had an inkling it would boil down to this. I have to admit, though, that even I was surprised by their blatant approach. I had expected a bit more finesse. Well, they are desperate, and desperate people tend to do stupid things."

Richard turned to Peter. "Do you think this is over now?"

"Most probably. There are still some formalities we have to take care of, but I honestly don't think they will take this to court. Trent most definitely won't. He's scared shitless of you, and he doesn't take on cases he can't win. The Connellys would have to find a new lawyer, and anybody who hears that they were dumped by Trent won't touch their case. At least none of the high-class lawyers. They recognize a dead end when they see one."

Dean snickered. "It's kind of funny to hear my parents referred to as a dead end."

Richard laughed. "That's what they are, boy. Most definitely."

Peter shook first Richard's and then Dean's hand. "Don't get the champagne glasses out yet, but I think you can start to relax."

"Thank you, Peter. You were great." Richard patted the lawyer on the shoulder.

Peter grinned. "Yes, I know. Although, in the end, you won the battle all on your own, General. No backstabbing involved."

Richard winked. "But we could have done it, if we had wanted to."

CHAPTER 33

RICHARD WAS just sorting through some documents in his office at Whisper when his phone rang. He furrowed his brow when he saw it was Peter. It had been three days since their fateful meeting at Trent Colby's office, and there still were some loose ends to be tied up. One of them being where the Connellys had gotten the pictures of him and Dean in their leathers. Since there were no pictures of them in action, the playrooms at Whisper were still safe. Because he and Dean only played at the club or at home, Richard wondered where the pictures had been taken. They were all direct shots, but the glimpses of background he could see on some of them suggested they were taken at the public area of Whisper.

Richard had already referred the problem to Martin, who was working on it. The safety of their clients' privacy was one of the top selling points of Whisper. If that safety had been compromised, they had to find the leak. Richard sighed and accepted the call. Always so much to do. "Peter?"

"Hi, Richard. I have good news and bad news. Which do you want to hear first?"

Richard growled. He hated games. "Just spill."

"Sheesh, are we grumpy today. Anyway, the good news is that the Connellys have abandoned the lawsuit because they have realized that at their age, they can't successfully take care of a child. That's the official version. So, congratulations. Now for the bad news. Their concerns regarding your sexual activities have reached the ears of some big shot at the Child Welfare Program. How that happened, I don't know. My guess is, somebody at admin was a bit overly enthusiastic. You will get a visit from Child Welfare tomorrow to determine if everything is in Emily's best interest."

Richard sat back in his chair. He was relieved that the Connellys had dropped the lawsuit. He would do anything to keep Emily, but it was nice to know he didn't have to spend the next six months in a courtroom. He wasn't particularly worried about the control visit. It was something he had expected from the moment this whole nightmare started. "Do you know who's coming? And do I have to worry?"

"They'll send a woman named Meredith Denton. You should know her already, because she was the one who took care of Emily until she was allowed to stay with you. And no, I don't think you have to be overly worried. Just make sure that the dungeon is closed and that Mrs. Denton understands the severity of your safety precautions. Then I don't see why she should take Emily from you, especially since she agreed to you having her in the first place."

"Except for the small fact that she hates gays."

Peter let out a heartfelt sigh. "If that's the case and if she takes Emily from you—and she needs to make it a case of gross negligence to justify it—I can always file a complaint and have somebody else come to your place again. You are in no immediate danger to lose Emily. The Child Welfare Program doesn't have the manpower to act quickly."

"Thank you, Peter. I'm going to tell Dean."

Richard disconnected the call and stared at the wall for a moment. Martin chose that moment to enter his office.

"Hi, Richard. Everything all right?"

"Yeah. More or less. Peter just called. We'll be getting a visit from the Child Welfare Program tomorrow."

"Oh man, I thought that was over."

"Apparently not. What can I do for you?"

Martin turned serious. He sat down and tossed Richard a file with a picture. It was one of the bar subs, a young man with pale skin, black hair, and huge green eyes. "That's Emilio."

Martin sighed. "That's our photographer. He confessed that he took those pictures of you and Dean. He had a small camera built into his collar. The one with the spikes."

Richard stared at the picture. He didn't know Emilio very well, but he was sure the young man would never do such a thing. "Why would he do that?"

"Here is where it gets ugly. You know Emilio is all alone. His parents died when he was fifteen. He lived on the streets for some time, and now he's trying to get his life on track. He rented a small apartment and is studying at a local community college. He needs this job here at Whisper to pay all the fees. Apparently a few months ago, a man approached him, beat him up, and threatened to kill him if he didn't take those pictures. He brought him the equipment and gave him very specific instructions."

"Do we know that man?"

Martin smiled coldly. "We do. He's the PI who worked for the Connellys. He's a brute, and I can understand why Emilio was afraid of him." Martin paused, a malicious smile on his lips. "He has left the state. When I explained to him all the unpleasant things we could do to him should he choose to stay, he couldn't pack his bags fast enough."

Richard grinned. "Good thinking. Now, what do we do with Emilio? I gather from your comments that you are inclined to forgive him?"

"Yes. The kid never had it easy, but he's smart and he has a chance to make it. After that PI worked him over, he even took pictures of all the wounds, just in case. And he never took pictures of you when Dean was naked. He only made shots where Dean wore enough to cover the crucial parts. Emilio knew those pictures would be used against you, and he figured that they wouldn't carry as much weight with both of you more or less dressed."

"I bet that didn't go over well with the PI."

Martin winced. "No. According to Emilio, he was threatened with another beating. But he managed to convince the brute by saying that you are too jealous to parade Dean around naked for everyone to see." Martin smirked. "I can't imagine why, but the PI believed him."

Richard shrugged. "No doubt because of my charming reputation. Why didn't he give Emilio more grief about naked pictures?"

"He somehow got his hands on our list of security measures. They're not exactly a secret, since we use them to advertise. That's how he knew that Emilio had no chance to get material from one of the playrooms. He probably figured that you and Dean in leathers would be enough."

Richard huffed. With the wrong kind of judge, it could have been enough. "I still don't understand why Emilio didn't come to us."

"We're a bit intimidating." Martin gestured first to Richard and then pointed at his own bulky frame. Neither of them was a small man or lacking in the muscle department. To somebody smaller and in a position of dependency, they did not appear reassuring. "And he was afraid we would see him as a liability and throw him out."

"This is a problem, Martin. Our employees should not fear us. They need to know that we are there for them."

Martin put his feet on Richard's desk. "A nice idea, Richard. Unfortunately, we have a BDSM club and most of our employees are subs. Subs without a Dom, as I may point out. To them, we are the top dogs. We are their masters and employers. We don't play with them, but we pay their checks. They have no reason to trust us with such information, because they don't know us."

Richard stared at the desk and Martin's feet. He knew his partner was right. No matter how often they stressed that the house subs could come to them with all their troubles, they didn't have reason to do so. This was one aspect where the Dom/sub dynamics didn't work in favor of a situation.

"They need somebody they can trust…." Richard noticed a dark spot on the sole of Martin's right shoe. "Somebody who has no problem talking to us, but who isn't intimidating…. Leeland! We could ask Leeland to become our middleman!"

The more Richard thought about it, the better he liked his idea. "He's a sub himself, he works here, the other subs like him, he's nonthreatening yet not afraid to stand up against a Dom, and keeps a cool head during crisis. He's the ideal candidate. What do you think?"

Now it was Martin's turn to stare into empty space. "Do you think he would be interested?"

"Most definitely. Especially if we offer him a pay raise."

"Should we both talk to him?"

Richard thought about it. "I don't think that's necessary. When I see him next time, I can make the proposal. Problem solved. What do we do with Emilio?"

Martin put his feet down again. "I say we keep him, but as punishment for not trusting us, he has to do one hour of dishwashing after every shift he works for the next month."

"Good idea! Are you going to tell him?"

"Yes. He's desperate, and I want him to know that it's over."

Richard winked at Martin. No matter how cold his partner sometimes appeared or how threatening he looked, he had a warm and caring heart. If only he would find the right sub to share it with.

CHAPTER 34

"GOD, I'M so nervous!" Dean was pacing the kitchen, unable to sit still if his life depended on it. They were expecting Meredith Denton any minute.

"It's fine, boy. Come here." Richard opened his arms to embrace Dean, and he let him do it for the duration of a heartbeat. Then he resumed his restless wandering. Richard couldn't blame him.

He, too, felt nervous, something he wasn't used to and didn't like. Even Emily had picked up on their strange mood and was softly crying in Aaron's arms. Richard took the girl from his father and held her close, letting the feeling of utter love he had for her wash over him. There was one last hiccupping sob, then Emily leaned her upper body back, stared at him with her incredibly blue eyes, and announced, "Dada! Woofie!"

Richard smiled and put her down. Donar and Thor were already waiting for their favorite playmate, wagging their tails in eager anticipation of the games Emily would come up with. She walked under the table— she was still small enough to do so—grabbed the two stuffed elephants Richard's father had bought for his dogs, and scampered toward the door. Donar and Thor followed with interest in their canine eyes.

Dean sighed and sat down on Richard's lap. "I just can't imagine her not being here."

He voiced his biggest fear, the one they all had locked deep inside their hearts. Richard kissed Dean on the lips, and his father patted his back.

"No matter what happens, son, we're not giving her up. Never. She belongs in this family, where she is loved and wanted, nowhere else." Richard threw his father a grateful look. His support meant a lot to them. The older man nodded and smiled.

The doorbell rang and Donar and Thor started barking. They viewed the house as their territory by now and defended it with the same vigor as their own home. Gently Richard pushed Dean from his lap. "Let's go and get this over with."

WHEN RICHARD opened the door, Meredith Denton looked almost exactly the same as when they had first met. He wondered if she only had this kind of sensible outfit. His gay-hater radar pinged like crazy, even though the smile on her lips when she took his hand was friendly.

"Ms. Denton. It's a pleasure to meet you again."

"Mr. Miller, I'd love to say the same, but we both know I'm not making a courtesy call." She smiled again and took some of the sharpness out of her words. "You don't want me to be here and the heavens know, I don't want to be here. When I left Emily in your care, I was convinced that my decision was right. I hope I don't have to regret it."

Richard hesitated for a moment and then decided to go with her straightforwardness. He liked to take the same approach in his dealings and appreciated it in others. "You are right, of course. We're not overly thrilled to have you here, so why don't we go inside so you can ask your questions, and then we'll show you around the house."

Meredith nodded her approval. "Sounds like a plan, Mr. Miller."

She entered and greeted Dean and Richard's father before she glanced around. "Where is Emily?"

At that moment, the little girl came barging out of the kitchen, closely followed by Donar and Thor, who had been banned there by Aaron. Meredith smiled at the picture.

"I see she has found some friends. And she looks great, Mr. Miller, Mr. Connelly."

Richard beamed with pride. "She's big for her age. Of course, the dogs helped getting her to walk because she wanted to follow them everywhere."

"Animals are good for children. Are those your dogs?"

"No, they belong to my father, Aaron." Richard nodded toward the general. "He stays here at least twice a week for babysitting duties, so Emily sees the dogs a lot. We have kittens."

Meredith raised a brow. "Isn't that a problem with two such big dogs?"

Aaron smiled warmly at her. "We thought so at first, but the kittens showed the dogs who's boss at the first meeting. They're thick as thieves."

Meredith actually laughed. "I would have loved to see that." She turned serious again. "Now please show me that 'horrible dungeon' the Connellys mentioned in their plea for custody."

Richard waved toward the stairs. "Please follow me."

Meredith inspected the door to the playroom as well as the locks and the security system. She seemed satisfied. "I'm not going to embarrass us all by asking you to unlock it for me. I can see that you have taken all measures to prevent Emily from entering here, which is more than I can say for the gun safety in some of the homes I've been to. At least whips can't kill you."

She straightened. "Let's go downstairs and do the paperwork."

After a tedious hour, where Meredith even made a sketch of the locks and the location of the playroom inside the house, she finally sat back. "I think we can call it a day."

"We can keep her?" Dean looked at her imploringly.

Meredith smiled. "Yes, you can keep her. I don't see a reason why not. You are caring, doting parents who take Emily's well-being seriously. I don't think she can do any better."

Dean laughed out loud and kissed Richard. He trembled with joy while tears streamed down his cheeks. Over the head of his excited lover, Richard looked at Meredith.

"I thank you. We are truly grateful." He hesitated a moment. "Can I ask you something, though?"

"Of course."

"I've gotten the impression that you don't like gays. My instinct in that regard is always dead-on, and I don't think I misread you. So what made you decide not to make our lives hell?"

Meredith shrugged. "It's true, I don't like gays. I also don't like onions, the color lime, and action movies with Vin Diesel. My dislike has nothing to do with your ability to take care of a child. For me, the only thing that counts is Emily's well-being. What you two do in the privacy of your home is none of my business. I may disapprove, but as long as you don't hurt anybody and behave like decent citizens, I have no reason to act against you."

Richard could only stare for a few moments. He had thought he'd seen it all, but Meredith had just managed to surprise him. "That's a very distinct view."

"It is. Which is kind of sad. But that's another topic." Meredith rose and offered Richard her hand. "I'm going to file the report, and then the Child Welfare Program is out of your hair. I wish you and your family all the best."

Richard smiled at her and shook her hand. "Thank you, Ms. Denton. Contrary to what we said before, it really was a pleasure to meet you."

She laughed. "You're just relieved. I'll find the door myself. Have a nice life."

When she was gone, Aaron whistled low. "She was one of a kind."

"Yes. Good for us." Richard kissed Dean once more. "Come on, boy. Tell the others the good news and invite them over. Spontaneous dinner here at eight. I'll call Mamma's."

Dean laughed and cried and did as he was told.

Later that night, after their friends had celebrated with them, Richard took Dean to the playroom and out onto the roof. He guided him to the deep lounge Peyton had set up there, and they both sat down. Richard still held Dean's hand, pressing soft kisses at his knuckles now and then.

"What a day." Dean leaned back and stared into the night sky. "I'm so glad and so exhausted." He paused for a moment. "We could have lost her."

On those last words, his voice started shaking, the full impact of what had happened only now registering.

Richard pulled Dean close. "But we haven't. She's here, in this house, in her room, sleeping soundly. Emily is safe, Dean."

A deep sigh was the answer. Richard stroked Dean's back until his boy had calmed down. It was time to address the other thing Richard had been thinking about. "There is something I'd like to discuss with you, boy."

Dean looked at him imploringly and nodded. There was a tiny hint of apprehension in his eyes that made Richard talk a little faster.

"It's something I've been thinking about since we got back together, and all that trouble with your parents and the Child Welfare Program has only strengthened my resolve."

Richard slid from the lounge and went down on one knee in front of Dean. "I want us to be a real family, boy. That's why I'm asking you, Dean Connelly, do you want to marry me?"

Dean just stared at Richard, his beautiful eyes blown wide, tears shining in them. Richard reached into the back pocket of his jeans and pulled out the engagement ring he had stashed there earlier.

He reached for Dean's left hand, ring between his thumb and index finger, and looked imploringly at his lover and boy. Dean made a choking sound, wiped at the tears with his free hand, and then managed to get the words out.

"Yes. Yes. I love you so much, and, yes, I do want to marry you."

With a satisfied smile, Richard slipped the ring, a simple silver band with their names engraved on it, over Dean's finger. Dean stared at it in wonder before he reached out for his Dom and kissed him hungrily. He was still crying, but that only added an interesting salty taste to their kisses.

Richard rose and sat back in the lounge with Dean cuddled between his legs. They sat there for another hour, gazing at the stars, basking in their love and happiness, and both insanely glad that they had found a home in the other.

EPILOGUE

"TODAY IS the big day, big sis." Dean was standing in front of Tricia's urn at its place on the shelf in the living room. He had made it a habit to talk to her as if they were on the phone, filling in the parts where she would have said something.

"I know. I wouldn't have thought so, either. But he's a good man. He's making me happy. And he's the perfect dad for Emily."

"Talking to Tricia, boy?" Richard stepped behind Dean and embraced him, leaning his chin on Dean's shoulder. When Dean had started his "discussions" with the urn, Richard had been worried. After a week, he had gotten used to it and was now at the point where he started talking to her as well. It was strangely soothing to talk to somebody who wouldn't answer.

"Yes. I wanted her to know how happy I am."

"Oh, I think she knows that. And I'm sure she's happy for you."

"Master—"

"Dean! There you are!" Aaron came barging through the door, glaring at his son. "Richard, you shouldn't be here and you know it! Get out."

Richard let go of Dean and hurried to get outside. Aaron had been flattered when Dean had asked him to walk him down the aisle, and the ex-general had made it his mission to organize a perfect wedding. For this herculean task, he had enlisted the help of Leeland and Peyton, who both proved to be even more relentless nags than Aaron. Thanks to their combined efforts, the wedding was going to be fantastic.

The yard was set up with a wooden dance floor, four huge round tables where the guests were seated, and a pavilion where the staff from Mamma's had been busy since the early morning hours with setting up a feast. Leeland had even organized a chocolate fountain, which they had to protect from Emily. She was sixteen months now, unbelievably fast on her little feet, and with a head full of the craziest ideas. That Thor and Donar were two perfect partners in crime didn't help matters. Currently, it was Julio's task to run after the trio and keep them out of everybody's way. Wilma and Fred were watching the action from high up a tree, unsure whether they should join the fun or keep a safe distance.

The wedding ceremony would be held under the biggest and oldest oak tree in the garden, whose branches were like a canopy. Everything was planned and perfect and beautiful. Dean gulped and reached for his collar to soothe his nerves.

Aaron patted him on the shoulder. "It's okay, son. Wedding jitters are normal." He looked at his watch. "Time to go. Your groom is waiting."

Aaron reached for Dean's hand and put it on his arm. Dean hesitated. "Aaron?"

"Yes, son?"

Dean smiled. "I like it when you call me that. Son. It feels right." He inhaled deeply. "I wanted to thank you. This is big for me. For Richard. You walking me to him means a lot to both of us. So, thank you."

Aaron embraced Dean and held him tight. "It's my pleasure, son. This means a lot to me too. There's nothing more important than family. Never forget that."

Dean glanced at Tricia's urn and knew Aaron was right. Family was the most important thing in the world. And it didn't matter if it was family by blood or by choice. Through Richard, he had not only found the bliss of a stable relationship, but also the joy of being a father and the happiness of having a group of close friends, all of whom were here today to celebrate his union with Richard.

Dean walked out into the yard on Aaron's arm, knowing he couldn't have come up with a better ending than reality had done for him.

Exclusive Excerpt

A Dom and His Artist

A Club Whisper Novel

By Xenia Melzer

Sometimes the perfect man can be found in the most unexpected place….

Martin Carmichael owns a security firm and is part owner of Club Whisper. He's a Dom in search of the right guy, and when his car breaks down on a lonely stretch of road, he thinks he might have found him.

Artist Collin Malloy is talented, easygoing, but somewhat insecure. Still, he has a big heart and is quick to offer help when he sees Martin in need. To thank him, Martin invites Collin to dinner, where the attraction between them becomes harder to resist.

But what will become of their budding relationship when Martin reveals that he likes his men bound, submissive, and in pain? Is it something Collin can accept… and possibly enjoy exploring? Even if he can, Collin has a secret of his own—a secret he doesn't even realize he's keeping.

Coming Soon to
www.dreamspinnerpress.com

Chapter 1

"Fucking son of a bitch!" Martin Carmichael flipped off yet another car that simply drove by, ignoring his desperate attempts to flag somebody down. He had gotten a sense of dread when his car started making funny noises on this street in the middle of nowhere, and he knew he was in deep shit when all the lights on the console lit up like a Christmas tree before winking out like dying stars. The engine of his brand-new, very expensive Cadillac Escalade had made a sad, hiccupping sound and then the car rolled to a halt. To add insult to injury, whatever had caused the space-age electronics essentially driving the car to quit working had also fried his cell, which had been plugged into the car's Wi-Fi system. Damn modern gadgets and their tendency to blow up in your face.

Martin had faced some dire situations in his life before, but he would have never thought getting stranded on a lonely street in the outskirts of Miami would actually be one of them. As an ex-military, the owner of a security firm that operated nationwide and on occasion even internationally, and as a Dom, Martin made a living of being intimidating. It was part of his very being, and given that he was six foot five, with the heavy build of a tank and the kind of muscle you only get when you actually work your body, he had intimidation mastered perfectly. Unfortunately, when you were stranded at the side of a road and needed the help of strangers, it didn't work in your favor when people were afraid of you. In the last two hours since his car had broken down, only about thirty other cars had come this way, and their drivers all ignored him, some of them even accelerating once they got a look at him.

Martin cursed again. He was even wearing a suit, for fuck's sake! Though, to be honest, said suit, although custom-made and perfectly tailored, gave him the air of a sophisticated mobster. Something he needed when dealing with the kind of customer he had just come from, but nothing that helped him getting assistance. If he couldn't stop a car in the next thirty minutes, he would have to start walking back home. The idea alone made him shudder in his very expensive designer shoes that were made for many things, but definitely not a long walk in the dust.

In the distance he heard the rumbling of a car and looked up just in time to see what had to be the oldest pickup truck in the States, signaling and then pulling up next to his car. The first thing Martin noticed about the truck, besides its age, was the paintings. The thing was covered in them. Snakes, lizards, geckos, salamanders. Some of them so lifelike it seemed as if they would crawl away any moment; others looked more like the paintings one expected to find on the walls of a cave. They all were done in brilliant colors, and Martin had to admit the truck looked stunning.

Now the driver's door opened, and Martin's breath caught in his throat. He didn't know what he had expected; he only knew it wasn't this. The man jumping down from the truck was five foot four and on the skinny side, but with lightly defined muscles under a shabby, dirty white muscle shirt. He had long black hair falling around his angular face in heavy waves. Part of it was held by a leather strap, but the man either didn't care about the wayward strands caressing his high cheekbones or had given up on taming them.

Martin liked twinks. No, he adored them. But he usually preferred them with a lot more makeup, perfectly groomed—he always thought some men were simply made for eyeliner—and with fashionable clothes. If they were kind of scatterbrained and needed somebody to rely on, somebody to dominate them, then he was the Dom they'd been looking for.

This man was not groomed. He didn't wear makeup, and even if his clothes had once been fashionable, they were just dirty now. He wore sneakers with holes in them, the skin on his hands looked rough, as if he didn't know what hand lotion was for, and there was dirt under his nails. Except for his height, the man ticked none of Martin's boxes, and yet he couldn't take his eyes off him. There was something about him, about the way he looked at Martin, without the fear and wariness people normally showed when they met him for the first time lurking in his deep green eyes. Martin was intrigued.

Now the man opened his gorgeous mouth. "Hi, I'm Collin. Do you need help?"

His voice was a bit deeper than Martin expected, but it sounded nice. He smiled. "Hi, Collin. I'm Martin, and yes, I need help. My car broke down and my cell is dead. Could you lend me yours so I can make a call and get somebody to pick me up?"

The beautiful face fell. Martin was wondering what he had done wrong when Collin started talking again. "I'm really sorry. I don't have a cell. You know, they're kind of expensive, and then you have to get a contract and you have to pay for that as well, and then people can always reach you, which can be a bit inconvenient, and they always come in boring colors, and there's so much you can do with them when all I want is to make a call, and I really don't understand those message thingies, and Jude said I would just lose it anyway, which is probably right because I often misplace things and then I can't remember where they're hiding and a phone is good at hiding, all small and slim and not making a peep when you forget to feed it, which I would, because I'm not used to having one and my place is kind of messy, what with all the things lying around, and I wouldn't want Dog to find it, because he would surely chew on it and then it would be dead, just like the hare he caught last week, and boy, was that messy and he wasn't sorry at all, even though there was blood everywhere and I had to clean up and the tiny bits of fur wouldn't come out of the cracks on the floor." He paused and then brightened. "But I did get a pretty decent skull out of it, so I guess it's kind of okay, although I'm not telling Dog, because then maybe he'd think he has to get me more hares and one is definitely enough, and did I mention that cleaning up was messy? Like, totally?"

Martin stared openmouthed at Collin. He had never heard anybody talk so fast and so much gibberish on one—no, two—breaths. It had to be a talent. Martin also started to suspect Collin was not necessarily playing with a full deck of cards, although he came across as charming rather than raving mad. At least to Martin, who had seen all kinds of crazy during his time in the military and now with his clients. He found that, very often, the line between batshit crazy and eccentric was defined by the number of digits in one's bank account. Collin surely didn't look like he had much to offer in that respect, and Martin wondered briefly if he even had an account. Still, he was sweet, with an openness most people lost once they left childhood behind. And he was the only person who had stopped and offered help.

"Well, that's too bad."

Collin seemed to be deep in thought for a moment. Then his eyes lit up and a smile appeared on his face. "How about I give you a ride into town? If you tell me where you want to go, I can drive. I have enough gas and everything and I'm a good driver. I swear!"

Collin's eagerness made Martin smile as well. Such unblemished openness was refreshing.

"That would be very nice of you."

Collin smiled, and the sun seemed to rise in his eyes. "Okey-dokey. Hop on in!" He turned around and went back to the driver's seat. Martin reached into his own car to retrieve the fried cell and then approached Collin's truck. He didn't think the data on his phone could be saved, but he had to make sure. Some of the addresses in there were worth quite a lot. When he tried to open the passenger's side door, it wouldn't budge. Martin tried again, and this time Collin leaned over and did something at the inside of the door, making a strange, clanking sound. Suddenly the door opened, and Martin got in. Collin was chewing his lip. "I'm sorry," he mumbled, suddenly no longer agitated. "The car is kind of old."

Martin felt the urge to punish Collin for the lip chewing and, at the same time, the insane need to reassure him. Both feelings were so strong it surprised him. He couldn't remember when he had last experienced such deep emotions—and with a complete stranger, to boot. Only Collin didn't feel like a stranger. More like—home. And that was really weird, because Martin wasn't into romantic shit like soul mates and love at first sight. Love was optional as soon as a contract was drawn up and signed. First came the rules, then everything else—if ever.

"There's water in the back. I'm afraid it's not cold anymore, but… well… if you're thirsty…" Collin trailed off, uncertainty tinging every syllable.

Martin cursed himself for letting his thoughts wander when he had to focus. Listening to Collin's insecure half sentences made him wonder what had triggered the sudden change and if it was his fault.

"Thank you, Collin. That is very kind of you. And I know how cars can act up on you. I mean, at least yours is still going. Mine is completely dead."

Martin watched Collin very closely and saw the young man's shoulders relax. He had to bite his tongue not to praise him. That probably wouldn't go over so well. Instead, he turned and searched for the water bottle in the small back space. When he looked into the bed of the truck, he saw old branches, stones, a piece of metal pipe, and the skull of a middle-sized animal, all in one messy heap. With the bottle in hand, he turned back to watch out the front window. After opening the cap and downing the lukewarm water in a few eager gulps, he dared to make a comment. "Interesting collection you got there." Martin indicated with his thumb.

Collin's cheeks reddened, whether from embarrassment or joy, Martin couldn't tell. He definitely seemed to be regaining his spirit, though, which was a plus as far as Martin was concerned. "It's for my new project. I collected them today."

"Project?"

The red deepened. Joy, Martin decided. Joy about his interest in something Collin did. If Martin had to bet, he would say that didn't happen to Collin very often. Which was a shame. "I'm an artist. Or try to be one. I'm not very successful or famous or anything, but I earn enough to make a living, and this is my new project. I was looking for dreams."

Martin could feel a mixture of insecurity and eagerness wafting from Collin. He was obviously deeply engaged with the subject, but at the same time unsure about Martin's reaction to it. Martin felt himself flinching. Nobody should ever feel uncomfortable speaking about their passions. Especially not dark-haired young men with the greenest, most beautiful eyes Martin had ever seen and a smile that made him forget his own name.

"Sounds interesting. May I ask what the skull of an animal has to do with dreams?" He laughed to take the sting he had just realized was there out of his words. "As you can probably guess from my question, I don't have a very active imagination." *Unless it comes to torturing cute little twinks, making them writhe and moan and beg under my whip and my hands and my mouth.*

Collin shot him a quick, darting look before he concentrated on the street again. "Actually, a lot. Shattered dreams, because a life has ended. The hope for a new life, because the cycle starts again. Time in the realm of dreams before the soul comes back to earth. The dreams of others, impacted by this death. The things the bones tell me. There's a lot. You know." Suddenly, as if some kind of switch had been hit, Collin fell back into the fast speaking rhythm he had shown before.

"People always only see what's right in front of them. They never look past the obvious. I mean, a skull is just bones, a reminder of somebody who's no longer there. A very biological thing, made of collagen and calcium and other bits that can withstand the elements for quite some time, but ultimately they vanish too. And then there's the story behind the bone, the force that drove it, the brain that lived safely inside, the soul that elevated it into being more than just a hard shell designed to protect something. Or take the metal pipe. I found it in the woods. Somebody had dumped it there, and I'm not sure what it was for. It's started to rust and there are things growing on it, I think moss and lichens, and there are little insects living inside and it has become kind of a city in its own, and now I've taken it away from the woods and changed its meaning again, and now the insects and the moss have to find a new place to live and that spot in the woods is going to change as well, and nobody ever sees the chronological side of things, the before and after, the things that make the current state possible and define it through what they have been. By collecting all these things, I've become a catalyst for various things and the possibilities stretch endlessly in front of me and it's all colors and choices and forms and kind of hard to understand because it's so brilliant and so bright and so confusing."

Collin took a deep breath of much-needed oxygen and glanced over at Martin with a wary look. "I'm talking too much again." He sounded very timid, and the fire and sparkle were gone. "I'm sorry. Jude says I shouldn't, but sometimes I forget and then—"

Martin couldn't stand it any longer. He held up his hand. "Stop right there, Collin. There is nothing you have to apologize for. I enjoy listening to you. I can tell how much you love your art, how deep your thoughts run. There's nothing wrong with being passionate about something you love. And if I make kind of a strange face now and then, that's not because you bore me, but because your ideas are very complex and it takes some serious thinking to understand them."

He smiled reassuringly at Collin and, when he saw the happy smile on the young man's face, decided to try a little joke. "Plus you can talk real fast, and that takes some getting used to."

Collin's cheeks reddened, but he chuckled, obviously understanding that Martin was trying to lighten the mood.

Collin drove at a moderate speed, and they could already see Miami in the distance. The mood in the car was now tranquil with an underlying tension. Martin could practically see the wheels in Collin's head turning as he tried to find a topic that would prevent him from babbling again. Since he was curious what Collin would do, Martin kept his silence. Finally Collin asked, "Why were you stranded out there?"

Given the complex time-and-cause speech Collin had just made, the question was logical, and it impressed Martin how the young man could keep the thread of the conversation even though he seemed to deteriorate from it by asking the obvious. Martin understood, though, that Collin wasn't asking about the car breaking down. Not really. He smiled and decided to play along. "I have a security firm, and one of my clients lives out there. He's just built a new house, and I helped him with the security system. Today was kind of a wrap-up, and I'm glad to say everything went smoothly."

"Is that why you're wearing a costume?"

The question startled Martin. "What do you mean?" His voice might have been a bit sterner than he had intended, because Collin's fingers gripped the steering wheel tighter.

"I'm sorry. I didn't mean to offend you. I can't always say what's on the tip of my tongue. I keep forgetting that."

"No, it's fine. You just surprised me. Few people would ask such a question. So, how do you mean it?"

Collin stared at the road ahead. "This is not you. This suit is somebody else, somebody who had something to do, but it's not you. At least, not all of you. The clothes you're wearing are part of a projection other people have of you, and you're using it. I'm just wondering why somebody as strong and independent as you would need a disguise."

Martin was speechless. Without any effort, Collin had seen past the designer wear and right into the heart of the matter. "Is that why you stopped for me? Because you saw that I'm not a gangster?" He had meant to make it sound light, but the truth was, sometimes it bothered him how people only ever saw the brute strength in him and were happy to assume the worst.

Collin glanced over before he concentrated on driving again. "If I were afraid of strength, I wouldn't have stopped. The person under the suit is much more dangerous than the one the suit is projecting. You know that. I can feel your confidence. It surrounds you like a halo, and that's what's driven me to you. Something I don't have." Collin smiled crookedly. "Besides, I know what it's like to be stranded at the side of the road."

There was a wealth of pain in that one sentence, and Martin felt the urge to take Collin in his arms and make all the bad memories go away. There was nothing he could do at the moment, though, not only because Collin was driving, but also because Martin hadn't yet verified his assumption about Collin being gay. So he just deadpanned. "I'm just glad you stopped for me, even though I was in costume."

That brought him a quick glance and a light chuckle, and the mood lifted again. As they neared Miami, Collin had to concentrate on traffic and the directions Martin was giving him, so their conversation lulled a bit. When Collin finally pulled over in front of the office building where Martin's company had its headquarters, Martin knew he had to either ask Collin out or forget about him. "Thank you very much for helping me, Collin. Do you have a landline where I can reach you? I would love to invite you to dinner as a thank-you."

Collin seemed a bit surprised at first, but then a smile blossomed on his face. "That would be real nice. And I do have a landline." He rattled off the number, and Martin quickly wrote it down on a piece of paper he found in the side of the passenger's door.

"Thank you again, Collin. I'll be calling you later and we can set up a da—" Almost too late, Martin realized the potential innuendo. Even though he was pretty sure Collin wouldn't recognize it as such, he still didn't want to take the risk. He would feel Collin out once they were on the date/thank-you dinner. "Um, day."

Collin still smiled, seemingly oblivious of Martin's almost slipup. He got out of the truck, patted the door, and wished Collin a good journey. Then he stood outside the building, waiting for the taillights of the truck to disappear into traffic. It was ridiculous, but Martin couldn't help it. There was something about Collin—he shook his head. He was acting like a lovesick fool just because some pretty piece of ass had taken him for a ride. It was high time for him to get laid. Only it wouldn't be that easy. Not with the image of Collin floating through his mind. Martin couldn't believe it. Almost thirty-five years, and now he was falling in love? Impossible. Richard would tease him into next year if he could see him now.

As it turned out, he didn't need Richard to hand his ass to him. When he entered the building and strode toward his office, his sister, Olivia, greeted him with a wolf whistle and a knowing look in her dark eyes, which were exact mirrors of his own and a heritage from their Native American grandmother. "Who was the hottie in that shitty truck, and why has he got you mooning like a teenager?" She furrowed her brows as she listened to her own sentence and then fired another question at him. "Why were you with hottie in the shitty truck in the first place? Where's your shiny new toy?"

Martin groaned. Crap. Olivia had been teasing him about his *cock enlargement*, as she so bluntly called his new car, since he had gotten it the week before. Now he had to admit it had broken down, which she would remind him of for the rest of his life. And such was his luck, his dear sister could chew two bones at the same time, which meant his predicament with the car wouldn't get him out of telling her about Collin. Why hadn't he stayed in bed today? No, stop. If he had, he wouldn't have met Collin.... Why hadn't Olivia stayed in bed today?

"Brother mine, I'm still waiting!"

"Can't you just go away?"

She grinned broadly. "Nope. Not until I've fulfilled my duty as your annoying older sister. Standards must be kept."

"First of all, I keep telling you five minutes is not enough time to make you a real older sister. It just means you were more determined to leave the womb. Second, you don't have to work at being annoying—it comes naturally to you."

"Still waiting."

Martin threw his arms up in a gesture of defeat. She wouldn't budge, he knew, so he surrendered. "Fine. My shiny new toy died on me, frying my cell in the process. I stood under the glaring sun for at least two hours and numerous people passed me by, not stopping or offering help, because, well, you know." He gestured down his massive frame. "I was getting ready to walk back, when suddenly this shitty truck pulled over and Hottie offered me a ride. And, yes, I'm going to invite him for dinner as soon as I have a nice long talk with my car dealer. I'm not entirely sure if he's gay." Martin listened to himself and added, "The hottie, not the dealer, but my gut says yes, so I'm giving this a try."

For a moment, Olivia didn't say a word. Then her lips twitched and she started laughing. When she calmed down a bit, she wiped her eyes with the sleeve of her blouse and stared at him, full of glee. "I'm going to get some mileage out of the car thing." She chuckled at her own pun. "And I can't believe you just tried to defend your choice of ass in front of me. You never do that." Her eyes narrowed. "You like him."

Martin shrugged. "And if?"

Olivia sighed, suddenly serious. "Then I'm of course happy for you, but also worried. You know as well as I do that fishing outside the scene can be a dangerous game and almost always involves heartbreak."

Martin sighed as well. Boy, did he know that. He'd seen it happen more than once—Richard and Dean so far being the only exception to the rule—and gone through it as well, back in the day, when he'd just started out as a Dom and had been young and foolish enough to think love could conquer all. As it turned out, love had serious problems conquering different opinions on the value of kink in a relationship. It was a place Martin had sworn to never visit again, and here it seemed as if he was sailing straight into the heart of the storm. "I know. And I do intend to have the talk with him as soon as possible. I'm not even sure what draws me to him. I mean, he's nice-looking, but I usually prefer my men better groomed and with less brain."

Olivia snickered. "Only God knows why that is. It would drive me crazy, having somebody who can't take care of themselves hanging on my apron."

"You don't wear aprons. And I'm not sure, but hanging on to a leather corset is probably not as easy. Besides—" Martin flashed her a crooked smile "—you know very well that it makes me happy to provide for others. Having a sub who caters to my every whim and needs my protection and guidance is the ultimate gift for me."

"Not all of us are mercurial." Olivia slapped him playfully on the arm. Martin's contradicting needs—the one to dominate versus the one to care for somebody—were a never-ending source of discussion between the siblings. Olivia was a good Dom, both for men and women, but she preferred her subs to be strong and self-reliant. She needed the constant challenge of a personality as stubborn as her own as much as the satisfaction of subjugating such a person. When somebody didn't put up a fight, Olivia wasn't interested. As similar as the siblings were in almost every aspect of their lives, this was one vast difference.

Martin's need for somebody to depend on him also set him apart from most of the other Doms. Not that there weren't Doms out there who demanded their subs to live with them or even give up their jobs. But usually those Doms wanted it because of the feeling of control they achieved through the act of having their subs under their rule. Martin did it because he felt good when he could take care of somebody who needed it. He even felt better—or would feel better—when that care came naturally and wasn't spelled out in a contract. So far, all he had gotten were contracts, and the kind of domestic fulfillment he was looking for was a distant dream he was thinking about giving up.

Martin had tried to have a live-in sub, and it hadn't worked out. He'd even tried a Master/slave relationship once, but that was so far removed from what he really wanted that he had stopped the experiment only one week into the trial period. Martin never told anyone, but with every failed attempt to find a long-term partner, he doubted more and more his own ability to decipher what he really wanted out of a relationship. What if it wasn't the twinks who were incompatible, but him? It didn't help that he had a certain reputation in the scene. His looks ensured that mainly pain sluts sought him out, and his money almost guaranteed nine out of ten of those pain sluts were also gold diggers.

No wonder had he been attracted to Collin, who knew nothing about him and at the same time more than any of the twinks in the club. Simply by looking past the obvious.

"I don't know, Olivia. I think he has potential. I would love to get to know him better." Martin felt a wolfish smile tugging at his lips. "I also would love to introduce him to BDSM. I bet that tight ass colors beautifully."

Olivia laughed. "You're such an ass yourself." She leaned in and placed a kiss on his cheek. "Go get him, tiger."

"Soon. First I have to make a call to the car dealer. I hope for his sake this is all covered."

"Have fun, little brother."

IT WAS after 11:00 p.m. when Martin finally got off the phone. He'd called the car dealer, who had tried to wiggle his way out of taking responsibility, claiming Martin must have mishandled the complicated electronics. It took massive threats, and finally a call from Martin's lawyer, before the dealer agreed to waive the cost for repairing the car. Son of a bitch that he was, he flat-out refused to tow the car in, so Martin had to find a company to do the job. That had cost him another hour on the phone. He would have loved to leave it to his secretary, but it was Jennifer's monthly evening off, when she went to dinner with her friends. The date was holy, and not even the apocalypse itself would keep Jennifer in the office on that day. And should the Four Horsemen think about making her stay, they'd find out pretty quickly there were worse things than death, famine, plague, and war—a cranky Jennifer at the top of that list.

Martin checked the clock. Quarter to twelve. No way could he call Collin at such a late hour. Promising himself he would secure his date first thing the next morning, Martin left the office and went home.

FOR THE hundredth time, Collin stared at his phone. It wouldn't ring. It just wouldn't ring. It was already past ten, and his common sense told him the hot guy wouldn't call, but his foolish heart kept hoping. Martin had been so nice. Which was probably why he wouldn't call. Collin tended to scare everybody away with his behavior and his tendency to talk more than was good for him. He sighed. It would have been so nice to make a friend. A good-looking friend. Then again, Martin probably wouldn't have appreciated a friend who kept ogling him and imagining what it would feel like to be kissed by him. Jude was right. Collin was hopeless.

With a deep sigh, Collin sat down on the old sofa he had found at a flea market. He'd crocheted new covers in the colors of the rainbow to make it look more inviting, and even if he said so himself, he'd done a great job. Dog came running with his stuffed bear between his massive jaws. Jude said it wasn't good to give Dog a toy and that he was there to guard the property, but Collin didn't see a reason not to spoil the beast. He was aware that other people feared the rottweiler as a dangerous creature, though Collin couldn't understand why. Dog was loyal and full of love and tenderness. He didn't like strangers on the property, but at least he didn't get out a gun and fire at anything that moved like so many other people. Okay, the thing with the hare had been gross. Collin wasn't even sure where Dog had found the animal, because hares weren't exactly common in the city. On the other hand, he understood the gesture for what it was—an attempt on Dog's part to make Collin happy and to provide for him. So being ungrateful was kind of shitty.

He patted the huge animal on the head. "He won't call, Dog."

Collin felt tears gathering in his eyes. He usually lived in a state of bliss. Driving with Martin for almost an hour had somehow fucked with his brain. For the first time in very long, he wished he were better at meeting people. Then he would have charmed Martin with his natural humor, his wit and clever remarks, and the man would have not only called the second Collin entered his studio, but they would now be kissing somewhere private.

As if sensing Collin's sadness, Dog jumped up on the sofa—again something Jude didn't approve of—and snuggled his massive head in Collin's lap, whining softly. Collin petted the soft fur and scratched Dog behind the ears. Sometimes it really sucked to be him.

THE NEXT morning Collin was awakened by Dog's enthusiastic barking and the ringing of his phone. He scrambled up from the sofa on which he obviously had fallen asleep and stumbled to the old phone on the wall. He picked it up and yawned. "Yes?"

"Collin? Is that you? This is Martin. Martin Carmichael. You helped me out yesterday."

All of a sudden Collin was wide-awake. A strange feeling sizzled through him, like an electric current, only nice.

"Yes. Yes, it's me. I…um…just woke up. Good morning." Collin rolled his eyes at himself. So much for dazzling Martin with his social skills. He sounded like an idiot.

Martin chuckled. "Good morning. I'm sorry for waking you. I know how hard it can be to have a conversation without a cup of coffee under your belt. Should I call again later?"

"No!" Collin blushed, glad Martin couldn't see him. He tried to get a grip on himself. "I mean, no, it's fine. I'm awake now and I don't need coffee. In fact, I steer clear of it because the caffeine does strange things to me and then I can't sleep and feel antsy all the time, and anyway, very often coffee is harvested by child labor, and who would want to support something so nasty when a glass of water is perfectly fine and doesn't make your skin crawl or your hands shake?"

Collin realized was babbling again when Martin's rumbling laughter echoed over the line. "I'll remember not to give you coffee, then. I'm calling about our dinner and wanted to know if you had time today."

"I thought you had forgotten!" Collin slapped his hand over his mouth. He'd spoken without thinking again. Martin's silence told him the man finally realized what a nut job Collin was. But when Martin started speaking, it wasn't the blunt rejection Collin expected.

"I haven't forgotten, Collin. And I apologize for worrying you. I most certainly didn't mean to. I was stuck on the phone, first with the car dealer and then with getting the SUV towed in. When I was finally finished, it was almost midnight. I didn't want to disturb you so late."

Collin felt a little better that Martin hadn't forgotten and at the same time bad for giving him a hard time. "I should apologize, Martin. Of course, you have more important things to do than phoning me. I didn't mean to nag."

Again came the warm, rumbling laughter that did funny things to Collin's stomach. "You're not nagging. I told you I would call and I didn't do it, so you have every right to question me. I promise, it won't happen again. Now, are you available tonight?"

That was a no-brainer. "Yes, of course."

"Then how about I pick you up at six and we'll have a nice dinner at one of my favorite restaurants?"

Collin felt giddy with joy until he remembered something. His face fell. "Um, I don't have the clothing for a fancy restaurant, and I don't want to embarrass you."

"Don't worry, Collin. The place I have in mind is cozy and not uppity at all. You're going to love it, and jeans are perfectly acceptable there. By the way, I do need your address."

Collin felt as if a lead weight had dropped from his heart. "Then I'm looking forward to tonight." He rattled off his address and added, a little shyly, "Thank you."

Martin chuckled again. "You've got it wrong, sweet one. I'm the one who has to thank you. See you tonight."

The line went dead, and Collin stared at the receiver for an eternity before he dropped to his knees and hugged Dog, who was sitting on the floor eyeing him with mild curiosity. "I think I have a date, Dog. I'm so excited."

XENIA MELZER was born and raised in a small village in the south of Bavaria. As one of nature's true chocoholics, she's always in search of the perfect chocolate experience. So far, she's had about a dozen truly remarkable ones. Despite having been in close proximity to the mountains all her life, she has never understood why so many people think snow sports are fun. There are neither chocolate nor horses involved and it's cold by definition, so where's the sense? She does not like beer either and has never been to the Oktoberfest—no quality chocolate there.

Even though her mind is preoccupied with various stories most of the time, Xenia has managed to get through school and university with surprisingly good grades. Right after school she met her one true love who showed her that reality is capable of producing some truly amazing love stories itself.

While she was having her two children, she started writing down the most persistent stories in her head as a way of relieving mommy-related stress symptoms. As it turned out, the stress relief has now become a source of the same, albeit a positive one.

When she's not writing, she translates other authors' manuscripts to German, enjoys riding and running, spending time with her kids. and dancing with her husband.

Website: www.xeniamelzer.com
Email: info@xeniamelzer.com

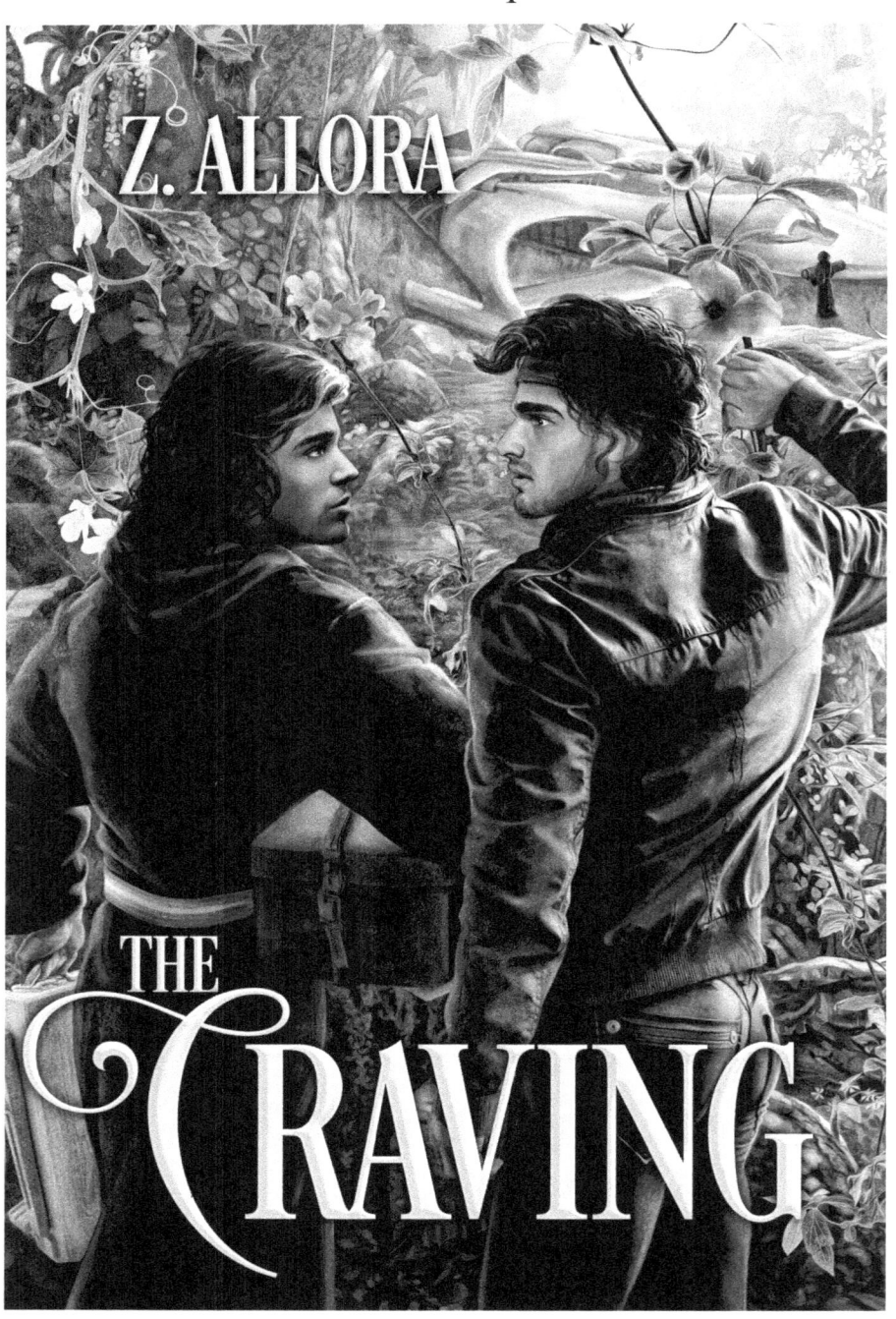

Z. ALLORA

THE CRAVING

Also from Dreamspinner Press

Tropical Depression

Stormy Weather: Book 2

BA TORTUGA

www.dreamspinnerpress.com

www.ingramcontent.com/pod-product-compliance
Lightning Source LLC
Chambersburg PA
CBHW060056260626
47160CB00005B/1685